RAG DOLL GIRLS

SYDNEY JAMES

LISA

AFTER MY TREK to the grocery store, I was so exhausted that I barely made it up the stairs. Two of the three weak light bulbs in the narrow staircase were out as I slowly climbed to the second floor. When I spotted the garish yellow eviction notice stuck to the door of my shabby one-room apartment, I missed a step and lost my balance. At the last minute, I managed to grab hold of the railing with fingers that were numb from the carrier bag's thin handle. The bag fell to the floor with a dull thud, but at least I didn't.

Part of me wanted to just let go. Perhaps breaking my neck tumbling backward down the steep staircase would be the best solution to all of my problems.

I didn't, though. Don't ask me why, because I couldn't tell you.

Somehow I found my balance, picked up my bag, and made it up onto the landing and over to the door, ignoring the big, bold letters declaring me to be home-less within the next ten days.

Ten days.

As if I'd be able to turn my life around in that time.

For the last thirty years, everything had been getting steadily worse, day by day, year by year.

But sure, I'd be able to turn everything around in a little over a week.

Optimist. Not something anyone had ever called me.

Not that anyone ever talked about me. If they did, they probably didn't use my name.

That pile of lard in apartment 2D, perhaps. The monstrosity on the second floor, maybe.

I didn't know and told myself repeatedly that I didn't care. Other people were not my business, not my problem. I didn't bother with them, and for the most part they didn't bother me.

I found the keys at the bottom of my oversized purse, unlocked the door, and squeezed in through the gap.

No, I wasn't so fat that I didn't fit through a regular-sized front door. But the door didn't open all the way. There were boxes stacked against the wall inside that prevented me from opening the door completely.

I really ought to move those boxes.

I had been told to move those boxes.

Those boxes were one of the reasons why there was a neon yellow eviction notice sticker glued to my front door.

Those boxes would never be moved. Not by me, at least.

Somehow I knew that.

In the same way, I knew that eating all the food in the bags that were cutting off the circulation to my fingers would do nothing to combat the clinical obesity weight issue that I'd been struggling with since my teens.

I wasn't stupid.

But I also wasn't very good at doing what was good for me. The right thing. Whatever you want to call it.

I made my way into the tiny kitchen and unpacked the groceries. The shop was just down the block, but I'd been gone for over an hour and a half, according to the red digits on the microwave. I was exhausted, and my 5XL sweatshirt was living up to its name, glued to my back with what I was sure was a large and very visible stain. A couple of hours. Two bags of groceries. And I'd spent all of my energy for the day. It was a little after eleven, and I was pretty sure that once I'd sat down on the sagging couch in my living room, I wouldn't get up again—apart from bathroom visits and to get more food —until it was time to go to bed.

Of course, I had things on my to-do list. Urgent things, even. Like getting hold of my social worker, Brenda, and telling her about the eviction. Not that she would do anything about that. Not even help me find another apartment. I'm sorry, Lisa, she'd say, but the social services are here to help people who are willing to do what they can to help themselves. Who have exhausted all other possibilities. You haven't stuck to a single one of the plans that you and I have drawn up. Your therapist tells me that you haven't been working on any of the routines that you've agreed on. I can't help you if you aren't prepared to do some of the work your-self. I'm sorry, Lisa, but my hands are tied. I've explained this to you. You are no longer eligible for any more assistance from this office. You will have to make other arrangements.

Stupid woman. As if I hadn't tried. As if I hadn't intended to do every one of the things that we had discussed. That my therapist had insisted would help me break my destructive patterns.

But in the end, every one of those little steps had proved to be too hard, impossible even. Going outside on a regular basis. Getting exercise. Losing weight. Finding a job.

How was I supposed to suddenly be able to do all of those things when I hadn't been able to do them before? When I didn't have the first clue as to how one actually did any of those things.

It might not look that difficult from the outside, but then no one else, not even my snooty social worker, had any idea on the toll it took just to get down the block and pick up some food. They had no idea how hard it was, what an effort it required.

It looked so easy when everyone else did it. But for me, it was extremely hard. Always had been.

Make other arrangements. I knew what she meant by that, but … no. Just no.

I popped a frozen pizza into the microwave and made up a tray to bring into the living room. I usually brought enough food to last me until bedtime, already at lunch. That's why I preferred processed stuff that didn't need refrigeration. Didn't need cooking. Potato chips didn't require peeling and boiling and preparing. You could just eat them right out of the bag. And if, on some infrequent occasion, I didn't finish the entire bag before I went to bed, they were still good for breakfast.

Why people bothered to cook at all was beyond me.

I carried the tray into the living room, switched on the TV, and made sure that I had everything I needed before sitting down on the sofa. The cushions had flattened after several years of use, but they were more or less perfectly molded to my wide behind, and I found it to be comfortable, even though it looked a bit sad. I'd be sorry to have to leave my sofa behind, but I couldn't take it with me.

Not when I didn't have anywhere to go.

I supposed that I would have to find a shelter of some kind. It would have to be a women's shelter because I would never stay in a place with men. That would be an absolute requirement.

Getting a new apartment, now that I'd been evicted, and after losing my disability pension, was going to be impossible. As if I was any less disabled because the root of all my problems was "the weight issue," as Brenda called it.

I didn't have a weight issue, I had told her. I don't have an issue with my weight. But you can barely walk, she'd said. I don't have anywhere I want to go, I had replied.

I sat for a while staring at the dark screen on the TV, remote in hand, thinking that I ought to do something. Make a plan. Get up and get cracking.

But in the end, I just switched on the set and started surfing the channels. Once the pizza had cooled off a bit, I heaped Doritos on top of each slice and ate them slowly; my eyes peeled to the screen while episode after episode of various daytime soaps played out. So much drama, every day. I was lucky to be living alone, with no family or business associates to plot and scheme behind my back. The human race was doomed; I knew that much, even though my own interaction with the rest of the humans was kept to the strictest minimum.

When a soft chirping sound penetrated my concentration, it took me a while to understand where it was coming from. But of course. The phone. Brenda must have found out about my eviction somehow, and now she was calling to tell me what she intended to do about it. Or perhaps I had won the state lottery. Yes, that was probably it. This had definitely been my lucky day, so far.

I wiped my Dorito-yellow fingers on my sweatshirt and found the phone behind a sofa cushion. The battery icon was blinking. Well, it must have been hiding behind that cushion for a couple of days. Since I ordered that Chinese food, I guess. It was the only thing I ever used the phone for, that and making appointments. No one ever called me. Not even my social worker, come to think of it. Brenda always communicated through the post.

"H-hello?" I said, stopping to clear my throat, mid-word.

"Lisa?" The voice sounded familiar, but I couldn't quite place it. It wasn't Brenda; I knew that much. The tone was all wrong.

"Who is this?" I said, lowering the volume on the TV.

"*Det är jag,*" the voice said, and it took me several seconds for my brain to switch back to the language I'd spoken as a child. It's me, she'd said. And with those words, she didn't need any further introduction.

I didn't know what to say. I just sat there with the phone to my ear, staring at the characters moving about on the screen in front of me. My ribcage started to constrict, and I felt myself getting light-headed.

A faded old memory appeared from somewhere in the back of my mind. A smiling, blond teenager, bouncing out the door to meet her friends while I sat on the sofa in our living room back home, a blanket over my legs and a bowl of ice cream on my lap.

I blinked rapidly to rid myself of the image.

"Lisa?" the familiar voice said again. *"Är du där?"* Are you there?

"Ja," I whispered. It was the first word of Swedish I had spoken in more than ten years, and it sounded strange, even to my own ears. I hadn't realized that I had stopped thinking in Swedish, but now my brain had to scramble to find even the simplest words.

There was barely any air in my lungs, and I suddenly couldn't remember how I was supposed to fill them. Some kind of survival instinct finally kicked in, and I drew a long, raspy breath.

"I'm sorry to call like this," Astrid said, "completely out of the blue, but I thought I should tell you that Mormor died."

The memory of the blond teenager was replaced by a quick flickering of images, like the pages in a flip-book: a little old woman, my mother's mother, a small cottage in the woods, woven rugs on the rough floor-boards, a slanted ceiling up on the loft, the winding trail down to the dock, the thick reeds surrounding our little stretch of sandy beach. No amount of blinking could stop the images from bombarding me. I hadn't thought about any of that for years. Decades. Lifetimes.

"Lisa? Did you hear me? Mormor is dead. And the funeral is Friday."

Friday. The word didn't mean a thing to me. I knew it was supposed to, but it didn't.

"I think you should come," this woman who was my sister said, and there was a definite undertone of annoyance in her voice. "Mormor was heartbroken that you never came to visit her; you meant the world to her, you know."

Did I?

"I … I can't," I stuttered. "There's no way … *This* Friday? No. Sorry."

As if any other Friday would have been different. But no. I could just as easily have hopped on a space shuttle and hurled myself into hyperspace as get on a plane and travel around the world, back to the country where I'd grown up. Where my grandmother had lived her entire life. Where the remnants of my family still lived. Where I was still a citizen, and my social worker insisted that I should move back to. Never. No way. I'd sworn, when I got on the plane to the States a few weeks after my eighteenth birthday, that I'd never set foot in Sweden again. And that was a promise that I intended to keep.

Astrid sighed, the same way she'd done a million times when we were kids. Or, I was a kid, and she was a miniature adult already at seven and a half, fixing me with her annoyed stare whenever I didn't behave in the way she expected from me. "Mom and Frank are on a cruise off Bali or wherever, and they refuse to leave the boat and get on a plane because they won't get a refund and they've been looking forward to this all year and … Honestly …" A deep breath and I could picture her rolling her eyes. Except, I pictured her at nineteen, the way she had looked the last time I saw her, even though it slowly dawned on me that she must be much older now. I guess she looked like Mom, now. She always had taken after her.

"Who's Frank?" I asked before I could stop myself.

The line went silent for a while. "Frank? Mom's Frank."

"Mom has a Frank?" Not that I cared. I hadn't spoken to my mother in more than ten years. Not since Dad died.

I hadn't gone to his funeral either. Why should I go to my grandmother's?

"I know you hate us and all that," Astrid said, and there was a tremble of emotions in her voice that I wasn't prepared for. "But I can't stand the idea of no one else from the family turning up for Mormor's funeral. I just can't." Another deep sigh. "I've never asked you for anything, but I am asking you now. You are all the family I have left, and I am asking you to please come home. Just for a few days."

"I don't hate you," I mumbled, embarrassed more than anything. Why would she say something like that? But when I thought about it some more, I realized that it might be interpreted that way. I'd left without saying goodbye, never called or kept in touch. "I just … It's not a good time."

"Why not? What do you have to do that is more important than your grandmother's funeral? Huh? Tell me, Lisa!"

I went silent for a while. "Well, I've just found out that I'm being evicted …" I began. "So I really need to focus on finding a new place …" I fumbled for the remote and muted the TV completely.

"Evicted?" Astrid said. "Why?"

I mumbled something that might have been interpreted as a surly teenaged *I dunno*, but just as when I was fourteen, Astrid didn't accept that as an answer.

"No, tell me," she said. "What on earth have you

done? Have you any idea how much it takes to get evicted, even in the States? And how difficult it is to get a new place once you've been evicted by one landlord?"

I mumbled something that even I couldn't tell what it was supposed to sound like.

Another one of those annoying sighs. "Well, then this might just be your lucky day," Astrid said, and there was a sharp edge to her voice. "Because I may be able to help you."

"You?" The disbelief in my voice was evident. "What can you do?"

"Well, if you'd kept in touch, you'd know that I am a lawyer now. I made partner three years ago, and I make a decent living. So does my husband." She paused for a moment. "Whose name is Fredrik, not that you care. But anyway. Mormor left her cottage to the two of us, and I would like to buy you out. It won't be a fortune, but it should be enough to help you get a new place. I can expedite the process and help you with all the paperwork and stuff if you do this one thing for me in return."

"What?"

"Get on a plane and come to Mormor's funeral. If her own daughter can't be bothered to show up, at least both of her granddaughters should be there."

2

ASTRID

I ENDED the call and put the phone down a little too quickly, a little too hard, as if the plastic had been hot or something. Fredrik looked up, the concern visible in his eyes and in that tiny wrinkle between his eyebrows.

"So ... your sister is coming for the funeral?" he asked. His voice sounded casual, but I knew he must have heard what I'd said and had a million questions. Questions I wasn't ready to answer just yet.

Instead, I just nodded and then turned away. I had to blink fast to keep the tears from welling up in my eyes. There was no reason to get emotional. It was just ...

Wrapping my arms around myself, I walked over to the window, looking out onto the garden. It was dark outside, and I couldn't really see anything, but I also couldn't quite face Fredrik. I knew that he could never understand. His family was so close, all of them. So perfect. Two brothers and a sister, all of them happy, successful, married with children. His parents were still together, for crying out loud. There were about a million of them at every holiday and other get-togethers, of which there were many.

I would be alone at Mormor's funeral, now that Dad was gone and Mom was off with Frank. Not entirely alone, of course. I'd have my own family with me, but … Still. It had felt so wrong.

Having to bribe Lisa to come had also felt wrong, and it had left a sour taste in my mouth. But if that's what it took, then that's what I had to do, I guess. She needed to be there.

"How long since you saw her?" Fredrik asked.

I finally turned toward him. "Almost twenty years," I replied, picturing the chubby girl from my distant memories.

His eyebrows rose. "So, she'd have been a teenager?"

I nodded. "Eighteen. It was just a month or so after her birthday."

"Did she go to the US as an exchange student or something?" He closed his book and got up off the couch. Time for bed.

I shook my head. Nothing normal like that. "No. She just … left."

He laughed. "Just like that?"

I had to blink again. "Yeah," I said and tried to laugh it off. "Just like that."

My sister and I had never been what you'd call close. Not like Fredrik and his siblings. But part of what I'd been working through with my therapist Anita had been the void that Lisa's leaving had created in my life. All through my childhood, I had been the older sister, one of two children, and then, in my second year at university, Lisa had disappeared.

I had tried to explain to Anita that it hadn't made

that much of a difference, her going away. I hadn't suddenly become an only child because I'd been a grown-up by then, and I'd had my own life. We'd never been close. We had always been so different. Lisa had been a troubled child, who had grown up to be a seriously messed-up teenager that the whole family had tiptoed around, and honestly, it had been a bit of a relief when she'd left. Anita hadn't believed me.

And judging by my reaction just now, she might have a point.

Reluctantly, I had to admit that it had hurt me when Lisa disappeared. And that I was angry with her. My harsh tone with her over the phone was a testament to that if nothing else.

I tried to tell myself that I wasn't angry with her on my own account. I was angry because of what it had done to our parents when she just up and left. I was furious because of what it had done to Mormor. Our amazing grandmother, who'd always been there for us.

Lisa had been such a … weird kid. And things had happened that had made that weirdness sprout in all directions.

Part of me was relieved that she'd be coming back for the funeral, but a large part of me was afraid, too. I didn't know my sister. Didn't know what issues she still clung on to.

Surely, she had put all of that behind her. Surely, she had matured by now, shed that baby fat, found love, friends, an identity that didn't revolve around her troubled childhood.

Whenever I'd thought about her over the years, I'd tried to picture her as happy. Successful. Perhaps even a mirror image of me. When I graduated from law school,

I wondered if she might be in school as well. When I got married, I pictured her in love. When I became a mother, I wondered if I had nieces or nephews somewhere on the other side of the planet.

I'd never thought of her as struggling. Hearing about her eviction had given me an uncomfortable knot in my stomach.

What if my baby sister hadn't been happy all these years? What if she'd been struggling all this time?

Pushing these disturbing thoughts from my mind, I told myself that it certainly wouldn't be my fault if this was the case. I'd been here, all this time. She could have reached out if she'd needed me. She had chosen not to.

She was the one who left. She turned her back on me, not the other way around.

Fredrik walked up to me and wrapped his arms around me. My first instinct was to shy away. I felt embarrassed, even a little ashamed, after that phone call. And tense like a coiled spring at the idea of seeing my sister again. I took a deep breath and allowed him to hold me. It was going to be fine. Everything would be different now. It had been almost two whole decades. We'd be able to start over from scratch. Clean slate and all that.

3

LISA

I HAD ARRIVED at the airport four hours before my flight was scheduled for takeoff, but that was two hours ago and I still hadn't made it through security. The automated check-in machine had been programmed by a sociopath, and somehow I hadn't been able to find the paper where I'd written down my booking number, even though the last thing I did before I left the apartment was to double-check that I had it. After pulling out almost all the contents of my large purse, I finally found it right in the place where I'd first looked. By then, my pulse was racing, my body was covered in sweat, and I didn't think I'd ever make it onto the plane.

I had kept an eye on the security checkpoint for a while now, sitting on a bench in the departures hall, but I still hadn't worked up the nerve to walk over and get in line. There seemed to be a steady flow of passengers at all times. I had hoped for a lull, that I'd be able to get through the inspection relatively unnoticed. Pass through the humiliation of having to take off my shoes and perhaps be made to stand there with my arms out while the guard waved the metal detector all along my flabby contours looking for weapons with a modicum of privacy. But there was no lull. The constant departure of airplanes meant a continuous stream of passengers. I would have to get up now and get in line, or I would miss my flight.

Oh, I would love to miss my flight, but I couldn't.

I had spoken to Brenda, and she had been over the moon when she heard about Astrid's offer. And of course, I should go, and family was so important, and perhaps I wouldn't even want to come back, perhaps I would want to stay in Sweden to be closer to my sister and …

No, I'd said. I'm just going for the funeral. Then I'm coming straight back. But it might take me more than ten days to sort out a new place, now that I'm going away, so …

Sure, Brenda said. She'd speak to the landlord and get the eviction pushed back a month. No problem. And oh, she was so happy for me.

Glad that someone was happy. I sure wasn't. And by the sound of it, it didn't seem Astrid was either.

Still, it must be nice to be able to do stuff like that. Make people do exactly what you want. Just whack them with a big money stick to keep them in line. I wondered what that felt like.

I took a final look at the large clock on the wall and got up from the bench, pulling my carry-on behind me over to the nearest line of people waiting at the security checkpoint. I did my best to look casual, as if I did this sort of thing all the time, but who was I kidding? No one. Everyone kept glancing at me, and I wouldn't have been more uncomfortable strapped to an anthill covered in honey. In fact, that was just one of the places where I'd rather be right now.

The person in front of me stepped through the metal detector, picked up their bag on the other side, and walked off. See, it looked so easy when other people did it. The guard beckoned me forward with a tired gesture. I panicked. I took one step toward her, but that was as far as I got. The guard held up her hand and frowned.

"Please place your phone, wallet, keys, and other metal objects in one of the trays and place your carry-on on the rollers," she said in a voice that suggested that she'd already said those exact words eleventy trillion times this morning.

I didn't have anything in my pockets, so I just placed my carry-on on the rollers and sent it through the x-ray machine. Then I stepped through the security portal. Even though I knew I didn't have anything metal on me, I still expected it to go BEEEP. It didn't. I put my shoes back on and looked around for my gate. It seemed to be in the corridor to the left. I grabbed my carry-on and started walking. Even though I was anxious to get to the gate, I walked straight to the nearest shop. It was a small space with barely room for a skinny child between the shelves. I peered down the narrow aisles at the soda fridges at the back and then glanced at the cashier.

"Can I help you?" he asked and gave me a strained smile.

"I'd like a soda," I said. "And some snacks."

"Allow me," he said, ducking out from behind the counter. "Which one would you like?" he asked when he was over by the fridge.

"A coke, please. No, two. And some Mallomars. And Snickers. King-size if you've got them. Five of those.

And …" I stopped when I saw the look on his face. "That's all," I said instead, even though I knew that this wasn't going to last me until the plane took off, much less until I reached my destination.

He hurried back through the aisle and dumped everything on the counter, starting to ring it all up. I reached inside the door to the shop and paid for my snacks, and took the plastic bag where he'd put everything. "Thank you," I mumbled and wandered off in search of my gate.

There were plenty of seats, but someone was sitting with a fairly regular interval everywhere, and I didn't want to sit next to anyone. I found a bathroom and went in there instead. The bathroom had room for a wheelchair and assistant, so I knew I'd fit in there. I made use of the facilities, since I probably wouldn't be able to use the bathroom on the plane. Then I pulled thick wads of paper from the dispenser and soaked it to give myself a sponge bath. The idea that the entire plane would be able to smell my B.O. made me sick. I had showered before I left home, but the stress of leaving my apartment for more than a quick expedition down the block to the supermarket made my sweat stink of panic and fear.

Once I'd washed off, I sat down on the toilet seat lid and waited. It was easier to sit in here. But then I started thinking that perhaps there was someone outside waiting to use the bathroom, and once that idea had stuck in my head, I couldn't let it go. In the end, I took my plastic bag and my carry-on and left.

A man just got up from one of the seats right at the end of a row over by the gate, and I hurried to sit down. Every two seats had an armrest, but I just about fit between the two armrests, taking up two whole seats. Thankfully, I'd been smart enough to book two seats on the plane.

Two pretty women in uniform appeared and started the boarding process. People got up and stood in line, right past me, but I stayed sitting. I didn't think I could manage to stand in line for too long. But instead of boarding the passengers, one of the flight attendants came over to me.

"Hello, Miss. Are you booked on this flight?" she said, bending down so that we were more or less eye level.

I nodded.

"May I see your boarding pass, please?"

I unzipped the pocket on the side of my purse and found them.

"And are these both for you," she said, her voice lowered out of consideration.

I nodded again, feeling the embarrassment making my cheeks burn. The people standing in line closest to me must have heard what she said.

THE FLIGHT WAS a grueling fourteen hours, but it felt even longer. The whole time, I couldn't even breathe properly. Despite having two seats all to myself, I was terribly uncomfortable, the tucked-away armrest digging into my spine so that I couldn't lean back properly. Being stuck in such a small space with so many strangers made me want to scream out loud. Every time the little cart passed down the aisle, I ordered something, anything, as much as I dared, but the looks I received from the flight attendants and the passengers sitting nearby made me cut my orders in half. Even though I was practically starving myself, people still seemed appalled, and I sipped my mini cokes to make them last and took small bites out of my chocolate bars and the food I ordered to try and calm my stomach.

When the seatbelt lights lit up, finally, I almost cried. But even then, it took forever before we had actually touched down and taxied over to the terminal. I had been boarded ahead of all the other passengers, and one of the flight attendants came over to ask me if I wanted to disembark first, as well.

I shook my head vehemently. "Oh, no. I'll wait until everyone else is gone," I mumbled. It had been a tight squeeze to get me into my two seats, and I did not want to risk getting stuck on the way out, with the entire flight full of impatient passengers staring at me.

She gave me a professional and entirely fake smile and hurried back behind the curtain.

As all the other passengers slowly made their way off the plane, I sat with my head turned away, staring out the tiny window at a section of gray wall and a drainpipe. Not exactly riveting, but better than seeing the curious stares from all the other passengers.

My stomach was growling angrily as the last stragglers passed me by, and I unbuckled the seatbelt extenders and started to get up out of my seat. The flight attendants were standing at the exit, fake smiles glued to their glossy lips and glancing at each other to try and get out of helping me. I ignored them and pushed myself out into the aisle and then sideways toward the exit.

"Goodbye," said the blond flight attendant. "Have a nice day."

I grunted something and swallowed my tears when I saw them grimace in the corner of my eye as I passed them. I bet all three of them and their best friends could have fitted in my sweaty dress.

Finally, I stepped out into the terminal and raced toward the nearest bathroom. Another makeshift sponge bath and an intense cry later, I stared at myself in the mirror, trying to get a grip. It wasn't working. The monster in the mirror, I couldn't quite comprehend that it was me. I bent over, washed my face, rubbing away the smeared mascara and the foundation that looked like yellow mud after the sweaty flight. The result was a pale and splotchy face, not much of an improvement, but I couldn't muster the energy to reapply makeup. And honestly, it wouldn't have made much of a difference. No amount of concealer would have covered up all that I wanted to hide.

I rummaged through my purse after something sweet, anything at all, but I'd already done that on the plane and eaten everything. Even the old emergency Snickers bar I'd found tucked away in a side pocket. Now there was nothing edible in there. Nothing at all. I felt weak, faint almost, and had to remind myself that I *had* eaten on the plane; I wasn't actually starving.

It just felt like it. I couldn't remember the last time I'd eaten this little in a day.

I grabbed my bag and started walking toward the exits, debating whether or not I had time to stop and buy a snack or even a meal, but as soon as I switched on my phone to check the local time, it started buzzing with notifications about missed calls from Astrid. She was probably already waiting for me in the arrivals hall. With a reluctant sigh, I made my way toward the escalators. The ads that papered the walls were in Danish, since the nearest airport for the south of Sweden was Copenhagen, but I could hear both Danish and Swedish being spoken around me. It felt strangely familiar and unfamiliar at the same time. The people around me weren't all tall and blond like the stereotypical image of a Scandinavian, but they were all slim or at least a lot slimmer than me. I'd been fatter than most back in the States, but here, I was a monster. An abomination. Even though the corridor was crowded, everyone made sure to give me a wide berth.

Passing through the automatic doors out into the arrivals hall, I was bombarded with faces, sounds, voices, cries. Everywhere I looked, someone was waving, shouting, greeting a loved one. It was overwhelming, and I felt myself getting confused and bewildered. How was I ever going to find Astrid in this chaos? Would I recognize her? Would she recognize me? I flashed back to my reflection in the bathroom mirror just now and thought that she probably wouldn't. I had barely recognized myself. There were no mirrors in my apartment back home. And I liked it that way. It was bad enough if I went out on a sunny day and happened to catch a glance of myself in the reflection of the storefronts lining the street where I lived. That horrible feeling when you see something that makes you recoil in disgust and then, just a moment later, realize that it's you.

And now I was going to see that same disgust in my sister's eyes. Not looking forward to that.

Not that I didn't want to see my sister. Of course I did.

I just didn't want her to see me.

I stepped through the automatic gates and looked around. Everyone else seemed to have found their loved ones, and everywhere I looked, people were hugging and smiling, so happy it was painful to look at.

I forced myself to look closely at all the faces that surrounded me, to try and find Astrid. She'd be older too. Not a teenager anymore. A lawyer. A married woman.

And then I spotted her. It felt like a punch in the gut, seeing her just a few feet away from me, up on her toes, craning her neck to see behind me, checking her phone, and then looking again. She was stunning. She always had been, of course, ever since we were little, but now, she looked like someone who could be in a commercial. Her hair and makeup were immaculate, her clothes were stylish and pressed and so well-fitting as if they'd been made just for her. I couldn't help but glance down at my dress, a polyester disaster that I'd bought and wore only because it was one of the few garments I'd been able to find in my size. I had actually tried to look nice for this moment. Oh, what a waste of money and energy.

I pushed myself through the crowds, mumbling apologies to everyone I came into contact with. And then I swallowed, and said her name.

"Astrid."

It was barely audible, my voice didn't carry at all, and the arrivals hall was so very noisy. I tried again.

"Astrid." A little too loud this time. Too high-pitched. She jumped and twirled in my direction, and I cringed when I saw the various reactions flash across her face.

"L-lisa?" The disgust. The disbelief. The confusion.

The panic. And then the get-a-grip face. A deep breath. And a forced smile. "Lisa! There you are!"

I just stood there, feeling stupid. Feeling awkward. Feeling like I'd rather be anywhere else in the world right now than right here. "Here I am," I mumbled. All of me. I didn't say that last part, but I couldn't help but think it.

"You came. I was beginning to think you wouldn't …" She bent forward, and I reacted instinctively by taking a step back, not realizing what she was trying to do. Then it dawned on me, and I let her give me a brief hug, cringing again when I felt her soft, dry skin against my clammy cheek. If she wanted to vomit, she hid it well; I'll give her that.

"Here. Let me take that," she said and grabbed the handle of my carry-on before I could protest. "I'm parked in the nearest parking garage; it's not far." Then a worried glance in my direction. "Are you alright to walk? Should I go and bring the car back here?"

I felt my cheeks burning. "I'm fine," I murmured, bracing myself against another stranger pushing past me in a hurry to get to somewhere fast.

"How was your flight?" She was smiling at me, and I tried not to let my frustration show. Small talk? Really?

I shrugged and focused on navigating through the crowds. Keeping up a conversation was way beyond me at this moment.

We left the arrivals hall and exited out into the midmorning sun, trying to keep up with the flow of passengers who all seemed to be in a hurry. I did my best but couldn't do it. Glancing around me, I spotted a small niche by an emergency exit and made my way over to it. Once I'd gotten out of the way of everyone, I leaned up against the wall, struggling to catch my breath. I tried standing tall, keeping my head high, but every time I looked up, I saw someone staring at me with such contempt, such disgust, that I couldn't stand it. It took so much energy to ignore those looks, and I didn't have that much to spare right now.

"Lisa?" Astrid was there, right in front of me. Her voice sounded concerned, but I was certain that what she mostly felt was embarrassment at being seen with this ... this beached whale. "Lisa, are you alright?"

I rubbed my hand over my face and tried to meet her eye. "Fine," I mumbled, not very convincingly. "I just need to ... catch my breath."

She unzipped her purse and pulled out a water bottle. Stainless steel with pretty flowers. "Here," she said. "Have some water. It's nice and cold."

I took a quick swig. The water wasn't just cold, it was freezing, and it made my teeth hurt. "Thanks," I said, handing her back the bottle. What I really needed was a gallon of coke. Lukewarm and flat. What I really needed was to be in my apartment back home, all alone, with my snacks and my microwave pizzas and my sodas and my TV. The intense longing for that safe space made my eyes sting.

I pushed myself away from the wall. "OK. I'm fine now. Let's go."

To my despair, she took my arm and squeezed it tight. "There's no rush," she said. "Just take your time."

I wanted to pull away from her, wanted to keep my sweaty and smelly body away from her pristine and perfect one, but she wouldn't let go, and I didn't have the energy to struggle.

In the end, I just let her help me all the way to her car.

THANKFULLY, Astrid's car turned out to be a large SUV, with plenty of room, even for me. It was a bit of a struggle to get into the passenger seat, but I made it, and I managed to get the seat belt across and fastened, even though my hands were clammy and weak by now. I was panicking but in a slow, low-key way rather than a full-on freak-out.

I didn't know how much longer I'd be able to keep this up without a break. When would I be able to get some time to myself? And get to a grocery store and stock up? Refill my purse with Snickers and Coke.

I should have brought a larger purse.

I clutched my almost empty handbag to my chest and fumbled with the clasp. My fingers felt numb and almost like they weren't part of my body.

"How far?" I mumbled. "To your house, I mean." It was embarrassing that I didn't know where my own sister lived. I didn't even have her address.

She glanced at me. "Oh. Well … I live in Bjärred now. It's about forty minutes from here. But we're not going to my place."

I stared at her hands on the steering wheel as she started the car and backed out of the space. There was a small screen on the dashboard that showed the images from a camera somewhere on the back of the car. I'd never seen that before. "Where are we going then?" I asked. The funeral was tomorrow; I knew that much. So we couldn't be going far.

She drove toward the exit, just giving me another

quick glance as she slowed down and stopped briefly, waiting her turn behind two other cars. She pressed a button, and the window on her side slid down. The car rolled slowly forward toward the ticket machine as the other cars moved off. She leaned out to insert her credit card. The striped barrier had just come down after the car ahead of us but bounced back up right away, and she pressed down on the gas pedal. The car moved gracefully out from the parking garage and slid effortlessly into the congested traffic outside. "We're going to Mormor's cottage," she said, and I felt the last of my stamina give way. My right hand reached for the door and started fumbling for the handle.

I heard a voice that sounded as if it came from far away, quietly wailing something that sounded like an extended Noooooooo. I guess it was my voice. I don't remember saying anything. My fingers found the door handle somehow, and the door opened, but then the seat belt caught me, and I was yanked back against the backrest.

"Lisa, no!" Astrid said, and she sounded just like Mom when she said that; I swear it was like I was instantly five years old again and had done something I wasn't allowed to. The car stopped with a jerk, and someone behind us sounded their horn loudly.

I tried to turn back and find the button to release the seat belt, but Astrid slapped my hand away. "Stop it, Lisa," she said, and this time she didn't sound annoyed. More frightened. "Close that door," she said, and when I didn't, she leaned over me and pulled it shut. Then she sat back up and pressed a button on her own door. I heard all the doors click shut at once. Had my sister just child-locked me into her car?! I was thirty-five, for crying out loud!

"I'm not going back there and you can't make me!" I cried. "I never agreed to that; that was never part of the deal, I would never have come—" The car that had seemed so roomy and spacious just a couple of minutes ago felt cramped and claustrophobic, and there was no air in here. I pounded the buttons on the door, and the window slid down half an inch or so. The air that welled in was thick with exhaust fumes and the stench of diesel. I choked but kept repeating my objections like a mantra. "Let me out, Astrid. I'm not go—"

Another horn sounded behind us, and Astrid checked her rearview mirrors briefly before stepping on the gas pedal again. This time the car moved forward with a jolt, and her movements when she turned the steering wheel to change lanes were not as calm and collected as before. I pressed myself against the door, clutching the seat belt, struggling to catch my breath.

"Just let me out, anywhere," I gasped. "Right here is fine. Or at that gas station." I raised a trembling hand and pointed, but Astrid drove past the exit and onto the highway. "Astrid, please!" My voice was thick with tears now, and I stopped pleading. Just sobbed quietly and stared out the windows at the strange sights and tall buildings zooming by. None of them had been here when I left.

Astrid didn't say a word. Just drove down into the tunnel toward the bridge, constantly checking her mirrors and nervously moving her hands back and forth on the steering wheel. After a couple of minutes in the echoing and claustrophobic underwater tunnel, we emerged on the man-made island in the middle of

Öresund, with the Öresund Bridge rising ahead of us. I could hear her breathing out slowly as the car started its ascent. Not me, though. I was still as tense, perhaps even more, seeing all the unfamiliar sights. The iconic twisted architecture of the Turning Torso building, not quite finished when I left. The bluish Kronprinsen. The churches that rose above the surrounding buildings in the city center over on my left. I'd thought that I'd never see any of this again, and I wished I hadn't.

Glancing over at Astrid, I could see she wasn't too thrilled to have me here either.

We finally reached the Swedish side, and Astrid slowed down as we approached the customs check-point. A customs official in reflective high viz clothes waved us through with a cursory glance inside the car. My sister raised a hand in a wave and accelerated onto the highway that circled the town.

"Why are we going to Mormor's cottage?" I asked, forcing myself to sound calm and collected. Reasonable. That was not what I was feeling, though, "Why can't we go to your place? Or a hotel? I can stay at a hotel if you don't have a guest room. I'll sleep on a park bench or anywhere at all. But I'm not going back there. I just can't."

Astrid shook her head. "Stop it, Lisa. It's just for one night. The funeral is tomorrow, and it's in the church right by her cottage. She'll be buried there in Linderöd, next to Morfar."

A gas station was coming up, with a rest stop, and I gathered all my remaining strength. "I need to use the bathroom," I said, trying to keep the panic from my voice. I had to make her stop this car. There was no way I was going back to Mormor's cottage.

I couldn't bear to look at her, but I heard her breathing in quickly through her nose. "Do you really?" she asked.

I nodded. "It was a long flight," I said, staring out the window on the passenger side so that she wouldn't see my face. My sister had always been able to tell when I was lying.

"Fine," she muttered, flicked on the turn signal, and slowly drifted into the exit lane. I held my breath until we'd gone past the point of no return, and then I sat up and reached for the seat belt again. She drove around the side and slid into a parking space right outside the restrooms. My seatbelt came undone, and I fumbled for the door handle, but of course, it was still locked.

"Could you …?" I asked and glanced over at her.

She looked a little embarrassed and pressed the button for the child safety lock. The door opened and I almost fell out of the car. The moment my feet hit the tarmac, I felt like a huge weight had been lifted off my shoulders. Free! I was free! And there was no way in hell I was getting back in that car. No way in hell was I going to my grandmother's cottage. Never. I staggered toward the restrooms but kept on going right past the doors and turned the corner just as I heard a car door open behind me.

"Lisa!" Astrid called out after me, but I didn't stop.

The automatic doors slid apart and I stepped inside the brightly lit little shop and stumbled toward the soda fridge. I got two 2-liter Coke bottles and as many chocolate bars as I could carry—mostly Snickers because they were my favorites and looked just the same as the ones at home. But I also got a couple of Kexchoklad and a Plopp, for old time's sake. I hadn't had one of those for years. I dropped everything on the counter and stared at the menu above the gas station attendant's head. They had hamburgers, and hot dogs and grilled panini, and …

I didn't even look at the attendant when he started ringing up my purchases. "I'll have a double bacon cheeseburger, with fries, And two regular cheeseburgers," I said and scanned the large, garish color images of the menu. I could stick the cheeseburgers in my purse for later. "And the panini, with pineapple, and … better make that two paninis." My eyes wandered along the lit-up display. "And a large strawberry milkshake."

Gas station food had certainly evolved while I'd been away. When I was a kid, all you could get at a gas station was gas and some sweets. Perhaps a stinky Wunderbaum and a CD with an outdated hits compilation. But this was almost like in the States.

I dared a glance at the attendant and realized that he wasn't even raising an eyebrow at my purchases. I looked around me and noticed that the other customers were primarily families. He must think that I was ordering for my entire family. Or, he just didn't give a damn. The relief after the judgmental looks from the flight attendants and everyone at the airport was immense. I looked around the store, feeling strangely liberated. "And half a dozen donuts," I said. "Half plain and half chocolate-covered. And two cinnamon rolls. No, make that four." Might as well stock up. I had no idea how I was going to get out of here or how I would get home. I couldn't even think about that now. All I could think about was the smell of the hamburgers on the grill behind the counter, and how those chocolate-covered donuts would taste when I bit into them.

I paid for my order and stepped to the side to wait for my food. Someone came up behind me, and I moved even further to let them pass.

"I thought you needed the restroom." Astrid sounded more weary than annoyed. I couldn't look at her. "And what are you doing buying all that …" I swear the word crap came all the way to the tip of her tongue before she managed to stop it. "Soda and candy," she said, shaking her head. "We'll have dinner once we get to Mormor's; there's no need to …"

The attendant came over with the rest of my order in two large brown paper bags. Astrid just stared at them.

I grabbed them, along with the two plastic bags with my soda and the candy, and walked toward the door. There were a couple of picnic tables on a small patch of grass over by the highway, and I made my way there. My sister followed me. I ignored her.

Or rather, It wasn't so much that I ignored her, as the fact that my entire body was trembling from exhaustion and stress. All I could think about was that I needed to eat, I needed to bite into that bacon cheeseburger, I needed a large drink of coke, needed to feel the carbonated bubbles tickle the roof of my mouth and give me that kick, that energy boost, that sweet sugary comforting feeling that I needed in order to figure out how to get myself home.

It must have been raining here earlier in the day and the benches were still wet, but I didn't care. I sat down and ignored the cold seeping through my dress and the creaking sound when the entire table-with-two-attached-benches structure tilted slightly in my direction. I pulled open one of the bags and grabbed my burger. With trembling fingers, I folded back the paper and took a bite. It was too hot, and the cheese burned my tongue, but I didn't care. I gulped that burger down so fast that I didn't even have time to taste it. In between bites, I took large gulps of coke, feeling the sugary bubbles spread throughout my body. I found the milkshake and sucked it up the thick straw. The cool semi-liquid soothed my scorched tongue. Without even a moment's pause, I ate two of the cinnamon buns and three donuts, one plain and two with chocolate. Every bite was followed by a large gulp of coke or another sip of the milkshake.

Slowly, as my stomach was filling up, I started to relax. Started to feel more like myself. Coming back down to earth. I wrapped the cheeseburgers and the paninis in napkins and stowed them away in my purse, along with the candy bars. Seeing the side of the purse bulging out made me feel calm and safe. I had hated feeling so hungry on the plane and not being able to do anything about it. This would see me through the next few hours, no matter what happened. The second coke bottle I kept in the plastic carrier bag, along with the cinnamon buns and the donuts. The trash went in the bin by the table. Only when everything was tidied away did I lift my head and look at my sister. She was standing on the other side of the table, staring at me. I forced myself to meet the stare. I wasn't a kid anymore. I didn't have to do what she said.

"Are you done?" she said, her voice both incredulous and annoyed.

"You can leave," I said. "I'm not coming with you."

Her left eyebrow did that thing it always used to do. It still pissed me off. "Oh, yes, you are."

I shook my head. "I'm sorry," I said. "I really am. Sorry I wasted your time and your money. I'll pay you back for the plane ticket, somehow." *Yeah, right*, the sarcastic voice in the back of my head said. *That's a priority, now that you're going to be homeless.* "But there's just no way in hell I'm going to do this." I took a deep breath. "I just can't. I thought I could manage the funeral if I really pulled myself together, but ..." I shook my head. "This is too much, Astrid. Going to her cottage?" I trembled. "I can't go back there, Astrid. I truly can't."

"But —"

"No, Astrid. No." I forced myself to look her in the eye. It was unbearable. She looked so much like herself as a little girl that I felt myself plummeting back through the years, shrinking to my five-year-old self right there in the gas station parking lot. "I can't ever go back there."

She was quiet for a long time. Then she sighed. "I understand," she said slowly. I opened my mouth to protest, but she cut me off. "Or perhaps understand is not the right word. Because I don't, really. I know you took it hard. And I can tell that it's still difficult for you." I opened my mouth again, but she still wouldn't let me speak. "But Lisa, honestly. What happened there ... It didn't just happen to you. I mean. She was *my* friend."

I closed my mouth firmly. Oh, no. We were *not* talking about *that*. Not now. Not here. Not ever. I wanted to slap my hands over my ears and babble to drown out the sound of her words, but I was paralyzed. Could not move.

"I understand that it must have been a traumatic experience for you, Lisa," she said, still with that weird almost-mom voice. "But Ellen was *my* friend. And what happened to her was an accident. It was terribly sad, and I felt horrible about it for the longest time, but …" She shook her head. "Life goes on, Lisa. Ellen wouldn't have wanted me to stop living because of what happened to her. Of course, I've felt guilty about it over the years. About the fact that I wasn't with you that day. If I had been, perhaps things would have turned out differently. Perhaps she'd even be alive today."

I could feel myself being sucked down into a narrow tunnel, a wormhole into the past. Into a past that I'd done my best to distance myself from over the past thirty years. Into a past where I was a chubby little girl with long dark hair, always tagging along with my older sister and her best friend in the whole wide world.

Ellen. The coolest girl I'd ever known. And the first person in my life who died.

4

LITTLE LISA

THE FIRST THING I became aware of as I drifted up from a deep sleep was whispering voices.

"Hush, you'll wake her," said my sister.

"No, she's sleeping like the dead," giggled Ellen.

And then the sound of bare feet across the floor-boards toward the steep stairs and down a couple of steps. I struggled out of my tangled sheets and sat up, pushing my mussed-up hair from my face just as they disappeared out of sight.

"Where are you going?" I called after them. "Can I come?"

Both girls exploded into muted giggles. Then Astrid hushed her friend and poked her head back up into sight at the top of the stairs. "Nowhere. Just out. Go back to sleep, Lisa. It's really early."

And then they ran down the stairs and out the front door before I could even get out of bed. I had been sound asleep just a moment ago, and I had managed to twist my nightgown around my torso in my sleep so that it was as tight as a straitjacket. While I unwound it,

I stumbled over to the window and watched the two girls disappearing along the path into the woods on the other side of the yard. My sister and her best friend. Off for a morning swim in the lake. And they hadn't wanted me to tag along.

I pulled off my nightgown and found my cutoffs and T-shirt on the floor where I'd dropped them last night. Buttoning the jeans was always a bit tricky, but once I was dressed, I climbed the stairs down from the attic and went into the kitchen. Mormor was sitting at the table, reading a newspaper and drinking her coffee. I walked over to her and slipped under her arm into her fragrant warm embrace.

"Good morning, pumpkin," she said, putting her coffee cup down to give me a proper cuddle. "Sleep well?"

I nodded. "Astrid wouldn't let me go swimming with them," I complained, bottom lip well protruding.

Mormor ruffled my hair and got up. "Can you blame her for wanting some time alone with her friend?" she asked and walked over to the small refrigerator.

I crawled up into the old kitchen sofa and pulled the rug over my bare legs while she made me breakfast. Her homemade bread in thick slices, covered with her own canned raspberry jam, made from actual raspberries that I had picked myself, well, me and Astrid and Mormor, during our last visit, a month ago. While I was chewing on the sandwich, big as both my hands, she put a small pot on the woodstove and made some cocoa. She poured it into a large ceramic mug, added a little milk to cool it down, and placed the cocoa in front of me. It was still too hot, despite the milk, so I let it sit. It was only just drinkable when Astrid and Ellen came back from the lake.

They burst into the kitchen, shrieking with laughter, their long blond hair dripping wet and their skinny arms covered with goosebumps. They looked more like sisters than Astrid and I ever had done. Mormor poured them some cocoa as well and opened the hatch on the stove to let the warmth out into the small kitchen. The girls huddled in front of the stove, wrapped in their large towels, and complained through chattering teeth about how cold it was.

I sipped my cocoa and tried not to think hateful thoughts about my sister, even though I would have given anything to be freezing over by that stove right now. But it wasn't Astrid's fault that I didn't have a best friend like Ellen. Mormor had said that we could both bring a friend for the last week of the summer break, so that we wouldn't get sick and tired of one another. She had probably not even considered that we wouldn't both be able to find someone to bring, or what would happen if only one of us did. As it were, I had been the third wheel all week, and now, with only a few days remaining before we went back home and started school, it didn't seem as if that was going to change.

I focused on my sandwich, on the soft bread and the sweet jam, textures so different from the store-bought bread back home, and the cheese or ham slices that my mom or dad put on our sandwiches. Everything was so different here at Mormor's, and I usually loved it, but usually, it was Astrid and me who ran down to the lake in the morning, just as the sun had risen behind the tall trees in the forest that surrounded Mormor's little cottage. It was Astrid and me who ran all the way to the end of the dock and jumped into the water, where a soft mist covered the surface as the cold morning air made contact with the warm water of the lake. My dad had said that there was a scientific explanation for the way the mist curled out of the dark water. Still, I wasn't entirely sure that there wasn't something to my grandmother's theory that had to do with fairies and magical creatures in the vast lake that was said to be bottomless in the middle of the deep, dark forest.

I shivered under my blanket and took another sip of the cocoa. It was barely lukewarm by now but sweet and fragrant. With one fingertip, I traced the pattern on the ceramic mug, large daisies with different colored petals and chunky leaves. Then I heard a soft patter against the window to my left. When I looked up, there were streaks of rain against the small squares of glass.

"It's raining," I said to no one in particular. Astrid and Ellen were huddled together over by the stove, talking in whispers, but Mormor looked up from the sandwiches she was making for them and nodded.

"So it is," she said. "And the forecast says that it's going to rain most of the day. We'll have to think of something to do indoors."

Astrid turned her head toward Mormor. "Can we go to the mall?" she asked eagerly.

I sighed. I knew what my sister's idea of a great indoor activity was. Browsing every clothing store in the entire mall for hours on end, trying on a million outfits, and then perhaps not even buying anything. It was my idea of purgatory, having to sit outside the fitting rooms and waiting for her to finish.

"Oh," said Mormor. "I don't know." She glanced at me. "That wasn't too fun for you last time, was it?"

39

I was torn. Astrid was staring at me with that beseeching look she got, and I wondered what it would be worth to her if I said I'd also like to go. And then I looked at Mormor, who looked understanding and kind, the way she always did. Too many looks. How was I supposed to be able to make up my mind when everyone kept looking at me like that?

I glanced down, and my eyes fell on the newspaper that Mormor had been reading. In the corner of the page closest to me were several large ads for different movies. The symbol above all the movie posters looked just like the sign outside of the mall. "Do they have a movie theater at the mall?" I blurted out.

Mormor came over to the table and looked down at the paper. "Yes." She glanced over her shoulder at Astrid and Ellen. "Can you find a movie that all three of you would like to see, do you think?"

Astrid and Ellen rushed over to the table, pulling the paper away from me and scouring the listings. "This one," said Ellen. "A couple of girls in my ballet class have seen it, and they said it was great."

Mormor took the paper and peered at the small print. "Looks all right to me," she said. Then she folded the paper and handed it to me. "What do you say, Lisa? Would you like to see this movie?"

I grabbed the folded-up paper and stared at the image. A pretty girl with dark hair in braids and a bird on a branch just above her. I had no idea what kind of movie this could be, but if Ellen wanted to see it, I was tempted to say yes, just to please her. "Sure," I said, and Astrid and Ellen bolted for the stairs.

"There's no rush," Mormor called out after them. "The mall doesn't even open for a couple of hours yet."

But they were already out of sight and thundering around up in the small room in the attic like a herd of stampeding elephants. She sighed. "What do you say, Lisa, dear? Would you like another sandwich?"

I was pretty full already, to be honest, from that first giant piece of bread, but I felt my chin move up and down in an eager nod, just the same.

"And some more cocoa?" she asked.

Another nod. I curled up underneath the blanket and tried to ignore the thumps and giggles from upstairs. The second sandwich was just as big as the first but tasted even better.

At least, that's what I tried to convince myself.

5

LISA

I PUSHED the disturbing images from my mind and grabbed my things.

"I'm not going to talk about that," I muttered. "As I said, I'm sorry about the inconvenience, but I have to go home now. I'll just get my bag."

I started walking back toward her car, looking around to see if I could find a bus stop or a map of the area. I could hear her footsteps behind me.

"What home?" she asked, and I gritted my teeth. "You were being evicted, wasn't that what you said? Do you even have a home to go to, Lisa?"

I kept going, but my steps slowed down a little. "I was given an extension for another month," I muttered. "My social worker spoke to the landlord."

But that extension had been granted because I had told Brenda that my sister would help me get another place, the horrible voice in the back of my head said. If I went home now, Astrid wasn't going to lift a finger to help me out.

I tried to convince myself that I didn't need her help, but my feet knew I was lying. They slowed down and stopped, right next to an air-conditioning unit that blasted my bare legs with hot air. I swallowed down the tears and what little pride I had left and turned toward my sister.

"A month," she said. "Will you be able to get another place in a month, Lisa? Because you weren't working, you said so. So you have no job, and you've been evicted. How are you going to find a new apartment?" She glanced at my bulging shoulder bag and the Coke bottle in the plastic bag that was cutting into my chubby fingers. "How are you even paying for … food and stuff?"

I could see how it disgusted her. What I had become. What I had done to myself.

Well, we couldn't all be Miss Perfect in our immaculate outfits and fancy cars with a video camera for a rearview mirror.

"A credit card," I muttered.

She shook her head. "So you're not actually *paying* for any of it," she said, and I could see that she struggled to keep the contempt out of her voice. "How were you going to pay for the apartment that I was helping you get?"

I shrugged. "I was on a disability pension. But they retracted that because I couldn't jump through all of their unreasonable hoops."

"What hoops?" she said, crossing her arms and then uncrossing them again. "Like, rehabilitation plans and stuff like that?"

I nodded.

"What was so unreasonable about that? Don't you want to get better? Healthier?"

I turned and started walking again. She couldn't even begin to imagine what it was like. Everything was so easy for her; she had no idea how hard some of the things they'd wanted me to do were for someone with my ... obstacles.

Your blubber, said the mean voice inside my head. *Everything is hard when you're hauling around a whole other person around your waist. A whale wrapped around your midriff.*

"Lisa, stop," Astrid said behind me, but I wasn't staying around to be judged by my perfect sister. I had to get out of here, had to find my way home.

I stepped off the curb, and suddenly my ears were filled with a screeching sound and a loud, angry car horn. Looking up, a car had stopped just a couple of inches from my right leg. I hadn't seen it coming. Hadn't looked where I was going. How was I ever going to get back home if I couldn't even get across the gas station parking lot?

"Lisa, for crying out loud!" Astrid grabbed my arm and pulled me back up on the pavement, waving apologetically to the driver, who was yelling something muffled from inside the car. She tore the plastic bag from my hand and took my arm in a firm grip. "Just come with me. Just get back in the car, where you'll be safe. We are on the highway, there's no way you're leaving here on foot, and if you think that I'll let you hitch a ride with some random stranger, you've got another thing coming."

She was dragging me back toward her car, and I

wanted to pull out of her grip; I did, but there was something about her almost-mom voice that made it very difficult to fight back. I glanced back over my shoulder at the cars swooshing past on the highway and realized that she was probably right.

"Not to Mormor's cottage," I whispered. "Anywhere but there."

She glanced at me. "Just get back in the car."

She un-bleeped the car doors and more or less pushed me inside the passenger seat, slamming the door shut with more force than was actually necessary. It still only made a soft thud. Then she kept her eyes firmly on me as she walked around to the driver's side and got in beside me. She breathed out but didn't start the car.

"You can't just run away like that, Lisa. You're not a kid anymore," she said, staring out the windscreen. "I'm not going to give you that old cliche about having to face your fears, but I will tell you this. Nothing will ever get better if you keep doing the same thing that you've been doing. And looking at you, and from what little you've told me, I don't think that what you've been doing has been working for you all that great."

I didn't reply, just looked down at my hands that were in my lap, not resting, just laying there all powerless.

"Tell you what," she said. "I am going to stick to my side of the bargain. I am going to help you get a new place. And I am going to do everything I can to help you get your life back on track. I know it feels insurmountable, but I promise you that it can be done, with help." She took a deep breath. "I understand that it must have been hard for you, all alone. But you are here now, and

I'm not going to let you disappear again until I feel certain that you are strong enough to make it on your own, if that's how you want it." She paused. "And all I want from you in return is that you stand next to me at Mormor's funeral tomorrow."

"That's not all you're asking," I whispered, my voice hoarse and weak. I forced myself to raise my head and look at her. "I said I would go with you to the funeral, but now, you want me to go back *there*."

She looked so sad. "You used to love it there," she said. "It's the most beautiful place in the world, and Mormor was the most amazing person in both of our lives, and you just turned your back on her, just …" She blinked rapidly a few times. "You broke her heart, Lisa. She thought that you blamed her for not keeping Ellen safe, or for not keeping *you* safe from having to experience all that, I don't know."

I frowned. Was that it? I didn't think so. "I never blamed her," I said, my voice unsteady. "It wasn't *her* fault."

Astrid stared at me. "Well, she was convinced that you did, and you let her carry that blame to her grave." She sat up, adjusting her jacket behind her back. "I think it would be good for you to spend one last night in her cottage with my family and me. Say goodbye to Mormor. Let her know that you didn't blame her. Let her go in peace." She reached out and placed her warm, soft hand on one of my cold, lifeless ones. "Don't you think that could be good for you as well? A healing experience, even?"

I couldn't see anything good with returning there, not ever. And heal? Not bloody likely, after all this time. But there was something else that she had said that

46

stuck in my brain like a burr. "Your *family*?" I said. "As in … children?"

She leaned back. "Elinor and Jonas. They're seven and five. You are an aunt, Lisa. You have a niece and a nephew."

I stared at her. "And they are there? At Mormor's cottage? Right now?"

I had no idea what my sister's kids looked like, but suddenly, my mind was filled with images of a little girl and a little boy that wore an uncanny resemblance to my sister and me when we were little, helpless little children in terrible danger. "How could you take them there? How could you *leave* them there?" I gasped, shocked at the idea.

She looked at me with not a smidgen of under-standing in her eyes. "It is the greatest place in the world for kids," she said matter-of-factly. "I've always thought so, and what happened to Ellen didn't change that." She squeezed my hand. "It was an accident, Lisa. Accidents happen, and as a parent, I've had to come to terms with the fact that I can't protect my children from everything. Of course, they're not allowed to go swim-ming in the lake without an adult present; I'm more strict than our parents were on that point. But apart from that, I'm happy that we'll be able to keep Mormor's cottage as a second home so that my kids can spend their summers there, just like we did."

I could barely breathe. She had no idea. She never knew. She had put her children in such danger because I had never told her. I had never told anyone what had happened that time with Ellen.

My hands fumbled after the seat belt, clicking it into place. We had to go. Had to go there now!

47

"It wasn't an accident," I said, but the words barely carried across the car to my sister. A lorry rumbled by, and she leaned closer.

"Sorry, what was that?" she asked, a slight frown between her perfectly plucked eyebrows.

"It wasn't an accident," I repeated, louder, but by now, the lorry had passed, and I ended up almost screaming into the muffled silence inside the car. "Ellen didn't drown. She was murdered."

THE LOOK in my sister's eyes when I said that cut me like a dull knife, straight to the heart. It wasn't just that she didn't believe me. And why should she, honestly? I had just told her something completely unbelievable that went against everything she had been told. But it was more than that. She wasn't sure if I was lying, exaggerating, or if there was something wrong with me.

She didn't just look at me with disbelief. She looked at me with suspicion. Worry. And perhaps even a little fear.

What had I become?

What had she brought into her life by paying for my plane ticket here?

I could see her struggling to find her footing, scrambling to find a way to sort this out, before she took me back to her family. She wasn't just very much like Mom. She *was* a mom, and her older-sister condescending attitude toward me had been supplemented with a lioness level of protectiveness.

"Why ... why would you say something so preposterous?" she said, her voice forced into levelness and calm.

My mind was a turmoil of confusion, fear, panic, and a desire to run for the hills. But I knew I wouldn't get far, so I stayed in the passenger seat, the seat belt cutting into my belly and across my chest like two pieces of piano wire.

I hadn't meant to tell her. The words had just popped out of me when I panicked at the idea of her children at the cottage.

"Never mind," I mumbled. "Just drive."

Her eyebrows rose half an inch. "Drive?"

"To Mormor's cottage," I said. "We have to go there now. Come on."

She didn't move. Just stared. Tried to figure me out but failed miserably. "Now, you want to go?"

I shook my head. "I don't *want* to go. I *have to* go. There's a difference. Come on. Just drive!"

I turned and stared out the window on the passenger side, clutching the seatbelt to relieve a little of the discomfort. I could hear her starting the car and backing out of the space slowly. I didn't look at her but was pretty sure that she kept one eye on me to see how I would react.

We got back on the highway and drove for a while, past the city and continuing north. I recognized some buildings but was still completely unprepared when the mall came into sight, on the left-hand side of the road.

The mall where I'd seen him for the first time. The steel-gray-haired man with his weird family.

I tried to push the memories back into the dark crevasses of my brain, where they had been hidden all these years. I couldn't think about that now. I couldn't think about that ever. I just didn't have that kind of strength.

Did anyone?

"Is it much further?" I asked, feeling antsy and restless.

"Don't you know where we are?" she said. "Didn't you recognize that mall we just drove past? We used to go there, remember? Go shopping, and even to the movies once."

I pressed my hands against my eyes to try and keep the images from popping up on my retinas. "Yeah, but I was five," I muttered. "I had no concept of distance. I didn't need to know the way. I just got in the back of the car, and after a while, that could have been five minutes or five hours, the door opened, and I had arrived at my destination."

She snorted a bit. "That's true. And sometimes, those five-minute trips could feel like five hours, and vice versa."

"Are we there yet?" I whined, mimicking our distant childhood selves.

"Exactly."

She went quiet for a while. Then, "Lisa, is there something I need to know? Before we get to the cottage?" She glanced over at me. "Are you on any kind of medication or ...? Do you have a doctor or a shrink that I could call if anything should ... happen to you?"

My sister was a wiz at diplomacy.

Someone else might have said it straight out: Have you gone stark raving mad since we last met? Should you be walking around without a minder?

Should you be sedated?

Oh, how I wished that I could be sedated.

Anything to get out of this nightmare.

I couldn't believe I was going back there. That I had told Astrid to drive me there.

To Mormor's cottage, that had once been the most perfect place to be, just as Astrid had said.

Until one day, when it had turned into hell on earth.

And nothing had ever been the same again.

6

LITTLE LISA

As I'D EXPECTED, being at the mall with Astrid and Ellen was a drag. Mormor noticed this time and offered me a treat while we waited for the girls to try on one outfit after another. I couldn't understand the point in trying on clothes that you weren't even going to buy, but as I bit into the giant, crumbly cookie, I didn't mind as much anymore.

Mormor sat next to me on the bench outside the shop where Astrid and Ellen were, but we didn't speak. She sat there, apparently quite content with looking at the people passing by, nodding at most of them, exchanging a few words with some who came over to say hi.

Just as I put the last piece of the cookie into my mouth, I noticed her eyes fix on a family coming out of a shop a couple of doors down. The man was tall and wiry, his hair steel-gray and his face set in a grim, almost cruel, grimace. His wife, I assumed, was as short as he was tall, as soft and round as he was gaunt and angular, and her features were blurred by a layer of fat.

Her eyes seemed remote, where his were piercing. Behind them came a girl, a year or two older than me, probably. Her long, straight hair was trapped in two braids, so tight that they almost bent from the tension, and she was wearing an old-fashioned dress with nylon stockings, even though it was the middle of the summer. On her feet were shiny Mary Janes that looked a size or two too small for her. If it wasn't the shoes that bothered her, something did, because she looked pained and kept her eyes down the entire time I saw them.

I assumed the girl was their grandchild, but when they walked past us, I heard the woman scolding the child for not keeping her back straight, and she replied with a cowed voice, "Yes, Mother," like some character from an old black-and-white movie.

"That was her *mother*?" I whispered incredulously to Mormor, who had opened her purse and was rummaging around with her head bent down as the weird family walked past. "She looks as old as you!"

Mormor glanced at me, a small smile playing in the corners of her mouth. "Well, she's not *quite* as old as that," she replied dryly. Then she looked after the family as they disappeared down the corridor toward the exits. "But she's old to have a daughter Astrid's age; you're not wrong about that."

"Her hair was all white!" I whispered, even though the family had disappeared out of sight.

Mormor nodded, still staring at the doors they'd left through. "It happens like that sometimes," she said absentmindedly. She turned toward me. "In olden days, they used to say that someone's hair could go gray overnight if they got really frightened." She smiled. "Perhaps she's seen a ghost."

I sat up, crumpling up the small paper wrapper that my cookie had come in. It still smelled of chocolate. "But there's no such thing as ghosts," I said. "Right, Mormor?"

Her smile faded. "No, there's no such thing as ghosts," she said. "But Vera must have had some fright because she is not the girl I used to know."

I looked over toward the exits. The doors opened and closed with a whoosh every time someone entered or left the building. "Did you know her when she was a girl?" The idea of that white-haired woman ever being a little girl felt alien, and I couldn't quite wrap my mind around it. It was like trying to picture Mormor as a child, quite impossible.

Mormor nodded. "She grew up on the farm not far from my cottage. She went to the same school as your mother, only a few years ahead. I knew her parents well enough, but after they died, and she married that man …" She shook her head. "They keep to themselves, is all," she said. "I haven't spoken to her for years. I heard that they had a child, but that's probably only the third or fourth time I've ever laid eyes on the girl, even though they are some of my closest neighbors. We don't bother with the Johanssons."

She took her purse and got up. "The movie is starting soon. Let's see if we can pry the girls away from that shop."

I threw away the crumpled paper in the bin next to the bench and grabbed her hand. "Can we get popcorn at the movies?"

Mormor laughed. "You just ate a cookie the size of your head!" She squeezed my hand. "Well, you'll be going back to school soon. What are grannies for, eh, if not to spoil their granddaughters?"

The movie was every bit as great as Ellen's ballet friends had said it would be. Lisa and Ellen liked it too, and for once, they didn't spoil it by whispering and giggling. We all sat transfixed by the images on the big screen.

The story was that of a Sioux girl, the girl in the ad, who had been separated from her family and the rest of the tribe when they were moving from their winter camp to their summer lodgings. She wasn't much older than me, but she was used to being out in the woods and such and wasn't frightened to be alone, not like me.

She had to fend for herself for several days while struggling to track down her family and catch up with them. She was very clever and resourceful, and her mother had taught her what plants were edible and how to make a shelter and stuff like that. It looked quite cozy when she snuggled down under a tree and covered herself with dry leaves. I would have been scared stiff by all the strange noises and the complete darkness, but that little girl was fine.

Until the Hunter came.

Just when the girl was starting to close in on the rest of her tribe, and we all thought that the movie would have a happy ending, a man appeared. He was not one of her people. His skin was pale, reddened by the sun, and his hair was that same metal gray as Mormor's neighbor. He had a gun, and the girl hid from him, just in time. Then she lay there, trembling, as he used that gun to kill a beautiful deer that the girl had seen drinking from the creek earlier that morning. It was so sad! The tears were streaming down my face, and I was

55

on the edge of my seat, frightened for the girl, worried that she'd never make it back to her family.

She did, of course. It would have been a pretty crappy movie otherwise.

We all agreed that it was the best movie ever, and in the car back to Mormor's, it wasn't just Astrid and Ellen babbling on about it; I was also part of the conversation, recalling the details from the movie that I'd liked best.

For the first time since we'd come to Mormor's, I felt included.

It was the greatest feeling ever.

OVER THE NEXT couple of days, our games were all based on the movie we'd seen. It was great. For once, Astrid and Ellen didn't seem to mind me tagging along.

We spent all day out in the woods surrounding Mormor's cottage, pretending to be little Sioux girls that had been separated from our tribe, trying to find our way back to our families.

Of course, it wasn't as bad since it was the three of us. Being lost in the woods with two other girls, that was no hardship at all. We played and played and didn't go back inside until our stomachs growled with hunger. The little girl in the movie had eaten all sorts of leaves and roots and berries, but we didn't find any leaves we wanted to eat, and anyway, Mormor had dinner ready, so why eat roots?

On the afternoon of the second day of our game, we spotted a man in the woods. One moment we were all alone, and the next moment, Astrid slapped a hand in front of my mouth and pulled me in behind a tree, away from the narrow path we'd been walking on.

My heart raced in my chest as I heard footsteps coming toward us. In the corner of my eye, I saw Ellen crouching down, burying her face against her arm to keep her giggles from carrying. How she could be laughing, I couldn't for the life of me understand.

Because there, just a few feet away from where we were hiding, came a man. I only caught glimpses of him at first. But one thing I did see was that he carried a rifle under his arm.

The Hunter! My mouth went completely dry, and I held my breath, just waiting for him to disappear so that we could run back home to Mormor.

But Astrid and Ellen had other plans. As the man disappeared out of sight, Ellen held up one finger in front of her lips, looking at me with a stern face. Then she sneaked onto the path and started to follow him. Astrid slowly let go of me and went after her.

I stood there, behind the tree, completely bewildered. I never wanted to follow him, but I also wasn't too keen on the idea of going all the way back to Mormor's on my own.

The Hunter might be a scary man, but I'd rather be with my sister than all alone.

It was a good thing that we had practiced how to move through the forest without making a sound, because that meant that the Hunter never knew that we were on his trail.

We followed him up to the edge of the forest, where a huge, red barn loomed in the shadows of the tall trees. There were wide doors on both sides of the barn so that I could see straight through the building. On the other side of the yard was a large white house that looked strangely nice, considering that the Hunter probably lived there.

We sat crouched down behind a fallen tree trunk for a long time, watching the Hunter working in his barn. Eventually, Astrid and Ellen got bored, and we left.

On our way back through the woods, Astrid and Ellen talked animatedly about the Hunter and all the animals he had killed with his rifle.

Animals and little Sioux girls, probably.

They were giggling a lot, but I didn't think it was very funny.

7

LISA

THE WINDING ROAD through the woods, the last stretch before the turn toward Mormor's cottage, was so beautiful, the trees standing tall and imposing and the sun slanting through them to create glowing streaks through the darkness. A magical place of trolls and fairies. I had always been so excited when we got this far, jumping up and down in the backseat. Soon! Soon, I would get to see Mormor. Soon, I would get to go out into the woods and play! Soon!

Now, I was clasping the seatbelt as if it was a lifeline, struggling for breath. The panic had closed in on me as soon as Astrid turned into the smaller road from the highway, and now, I wasn't sure if I was going to make it all the way to the cottage.

But I had to.

Those two innocent children. My sister's children.

I was the only one who could save them.

Save them from the nightmares that lived in the woods surrounding Mormor's cottage.

The images that flashed before my eyes were

disjointed and confusing, but one thing was clear. One thing I knew for sure. Ellen's death had not been an accident. Someone had hurt her.

The Hunter.

The cowboy from the movie screen appeared on the inside of my retinas, turning toward me and spitting tobacco from the corner of his mouth. He raised his gun and pointed it, not at me but at something down by the river. The little Sioux girl had bent down over the water, cupping her hands to drink. I tried to scream, but the panic had squeezed all the air from my lungs, and I couldn't make a sound. The girl got up and turned toward me. But it wasn't the Sioux girl from the movie.

It was Ellen.

A shot rang out, and I jumped.

Astrid put her hand on my arm, stroking it. "We're nearly there," she said. "Are you OK?"

I shook my head. It felt as if I was going to be sick. Or die. Or spontaneously combust.

I'd had panic attacks before, but it had been a while since the last one. I had learned to avoid them. Learned to arrange my life so that I didn't expose myself to triggers.

If I just stayed in my apartment. If I had plenty of food and snacks at hand, and my TV on, my boring, repetitive, predictable shows, hour after hour, to keep my brain from trying to come up with thoughts of its own. Then I was fine.

But this? Getting on an airplane. Traveling back across the Atlantic to see my sister, that I hadn't seen in almost two decades. Going back to Mormor's cottage, where I had sworn that I would never set foot again. Meeting my brother-in-law and my sister's children and seeing the looks in their eyes … I already knew how they were going to react when they saw me; I had seen it too many times before to even dare hope that their reactions would be different.

Why was I doing this again?

I turned my head slowly and stared at Astrid. At her strained expression. Her tight grip on the steering wheel. Still pretty calm and collected, even though she had been confronted with so many unpleasant revelations over the last couple of hours.

That her baby sister had turned into a grotesque monster.

That her childhood friend had been murdered.

And/or that said sister had gone completely insane.

It must be difficult for her, I realized. This was not what her life was usually like. She didn't spend her days trying to avoid disasters, if you didn't consider a spilled glass of milk, being late for an appointment, or a flat tire a disaster.

I didn't.

My disasters were on another scale, entirely.

When my kind of shit hit the fan, I almost died.

———

THE YARD in front of Mormor's cottage looked just the same as when I'd been here last, only several sizes smaller. It threw me for a while, and even though I was almost choking in the passenger seat, I couldn't get out of the car.

Astrid switched off the engine, and everything went quiet, except for a slow ticking sound from somewhere under the hood. I focused on my breathing, on telling myself that I could handle this, that this was too important to let my fears and phobias take over. There were two little children at risk, and somehow I had to convince my sister that she had to get her kids out of here. That she must leave here at once, sell this place, and never ever come back.

Better yet, burn it to the ground.

Suddenly, I saw tall flames reaching for the night sky, sparks like fireworks in all the colors of the rainbow, and there was no air at all in the car. Not one molecule of oxygen. I fumbled for the seat belt, managed to get it undone, and then the door handle. If it hadn't been such a tight squeeze, I would have fallen out of the car, onto the grass. Now, I managed to stay on my feet, but only until I had staggered over to the stone steps leading up to the kitchen door. I sank down and felt the chill of the stone through my polyester muumuu and my clammy underwear. I felt sick, and the air around me seemed unable to quench my choking sensation, even though I took deep breaths, forcing myself to breathe in through the nose and out through the mouth.

Some of the things all of those stupid therapists had tried to teach me over the years seemed to have stuck, at least.

Something blocked out the sun, and I looked up at the silhouette of Astrid, standing over me.

"Lisa ..." she said, and there were so many undertones in her voice that I couldn't even name them all. Fear. Worry. Perhaps even a little confusion.

"Just give me a minute," I croaked, grabbing hold of the metal railing and pressing my hot forehead against it. "I just ... need a minute."

To her credit, she gave me several. And not once did she shift her weight from one hip to the other or sigh that annoyed sigh that she always used to do whenever I was frustrating her. She just stood there. Waited.

After a while, I could feel the worst of it pass. Another couple of breaths, and then I could sit up straight, wiping the sweat from my face, forcing some kind of smile onto my lips.

"OK," I said. "I'm fine." I looked around the yard, at the apple trees and the tool shed and all of it. So familiar, but still so alien. "Everything has shrunk," I said and then forced myself to look at my sister. Everything but her, that is. Astrid was tall and strong and all grown up. A mom. My sister was a mom.

A faint smile appeared on Astrid's stern lips. "Yes. I guess it must seem that way to you. You haven't been here for ... what? Thirty years?"

I stared at her. "And you have?"

She frowned. "Of course. Every summer." And then she saw the look on my face. "Come on, Lisa. You must have known that we kept coming back?"

But I hadn't had a clue. "We never came back here again. I made Mom and Dad promise. Instead, we went to all those summer camps and on road trips and ..." I said, searching through memories stowed away so far back in my brain that I didn't even know where to begin to look for them.

Astrid shook her head. "That was just what they told you, since you freaked out so bad whenever anyone even mentioned coming here." She looked closer at me. "But you must have realized, surely? You didn't honestly think that Mom would never visit her own mother again, just because you threw a fit anytime anyone talked about coming here?"

I stared at her. I didn't know what was worse, that the whole family had lied to me for years, or that I had believed them. Looking back, this explained why our parents had split up their vacation time and gone on separate holidays every year. Most of the time, as I recalled, I had gone off somewhere with Dad, while Mom was working and Astrid was at camp, and then, when Mom was off from work, she and Astrid would go on a trip somewhere, while I was at some camp or other.

Had they come here, every summer? A weird sense of retroactive panic filled me.

"All that time …" I stammered. "You came back here?" I gasped for air again, feeling my chest constricting, forcing myself to breathe properly. "And you were here? You and Mom?"

Astrid nodded. "And I've kept coming back here, every year. First on my own, and then with Fredrik, and eventually with the kids." She looked around the yard. "This place was the best thing about my childhood, and I wanted my children to have this experience growing up as well." She looked at me again. "So you see, I'm not selling this place. Mormor left it to both of us, but since you don't want it, I can buy you out. It won't be much, there's not much land, and the property values around here are pretty modest, but I'm prepared to be generous." She swallowed and then forced herself to meet my eye. "I can tell that these years have been hard for you, and I'm hoping that this can be a turning point." She looked down, then back up again. "I want to try and patch up our relationship—" I opened my mouth to

64

speak, but she cut me off. "I don't know if we can ever be ... close, or whatever, but I'd like us to not be completely cut off from one another. I want to know what's going on in your life, and I want my kids to know their aunt." She paused for a while, brushing away an invisible speck of dust from her immaculate blouse, that was somehow not even a little wrinkled from sitting in the car. My dress looked like an accordion. "We don't have a lot of extended family, and I ..."

I didn't know what to say. I hadn't even known that I had a niece and a nephew until an hour ago and had no idea what it meant to be an aunt. But the wild protectiveness that had surged through me when Astrid told me about them, told me that they were *here*, had made it obvious that they meant something to me, even though I had never met them.

I just couldn't wrap my mind around the fact that they had been here all this time. That Astrid had been here, all those summers during our childhood and teens, and then as an adult, with her own children.

Astrid had no idea.

I had to remember that. She couldn't imagine what my life was like because she had probably never experienced anything like this panic attack.

And she had never experienced anything like what had started my panic attacks in the first place.

She wasn't there.

She was home sick.

8

LITTLE LISA

MORMOR TUTTED when she saw Astrid at the breakfast table the next morning.

"What's the matter, sweetie?" she said, pushing the hair from Astrid's face. "Are you not feeling so good?"

Astrid looked up at her, and I could tell that something was wrong. Her cheeks were all red, and her eyes shiny, even though she wasn't crying. "I'm fine, Mormor," she said wearily.

Mormor put one hand on her forehead and tutted. "Oh, no, you're not. You're burning up." She poured some hot chocolate into the mug standing in front of her. "Try and eat some breakfast, and then I think you should go straight back up to bed."

Ellen leaned over and squeezed Astrid's arm. "Oh, that's too bad," she said. "We were going swimming today."

Swimming? I looked back and forth between them. What was this? No one had said anything to me about going swimming.

"Oh, no," said Mormor. "You're not going swimming with a temperature. That is out of the question."

Ellen complained a little, but then she saw that Astrid didn't even have the energy to protest, so she gave up.

After breakfast, Astrid was sent back upstairs to bed.

"I'll come with you," said Ellen. "I can keep you company. We can talk. It'll be fun."

Mormor shook her head. "I think it's best if Astrid tries to take a nap. You girls go out and play. It's a lovely day. No point in wasting it inside."

I could tell that Ellen didn't really want to, but there was no arguing with Mormor. Ellen put her dirty dishes in the sink and walked toward the door. "Sleep tight," she said to Astrid, who was on her way up the stairs. "See you later."

She sounded really sad. As if they would never see each other ever again. Astrid was only going for a nap, for crying out loud. I sighed and followed Ellen out the door.

"Wanna go climb the apple trees?" I said as soon as we got outside. Seeing the darkness among the tall trees across the yard brought back all the scary memories of the Hunter from yesterday, and whatever we did, I did not want to play in the woods today.

Ellen wrinkled her cute little nose. "Not really."

I hung from the banister on the outside steps, trying to look as if I didn't care either way. But the disappointment hit me hard. If Astrid hadn't gotten sick, would she and Ellen have gone off and played on their own again? I had thought that we had been having fun, all three of us. And now they wanted to be rid of me?

Suddenly I was glad that Astrid had gotten ill. I

knew that was bad; I knew that. But I couldn't help it. If Astrid was asleep upstairs, at least I'd get to play with Ellen. She'd have to play with me now, wouldn't she? I had to be better than *no one*, right?

Right?

I was afraid to suggest anything in case Ellen said no again. In case she decided that, in fact, no playmate at all was better than her friend's stupid little sister, who only suggested lame little girls' games.

"Were you and Astrid going down to the lake?" I asked, as casually as I could manage, not looking at Ellen.

"Uh-huh," she said, kicking at some gravel. She looked really disappointed.

"Swimming?"

"Uh-huh," she said again.

"Perhaps … we could go?" I suggested, trying my very best to sound indifferent.

She shrugged. "Okay," she said, and I did my best not to notice the resigned sigh that followed the word.

"I'll get my bathing suit," I said.

She nodded and followed me inside. Our bathing suits were hanging on the drying rack above the wooden stove, along with the large towels that we had used last time. I grabbed my suit and then struggled to fold up the large towel into something manageable that I could carry without dragging it on the ground. When I looked up, Ellen was standing there, with her towel folded into a neat roll tucked under her arm, looking at me with a doubtful look. As if she was already regretting saying yes.

I gave up trying for a neat fold and just bundled the fluffy towel under my arm. "I'm ready to go," I said.

She made a small noise in recognition and set off toward the door. I followed her. As we crossed the yard, she looked up at the small window to the room in the attic where we slept. I forced myself not to look up, just hurried my steps so that I was walking alongside Ellen instead of tagging along like a puppy on her heels.

In case Astrid was watching from the window.

The path down to the lake was shrouded in semi-darkness, as the sun couldn't reach the soft, needle-covered ground through the branches. It wasn't particularly warm yet, and I could feel goosebumps spreading over my bare arms. I shuddered and forced a smile onto my lips.

"I take swimming lessons at the pool back home," I said, glancing up at Ellen. She was a head taller than me and felt eons older.

"Uh-huh," she replied, not looking at me.

"I'm a pretty good swimmer."

Still no reply.

"Do you have any other activities, apart from ballet?" Ellen was in the same ballet class as Astrid every Tuesday after school. I knew that because Dad came to pick me up from the after-school program every other Tuesday when Mom and Ellen's mom took turns driving Astrid and Ellen to ballet.

Ellen still didn't look at me, just kept her eyes fixed on the trail ahead. She spotted a slug and took an extra-long step to avoid it, wrinkling her little nose in disgust. "I take swimming as well," she muttered.

I lit up. Yes! Something that we had in common. "On Saturdays?"

She shook her head. "Thursdays, after school."

"With Miss Gunnarsson?"

Another headshake. "Mr. Strömstedt." She paused for a moment before continuing. "He's a former champion, you know. Has won several medals. He brought them to the pool and showed us once."

"Wow!"

My wide-eyed response finally brought a smile to her lips, and she glanced at me. "He says that if I keep up the training, I should be able to qualify for the district finals next year."

My eyes got even wider. "Wooow!"

She giggled.

And that was that. The ice was broken.

We stepped out from the woods into the sunlight, dropped our towels on the pier, and changed quickly into our bathing suits. Then we plunged right in, screeching at first from the cold and then from laughter at the ruckus we were making. I don't remember exactly who said it first, but I think perhaps it was Ellen who mentioned something about swimming like a mermaid, and that was enough. In an instant, we were transformed into mythical underwater creatures who lived in a castle at the bottom of the lake and were hiding from our father, the King. There was something about a pearl that we had been playing with and lost and now had to find before we could go back to the castle, or our strict father would be terribly angry with us.

We floated around in the shallows, feeling along the bottom for stones that were smooth and round enough to pass as a pearl. I found one that was almost perfect, but only from one side.

"That's it!" Ellen exclaimed. "You found it! Wonderful! Now we can finally go back home to our palace."

She rolled over on her back, floating with her arms stretched out.

I laughed, but just as I was about to do the same, I noticed something at the edge of the forest. I froze and sank lower into the water.

"Ellen," I whispered. She didn't seem to hear me, just stared up at the sky. "It's him!" I grabbed her arm and pulled her toward me, and she yelped when some water splashed in her face. "The Hunter!"

9

LISA

I HEARD THEIR VOICES FIRST. High-pitched children's voices echoed between the trees across the yard. Then they appeared. A little boy first, with a hop and a skip in his step, and his towel hung like a cape from his shoulders, almost all the way down to the ground. His hair was rumpled and half-dried into a tousled mess and probably looked darker than it actually was in its semidry state. He was wearing swim trunks of the surfing variety, almost to his knees, and brightly colored in shades of blue and pink that weren't found in nature anywhere on the planet. He was a little chubby and very tanned. Jonas, I thought. My nephew Jonas. It was the strangest feeling. No words could describe it.

Behind him came his sister. Elinor was older and almost two whole heads taller than her little brother and as skinny as he was round. Her hair was braided into two thick braids, one behind each ear, but strands of hair had escaped and curled around her face. She looked so much like Astrid at that age that it made me feel a bit sick. I searched both children's faces for traces of my own childhood appearance but didn't find any, thankfully.

Then a man appeared on the path, laden with a picnic basket, a bright yellow cooler, a couple of large bath towels over one shoulder, and a pair of striped swim trunks on his head, both legs flopping down over one ear. He was dressed in a white T-shirt and a pair of khaki shorts that were frayed around the edges but not from wear. I guessed that they were pre-distressed in some factory or other. I never could understand the point of that kind of fashion, but then, fashion wasn't really my thing, now, was it?

My eyes wandered back to the children again, and I realized that the little boy had stopped and stared at me. His sister caught up with him, noticed his tense stance, and followed his stare. She, too, came to a sudden halt.

"Hey, Mom's here," said the man cheerfully behind them. "I wonder if she —"

And then he, finally, also caught a glimpse of the person sitting on the kitchen steps, slightly concealed behind his lovely wife.

I forced myself to get up, pulling myself off the cold stone steps with both hands and taking a couple of steps toward Astrid's perfect little family. This shouldn't be this hard, I admonished myself. They were family, sort of. Practically. Actually.

At least the children.

I didn't know any children. Couldn't remember hardly anything about being a child. Kids were just these little aliens who said strange things and stared at me wide-eyed and completely without inhibition on the street or at the supermarket.

"Hi," I said, or croaked, or … hissed perhaps. My

voice didn't sound even vaguely normal, but at least I had tried.

Astrid came up next to me. "Jonas, Elinor, this is my little sister, Lisa." She placed her hand against my back, and I guessed that it was meant as a show of support, but in reality, it only made me feel even more self-conscious and icky about the fact that I was sweating profusely. To her credit, Astrid didn't pull back. She left her hand, her soft, dry hand, against the damp polyester, and I felt vaguely grateful, underneath all the other layers of panic, fear, discomfort, and nausea.

The children didn't speak. Just stared (Jonas) or looked embarrassed (Elinor). Their dad caught up with them finally. He dropped all the things he'd been carrying and came around them, reaching out a hand toward me. I took it and shook it briefly. His arm was tanned and muscular, and his grip was firm and strong. Then he seemed to realize that he was wearing his swim trunks on his head. He tore them off and gave me a sheepish grin.

"Hi, I'm Fredrik," he said. "So great to finally meet you."

It actually sounded as if he meant it. I had to really focus to keep on my feet and swallowed hard to stop my stomach juices from welling up in the back of my mouth.

"How was your flight?" Fredrik asked, and I mumbled something that could be interpreted as OK. Small talk? Really? Was I expected to be able to do that? Yes, probably.

Astrid came to the rescue. "Jonas, why don't you go upstairs and change out of those wet swim trunks before you catch your death? And Elinor, could you hang the wet towels on the clothesline, please? I need to get started on dinner." She turned toward me. "I've made up the bed in Mormor's room for you. Fredrik and I will bunk with the kids upstairs."

I couldn't speak. I just nodded and stepped to one side to let the others pass.

"Let me get your suitcase for you," Fredrik said and hurried over to the car. He carried it easily up the three steps and disappeared into the kitchen. Reluctantly, I followed him.

It looked just the same, only smaller. Much smaller. Like a doll house.

And just like in a doll house, there was no room for a woman of my size. I remembered my grandmother's slight figure. Even though I, as a child, had thought of her as round and soft, she must have been a third of my size, and the kitchen wouldn't have felt like a vast ball-room for her either. As it was, I could just barely squeeze past the kitchen table and continue out into the hallway. Fredrik had put my carry-on on the bed and came back out, giving me a brief smile before disappearing up the steep staircase to my left. The creaks sounded so familiar, and it was all I could do to stagger into Mormor's old room and close the door behind me. The bed creaked ominously when I sat down, but it didn't break. Something to be grateful for, at least. Mormor had kept her and Morfar's double bed, even though she had slept alone in this room for decades. I could never have fit into one of the narrow cots upstairs.

How could I not have thought about where I was going to sleep?

Well, I hadn't thought. I hadn't been capable of

thinking. I had been completely stressed out, panicked about losing my apartment and about Astrid's phone call, about Mormor dying and all the memories that assaulted me when Astrid spoke about this place and about Mormor, and how I had refused to come back here after what happened.

I looked around the small room. Poor Mormor. She had never known the true reason why her granddaughter had refused to come and see her. She might have had an idea, but none of them could have been anywhere near the truth. Whatever that was.

The guilt cut me like a knife somewhere underneath the damp polyester, but there was nothing I could do about it now. Mormor was gone. And the little girl who had loved to come here every summer, she was gone too.

Just like Ellen.

I STAYED in Mormor's room, trying to block out the sounds of Astrid's happy little family coming from all corners of the small cottage. The walls were so thin; it felt as if they were right there next to me, even though the door stayed firmly closed.

I could hear Astrid rummaging in the kitchen across the hall, and after half an hour or so, there was a light knock on the door.

"Lisa?"

I stared at the door and pulled the blanket closer. "Yes?"

"Dinner's ready."

I could tell that Astrid was trying real hard to sound as if this was all normal, that this was all exactly how she had pictured it. Our first meal together again, after all these years.

"No thanks," I replied. And then, before Astrid had time to say anything, "I'm really tired after the flight. I'm just going to take a nap if that's okay."

A long silence.

"Sure." Another pause. "See you later then."

"Sure," I echoed and shifted slightly underneath the blanket. The paper wrapping the cheeseburgers made a distinct crinkling sound, and I froze. Had Astrid heard that?

If she had, she didn't comment on it. Instead, she called out to her family upstairs, and they all came bounding down the stairs right outside the flimsy door to my room. I held my breath until they were all seated at the table in the kitchen, but no one else came knocking.

I took another bite of the cold cheeseburger and washed it down with some Coke.

I wished I could close my ears to their voices, but it was impossible not to hear Jonas asking loudly why Aunt Lisa wasn't going to eat dinner with them. Astrid hushed him, saying something about my very long flight and how tiresome traveling was.

The whole family kept their voices low after that, just high enough for me to hear that they were talking, but not loud enough that I could hear what they said.

I didn't know what was worse.

The grilled panini tasted like cardboard and rubber, but I ate one of them anyway, in big gulps at first, but then smaller and smaller bites. I had to make this last. I didn't know when I'd be able to get out of here.

If I ever made it out of here alive.

My heart hadn't stopped racing since the airport back home, and I was seriously worried that it wouldn't be able to hold up to the stress. My doctor had warned me, but I'd never taken her seriously. I was only thirty-five. Thirty-five-year-olds didn't have heart attacks.

But right now, I wasn't as confident in that conviction.

I ate a Snickers in little mousy bites, letting the chocolate melt on my tongue as I stared at the ceiling, trying to think straight.

It didn't come easy to me. I was restless and jittery from the anxiety, and the food didn't seem to be helping. Mormor hadn't had a TV at all, let alone a TV in her bedroom, so that wasn't an option. Then I realized that more things had changed in the last thirty years, apart from my size. I pulled out my phone and plugged in the headset, opening the YouTube app. I had a playlist of old sitcoms and cooking shows and stuff, for when I had to wait for the bus or at the doctor's. The battery was low, and I hated to think what this would do to my phone bill, but I pulled out the plug for the bedside lamp and plugged in my charger instead. With my phone slowly charging on the nightstand, I leaned back against the headboard and ate the other panini while my head was filled with canned laughter and lines that I knew by heart. If I soaked each bite in a mouthful of Coke, it wasn't too bad.

Dinner out in the kitchen seemed to be over, and the kids disappeared up the stairs again. I removed one of the earbuds and could hear Astrid and her husband out in the kitchen across the hall, speaking softly. I couldn't hear what they were saying, but Astrid sounded sad. Poor Astrid.

But honestly, poor me, as well.

I put the earbud in again and closed my eyes. I needed to calm down. I needed to be able to think straight. Another gulp of Coke, and then I took a deep breath, letting the air out slowly through my mouth. See. I could do this.

I still couldn't wrap my head around the fact that Astrid had been coming here all these years. And that her children had spent their summers here, all their lives. That did make it difficult to convince Astrid that this place was dangerous, that she had to leave and never come back.

Was it possible that I'd been wrong all this time? Had I imagined it?

I wasn't even sure anymore what it was that I had imagined and/or witnessed. There were so many layers of confusion and nightmares when it came to what happened to Ellen. I had only been five when she died, and it had been a very traumatic event, I knew that much. I also knew that I had been a messed-up kid, lying and stealing and bunking off from school for as long as I could remember. Had I been like that even before that last summer we'd been here? I couldn't remember. Maybe. Probably.

And what part of the mess that was my brain now, as an adult, could I actually trust? There was so much that didn't seem real, so much that I didn't know if I could believe in anymore.

So much that I'd never wanted to remember in the first place.

On the contrary, I had done my very best never to think about it.

But now, here I was. And if there was any reason my

niece and nephew were in danger here, and I didn't do everything in my, albeit limited, power to keep them safe …

I would never forgive myself if anything happened to them.

Just as I had never forgiven myself for what happened to Ellen.

The look on Astrid's face when I'd told her that her friend had been murdered had made me doubt myself. The words had just blurted out of me before I knew what I was saying. And a huge part of me was screaming no, no, no, and just wanted to retreat back into the TV, sugar, and fat coma that had been my life for decades. It was the only way I knew to make it through the day.

Maybe I'd just made it all up, somehow. There were parts of those memories that I knew for a fact came from a movie. Maybe all of it was just fiction.

And maybe it wasn't.

I had to find out for sure, if not for me, then for those kids up there.

The walls of the small room seemed to creep up on me, and I raised the volume on my phone, forcing myself to take deep breaths. Another bite of Snickers and my pulse returned to manageable levels.

I rubbed my face. I could do this.

Just for one night.

Tomorrow was Mormor's funeral. We'd have to leave here for that. If I could just make sure that Astrid and her family were safe here, I'd be able to go home straight after the funeral. Tomorrow night, I could be on a plane going back home again. I just had to hang on another twenty-four hours. Surely, I could do that?

The thought of my apartment, my sagging sofa and

TV made my eyes sting. But I was doing great where I was. I was making do.

I would just have to do one more thing before I went to sleep.

I had to speak to my sister and try and work out which parts of my memories of that nightmare were real.

If any.

THE NEXT TIME I pulled out the earbuds, I couldn't hear any voices from the kitchen. Just the rustle and clang of someone doing the dishes. I desperately needed the bathroom, and then I needed to speak to Astrid. Alone.

I got up off the bed and was on my way over toward the door when I heard Fredrik's voice right outside the door.

"Kids? Time to get ready for bed."

I stood completely still while they came tumbling down the steep stairs, and I closed my eyes and rested my forehead against the door as I remembered all the times Astrid and I had done that same rush when Mormor had called out to us.

How we'd pushed and shoved at each other in the small bathroom, taking turns spitting out our toothpaste in the minute, semicircle basin. I could picture us so clearly, in our nightgowns and bare feet, little me and tall Astrid.

And then the dash back up the stairs and the cold sheets before my body heat had warmed up the small space underneath the covers. The stories Astrid used to tell me. The stories I'd made up in my head.

Warm tears ran down my cheeks as I got a glimpse of the girl I'd once been.

Before.

Astrid had been right about one thing. I had been happy here. Once upon a time.

And I didn't know if I was more angry or sad about that. Bitter, probably. Numb. Glancing back at the bed and all the empty wrappers, the almost empty bottle of coke, I felt a twinge of regret. Perhaps this wouldn't have been my life if that thing with Ellen hadn't happened. Perhaps I could have been like Astrid, happy and carefree and with a perfect little family.

A perfect little life, if it wasn't for her long-lost sister.

I could feel how my presence in her life must be disturbing. I could understand that. But it was her own fault. She had wanted me to come here.

And because of that, she would have to listen to what I had to say. And she would have to believe me. I wouldn't rest until she knew the truth.

I just had to figure out exactly what that was first.

I heard Fredrik's voice again, something about a story. And then his heavy footsteps on the stairs on the other side of the wall. If he was going upstairs to read to the kids, I could have a moment alone with my sister.

I slowly opened the door and glanced out into the hallway. It was empty and semi-dark. Light spilled out from the kitchen onto the woven rug that looked just like the one that had been there when I was a little girl. Perhaps it was the same one. This place was like a time capsule of my childhood. If you overlooked the shrinkage.

Walking quietly over to the bathroom, I discovered

that it too had shrunk. Perhaps even more so than the rest of the cottage. *Oh, Mormor!* I thought and pushed myself in between the small basin and the washing machine to pee. The hand basin dug into the left-hand side of my chest, and I was squatting half on, half off the toilet, but I managed to empty my bladder at least. And the massive old roll-top bathtub was the same, with a hand-held shower, so I should manage to wash up later, thank goodness.

But first, I had to speak to Astrid.

She wasn't in the kitchen, but the kitchen door was open, and I could see her silhouette on the stone steps outside. I made my way past the kitchen table and squeezed past the wood stove. The small enamel pot that Mormor had used to make me hot cocoa stood on the stove, in its usual place, and I could taste the cocoa just by looking at it. The whole cottage was like that.

Astrid must have heard me coming because she turned her head toward me. She even managed a smile. "Hey," she said. "Are you hungry? I saved you some food."

It was such a mom thing to say, and I felt tears sting at the back of my eyes again. I couldn't remember the last time anyone had cared if I ate or starved.

"Thanks," I mumbled.

She got up from the stairs and came back into the kitchen. She had a wineglass in her hand but put it on the kitchen table. I moved into the corner to let her pass. She got a plate from the fridge and slipped it in a microwave that hadn't been there in Mormor's time. We both stood there silently while the plate spun slowly round, round, and the numbers on the digital display counted down to zero. Astrid got the plate and put it on the table. Then she poured a glass of water from a jug in the fridge for me.

"Do you want some wine?" she asked.

I didn't know what to say. I'd never been much of a drinker. Didn't like the taste. That said, I hadn't tried any since my teens, and the plonk that was handed about at those parties I had gone to might have been a different brand than the stuff that my sophisticated sister drank.

"Sure," I said and watched as she poured me a glass.

Then she sat down opposite me at the table and pulled her own glass toward her. Her fingers moved restlessly around the base and stem, but she didn't drink anything. I tried a sip. It wasn't as good as Coke, but it had a nice edge to it that I needed right now. I took a fork from the holder in the middle of the table and tried the food. It was some kind of chicken casserole, and it was surprisingly tasty.

Even though I had already polished off most of the stuff I'd got from the gas station, I was ravenous, and the large portion disappeared off my plate in no time. The water tasted strange, and it took a while before I realized that it probably tasted like water had always tasted. I just never drank water these days. That something that was missing? Sugar and carbonation.

"Thank you," I said, pushing the plate away from me.

Astrid smiled faintly. "You're welcome," she said. Then she took a sip of her wine.

I pulled my glass toward me and mimicked her action. The wine tasted better the second time around, or perhaps it was just that I was getting used to it.

"I can't believe you've been coming here all this time," I said.

Astrid leaned back, her glass still between her hands. "I can't believe that you didn't know." She shrugged. "But of course, we came here. Mom wasn't going to turn her back on her mother, just because you started throwing hysterical fits every time she mentioned her or this place."

I shook my head. I had thought that Mom had understood, somehow. Even if I hadn't been able to tell her what had happened. Even if I hadn't been able to communicate what was going on in my head, I had still believed that my mother understood on some level how important it was that we never, ever came here again.

But instead, she had just lied straight to my face, year after year. Just to keep me from freaking out. I didn't understand. But then ... I didn't have any children.

As if Astrid could read my mind, she said, "There was always something with you, you know. You always had to have everything just so, or all hell broke loose. In the end, it was just easier to pretend to give in. If you believed that you got your way, we could go on with our lives."

I stared at her. "So you all just lied to me, day in and day out. For years." It was a level of deceit that I couldn't quite wrap my head around.

She shrugged again. "It was the only way we could function, as a family." She glanced at the ceiling. "It's like with Jonas. This last year, he has suddenly developed a terrible fear of fire. It's apparently typical around his age. It's really bad. We had to remove the candles from his birthday cake when he turned five. And I like my scented candles, so this was a problem. Whenever he'd come into the room and discover that I'd lit a candle, he'd throw a fit, just like you used to do." She smiled wryly. "So I made a deal with him. I wouldn't light any candles, but since I still wanted to use my scented candles, he'd have to light them for me. And it turns out that it works. It's probably some control thing. When he lights the candles himself, he feels in control." She took a sip of her wine. "It's a work-around. And sometimes it's annoying because I have to go and get him if I want to light a candle. But you get used to it. And in the end, it makes life so much easier. Those freak-outs take a toll on you as a parent."

"They aren't that much fun on the kid either," I muttered. She was even more like Mom than I'd thought.

Astrid smiled a little. "No, I'm sure they're not. But for now, we've put away all the matches and candles, both here and at home. I'm sure he'll grow out of it, eventually. Kids do."

I stared at her. "I didn't."

She looked startled. "Of course you did," she said. Then she looked down at her wineglass, twirling it slowly between her hands. She frowned. "Didn't you?"

I leaned forward. "I didn't just freak out for the sake of it," I said slowly. "My fears were real. What happened to Ellen was real."

She looked straight at me. "What happened to Ellen was an accident," she said. "It wasn't your fault. You need to let it go."

I shook my head slowly. "It wasn't an accident," I said. "But it wasn't my fault." I looked down at the dark red liquid in my glass. "At least, I don't think so." I rubbed my face with one hand. "I don't know what to believe anymore. It was such a long time ago."

She leaned forward. "You were only five," she said. "Just like my Jonas is now. He's not much more than a baby, and I don't know how much of this summer he'll remember when he's grown up."

I looked at her. "If he'd seen what I saw," I whispered, "he'd remember it for the rest of his life."

She stared at me. "What did you see?" she said, her voice hoarse. "Tell me."

My brain exploded with images, some true, others not. The problem was telling them apart. I rubbed my face again, with both hands this time, groaning at the strain of it all. When I looked up again, Astrid was still staring at me. She looked afraid.

"Did you see Ellen drown?" she asked, her voice not much more than a whisper. A single tear ran down her cheek. "That must have been horrible."

I felt my head turn from side to side. "I told you already," I said, and my voice sounded as if it came from a place far away. "She didn't drown."

10

LITTLE LISA

I DON'T KNOW where he came from, but one minute, we were all alone by the lake, and the next, we weren't. I thought that the sun must have disappeared behind a cloud or something because I suddenly felt cold, but when I glanced around, I could see the golden glitter of the bright morning sun on the water around me.

Ellen rolled over and looked back toward the trees. "Oh, him?" she said, under her breath. She didn't seem worried at all. "Don't worry, Lisa. It was just a game."

The water surrounding me suddenly felt like ice, and my teeth started to shatter.

"Look at you, Lisa," Ellen said. "Your lips are blue. We'd better get back to your grandma's and get you warmed up." She stood up, the water only reaching somewhere just above her knees. "Come on!"

And then she started walking back to the shore, wading up onto the small stretch of sand that we called our beach, and walked back up onto the pier where we'd left our clothes and towels. She shook out her towel and wrapped it loosely around herself, drying her face and the ends of her hair. Her two-piece bathing suit was clinging to her skin, and the bow on one side of her hips had come undone, the ribbons plastered against the top of her thigh.

I glanced back over at the Hunter. He was looking at Ellen. If I had been scared before, that was nothing compared to the dread that came over me now. I wanted to get up and follow her, I did, more than anything, but it was as if I couldn't move. As if the water surrounding me had frozen into a solid block of ice, and I was trapped in it forever.

Ellen let go of one end of the towel and bent over to dry her hair with the other. I saw the Hunter lick his lips, not taking his eyes off her. It turned my stomach. It was just like the Hunter in the movie, moving in for the kill of that sweet, precious deer.

The fact that he didn't even have a gun with him this time didn't register until much later. Right at that moment, all I could think about was the danger we were in. Or perhaps mostly Ellen. Because he didn't seem to notice me at all.

I sank deeper into the water, feeling the cold water cover my chin and my lips, just barely keeping my nose above the surface to breathe. Perhaps, if I just stayed here, he would go away. If I didn't move or did anything to attract his attention. If I just sank slowly to the bottom of the lake. If I held my breath for hours and hours.

Perhaps then, everything would be back to normal once I surfaced again.

But then the Hunter took a couple of steps toward Ellen, and I knew that playtime was over. I had to get out of the water. I had to do something.

I couldn't leave Ellen alone up there with that scary, scary man.

Somehow, I stood up. The water dripped from every part of me, and I started wading as fast as I could toward the ladder at the end of the pier, scrambling up it. My bare foot slipped on the middle tread, and I cried out when my shin banged against the sharp metal edge.

Ellen looked up, pulling her hair to the side to look at me. "What happened, Lisa?"

I scrambled up onto the pier and hurried toward my bundled-up towel, feeling tears sting my eyes, a dull throb on my left shin, and the cold air making my goosebumps turn into porcupine needles.

"I hurt my leg," I whined, wrapping myself tight into the towel, biting into a corner of it to keep my teeth from chattering and the sobs from being audible. When I bent over to look, a red line had appeared on my suntanned leg, an oblong drop of blood swelling up from the left side of it. "And I'm bleeding," I cried helplessly, looking up at Ellen.

She came over, looking at my leg. "It doesn't look too bad," she said in a comforting tone. "Let's get you back to the cottage. I'm sure your grandma has a band-aid for you."

I stifled a sob and then almost choked on it when a shadow fell over my face. When I looked up, the Hunter was right next to us, his back to the sun. All I could see at first was the imposing silhouette of him, towering over Ellen.

"What's the matter?" he said, his voice like icy gravel.

I didn't reply; I couldn't. I just stared at him, completely frozen.

"She banged her leg on the ladder," Ellen said. "It's not a big deal. But we'd better get back."

"That useless ladder," he grunted. "I told the council they need to do something about those sharp edges." Then he bent down. "Let me take a look."

I was a statue. An ice statue, frozen solid on the dock, unable to move, unable to flee. He grabbed a corner of the towel and pulled it to the side, baring my chubby thighs. Another grunt. "That's nothing. Just a scratch." He stood up, letting go of my towel. "It's already stopped bleeding."

"You hear that?" Ellen said. "That's good, isn't it, Lisa?"

The man took a step back, but he didn't leave. Ellen came over and rubbed my arms through the towel. "You need to get out of that wet bathing suit and get some clothes on." She giggled. "I bet your grandma will be mad at me if I bring back a little Lisa-popsicle, don't you think?"

I didn't laugh with her. I couldn't. I also couldn't even imagine getting out of my bathing suit while the Hunter was standing right there. No way.

Ellen picked up my sundress and held it out to me. When I still didn't move, she came closer. "Come on now, Lisa. You'll catch your death."

I grabbed the dress and pulled my arm in underneath the towel again. My bathing suit was dripping wet and clung to my skin, but somehow I managed to get the shoulder straps down my trembling arms and roll the bathing suit down to my waist under cover of the towel. Then I wrapped the towel around me, just under the armpits, and tucked one end inside to keep it in place while I pulled my sundress over my head. As soon as I'd got the sundress on, I felt a little better. With the large towel over my shoulders, I tugged the bathing suit off completely. I was still very cold, but at least I wasn't getting colder by the minute.

Ellen nodded, pleased that I was finally moving, and pulled on her own dress on top of the two-piece. Her bikini left a damp imprint across her chest, even though she undid the bow at the back of her neck and pulled it off almost right away. When I glanced at the Hunter, I could see that he'd noticed it too. I walked over and tried to block his view, but he was so much taller than me. I wanted to hold up my towel to shield her, wished that I had the courage to tell him to leave, to stop staring, to leave us alone. But he was the scariest man I'd ever seen, and I couldn't say a word. He was a killer. I'd seen his gun with my own eyes.

"You forgot something," his gravelly voice said behind my back.

I jumped and turned, following his stare to the wooden boards of the dock where a pair of panties lay. White, with pink trim and a disproportionately large washing care label that poked out.

With glowing cheeks, I hurried over and snatched them up, hiding them in my fist. Then I scurried back to Ellen, grabbing her arm. "Let's go," I whispered, the pleading in my voice obvious. I didn't even care if he heard me. I just wanted so desperately to get away from him.

"Yeah, yeah, we're going," she said, stepping out of her bikini bottoms and pulling on her underpants in one swift, unselfconscious move. Then she picked up her towel and draped it around her shoulders. She nodded toward the Hunter and started walking back toward the trail.

"My cat got a full litter the other night," he said, and I walked straight into Ellen's back when she stopped suddenly. "You girls wanna see 'em?"

"No, thanks," I said, at the same time as Ellen replied, "Kittens? Really?"

11

LISA

Astrid looked as if she wanted to get up and leave, but I had to hand it to her. She stayed seated. Kept looking at me. But her fingers on the glass stopped moving.

"You're going to have to tell me," she said, her voice strained, "what you believe happened to her." She shook her head slowly, not taking her eyes off me. "You were only five. I'm sure there are things you're getting muddled up or things that no one ever told you so that you had to make up stuff to fill in the blanks. Kids do that all the time."

My eyes stung, but no tears came. Perhaps I didn't have any left? "I was there," I croaked. "You weren't."

She looked hurt. Then tired. "I was sick."

I nodded. "You had a temperature. Mormor wouldn't let you go swimming."

"It was just a twenty-four-hour bug," Astrid said. "I was fine later that day. If you'd just waited …"

I frowned at her. "Mormor told us to go outside and play. To let you rest. We went down to the lake for a swim. You and Ellen used to do it all the time."

She looked up at me. "Ellen was a good swimmer," she said, and there was an edge to her voice.

I nodded. "Yes, she was."

A small frown appeared between her eyebrows. "So what happened?"

I sighed. "I told you. She didn't drown. We got out of the water when the Hunter came?"

The frown deepened. "What hunter?"

"*THE* Hunter!" I leaned forward. How could she not remember him? He had plagued my nightmares for decades. And she had just … forgotten about him? It didn't seem possible.

She shook her head slowly. "I have no idea what you're talking about."

"The Hunter," I croaked. "When we were playing Sioux girls. He had a gun."

Astrid stared at me. "I remember us playing that game," she said slowly. "Because of that movie we saw." Her eyes narrowed. "The hunter was in that movie, Lisa," she said slowly. "He wasn't real. You're getting things mixed up. I told you—"

"No!" Or was I? No. I couldn't be. "Not the hunter from the movie. The one who was here, in the woods. He had a gun. We followed him back to his barn. Don't you remember? We hid among the trees, watching him working inside his barn."

Astrid shook her head slowly. "But that was just some old man, Lisa," she said. "Just one of Mormor's neighbors." She glanced over toward the window. It had gone completely dark outside. "I'd forgotten about him." She looked back at me. "But I think I know why you're mixing him up into all of this. Because he died too, didn't he?"

She looked relieved, and I wanted to scream out loud. This was so frustrating!

"What? No. He wasn't dead. He was there when we were swimming. And when we got out of the water—"

But Astrid had stopped listening. "I remember Mormor being so upset. But she only found out that next morning, when Mom and Dad came to get us. Everyone was so upset, and Ellen's parents came and—"

I stared at her. "They did?"

She rubbed her hand over her forehead, pushing her hair back. "Yes. It was awful. Her dad was so mad, and her mom was just …" She shook her head. "I can't even imagine what they must have gone through." She gestured toward the yard. "And then that policeman who'd been here the day before, he came back. And he spoke to Mormor outside, and she came back in here all gray in the face, saying there'd been another accident."

"Another accident?" I said, but I could barely hear my own voice. My head was filled with images that I couldn't get a grip on. Bright sparks against the night sky. Hot flames.

"Yes," Astrid said. "There was a fire on a neighboring farm. Their barn burnt down, and someone was killed. It was him. I didn't know that then, but I found out later."

Fire.

Suddenly I remembered the crackling sound of Mormor's wood-burning stove, and I turned and stared at it. At the small metal shelf on the wall next to it, where a box of matches had always been. It was gone now. Because of Jonas, probably. I hadn't been afraid of fire. Not like Jonas. Astrid had said that it was common among children his age, but I didn't remember ever being afraid of fire.

Fires were beautiful. Powerful. Cozy. Mormor had let me light the crumpled-up newspaper, and I'd hunched down and stared at the paper as it smoldered and ignited the edges of the firewood, the bark catching fire first with little gleaming embers moving across the surface. But those fires were small. There had been a big fire, though. I kept remembering a big fire.

Leaning back on the chair, I stared at the wall above Astrid's head. "I think I remember that fire," I said. "It was … huge. Angry. It was so *loud*. You don't think about fire as being loud, but it was deafening."

Even as I was sitting there, I could feel the heat of the flames against my face. Hear the roar of it blasting my eardrums.

Astrid snorted a little and shook her head. "That's exactly what I mean," she said. "You can't possibly remember that fire because you weren't there. But you must have overheard something that was said about it, something you didn't understand. And then it got all tangled up in what had happened with Ellen—which I'm sure was horrible and traumatizing for you—and then, since you never talked to anyone about it, you got … confused."

That wasn't the word she'd intended to use, I could tell.

But I had been confused. She was right about that. Everything in my head was such a mess.

"I *was* there," I said. "I remember it clearly."

She shook her head. "No, Lisa. You weren't. You can't have been."

I sat up. "We were in that barn," I said. "That's where the kittens were."

She frowned. "What kittens?"

"The ones that Ellen wanted to look at," I said, and the memory of squirming little rat-like creatures made my stomach turn. "The Hunter told us that his cat had kittens, and Ellen wanted to see them."

Astrid emptied her wine glass and put it down a bit too hard. "There were no kittens, Lisa. You're making it up." She stared at her empty glass. "You were never anywhere near that barn. We followed that man through the woods, I remember that now, when we were playing. And then we watched him for a while. We were fascinated by the fact that he had a gun, that was all, but then we got bored, because he was just working, so we left. You were never inside the barn. That part you are making up. And I need you to understand that I will do everything in my power to make sure that you get the help that you need." She looked up at me. "But you also have to … snap out of it. Those things you think you remember ... They're not real, Lisa. You've got it all muddled up."

But no. That part I wasn't confused about. I remembered the kittens. I definitely remembered the kittens.

Heavy footsteps moved across the ceiling, and I froze. I'd almost forgotten that we weren't alone in the cottage. Pushing back the chair, I stood up, just as Fredrik came down the stairs. He waved cheerfully as he passed the door on his way into the bathroom.

"I'm going to bed," I said.

"Lisa …" Astrid's voice sounded pleading.

I pushed past the table and moved toward the door out into the dark hallway. I turned and looked back at her. "I'm not crazy," I said, and it might have sounded a bit more convincing if my voice hadn't cracked at the end of the sentence. "I know what I saw. I was there."

I didn't wait for a reply. Just hurried into Mormor's old room and closed the door behind me.

As soon as I was alone, the tears came. The ones I'd thought that I had run out of. Oh, how wrong I had been.

I hadn't made it up. The Hunter had been real. And the kittens.

And the fire.

The fire had been very real.

Hadn't it?

EVEN THOUGH I'D had a large dinner, I ate everything I had left from the gas station, but even when it was all gone, I still felt hollow. I knew that I wasn't hungry, but there was this vast empty space inside of me that I didn't know how to fill.

What was supposed to be there? It couldn't be just Snickers and pizza, could it?

Outside in the hallway, I could hear Fredrik and Astrid getting ready for bed and then their steps up the stairs. They didn't speak up there, at least not in voices that carried, and the cottage went quiet. I kept my earbuds in anyway, for another couple of episodes.

When I pulled them out, it was getting close to midnight. I had nothing left to eat. Nothing to drink. And the old TV shows on YouTube weren't calming me down like they used to. I was bone-tired, and my eyes stung from all the tears. I rubbed them, getting up off the bed, gathering all the trash in the carrying bag from the gas station. Then I took the empty coke bottle with me out into the kitchen, filling it with water from the jug in the fridge. Then I refilled the jug from the tap and put it back.

The fridge was stocked but I didn't dare touch any of the food. I knew myself well enough to know that if I ate any of it, I would eat it all. And then there wouldn't be any breakfast for anyone.

Instead, I took my bottle and moved over to the kitchen door. It was locked. Strange. I couldn't remember it ever being locked, but I guessed times had changed here as well.

It was the weirdest thing, coming back to a place where you hadn't been for decades. I wasn't sure if it was the things that had changed that disturbed me, or the things that were exactly the way I remembered them.

I kept expecting Mormor to appear wherever I turned. It was strange to think that she'd been here all this time. In a way, it was as if she'd died a long time ago, too, when I left here after what had happened to Ellen.

What *had* happened to Ellen?

I had tried so hard not to think about that. Done my very best. But now, I had to admit that it hadn't worked. Everything was still there, at the back of my mind. Making me afraid of the dark. Making me afraid of all kinds of things. People, most of all.

And that hollow darkness inside of me that no amount of food ever seemed able to fill.

I turned the key in the door and opened it. I had expected it to creak, but it moved silently on its hinges. The darkness outside was compact. Intense. Almost blinding. I stepped outside onto the steps and felt it pressing down on me. I clung to my water bottle and kept one hand on the door handle, afraid that if I let go, I would get sucked out into that inky blackness.

And then what would happen?

I didn't know.

Fear was a strange thing. You didn't actually have to be afraid of any particular thing for the hairs on the back of your neck to stand up straight, like an animal bristling at the sight of an enemy or a threat. Every part of me wanted to duck back inside and lock the door, but I forced myself to stand there for another couple of minutes, staring out into the darkness.

There *was* something to fear here; I knew that. The fact that my sister and her family had been happy here for years didn't mean that I was crazy. It didn't mean that I was making things up or misremembering what happened. It was possible that darkness and danger could exist in a happy place like this; I knew that.

But what was I going to do about it?

I wanted nothing more than to get back on a plane and return to the safety of my couch, but I knew that wasn't an option anymore. Once I had started remembering, stuff had welled up from the deepest recesses of my mind, and there was no way I would be able to cram it all back out of sight again. Not now, not when I'd come back here.

There was only one way out of this nightmare, and that was to make myself remember it all.

I had to know for sure what had happened; otherwise, I couldn't leave here. If anything should happen to Elinor and Jonas, I wouldn't be able to live with myself.

I mean, I could barely live with myself as it was.

Glancing down at my round belly and the Coke bottle that I was clutching like a flotation device, I felt an intense sadness envelop me.

It hadn't been my fault. I had only been five. Seeing Jonas had made me realize how little that was. The fact that I'd been running around in the woods alone at that age was insane.

But I hadn't been alone. I'd been with Astrid. Or with Ellen.

Except for that one time.

With one last glance out into the darkness, I stepped back inside the kitchen and closed the door. I turned the key and then checked to see that the door was really locked. It was.

I returned to Mormor's room and crawled into the bed, pulling her thin blankets over me. The room was cold and a little damp, but the chill I felt came from a place inside. From the realization that I would have to remember it all if I was ever to be able to forget about it and put it all behind me.

LITTLE LISA

I TUGGED at Ellen's arm. "Come on," I pleaded. "We need to get back. My leg, remember."

She barely glanced at me. "It has already stopped bleeding, Lisa." Then she took a step toward the Hunter, her wet bikini and damp towel dangling from one hand. "I'd love to see them. I looooove kittens."

The Hunter grunted something unintelligible. Then he moved past us and started walking along a second path that I hadn't noticed before. Lisa hurried after him with bouncy, excited steps.

I stared longingly at the path back to Mormor's cottage, wishing I could just run back there, as fast as my feet would carry me, throw myself into Mormor's arms and stay there until Mom and Dad came to get us next week. I didn't want to be here anymore. I wanted to be at home, in town, where the dangers were more normal, like cars not stopping at the crosswalk or the scary drunk men at the park.

This was a new fear for me, and I didn't know that I could handle it.

But Ellen was just slipping out of view behind some trees and I couldn't let her go alone. On numb feet I staggered after her, a sob stuck painfully sideways in my throat. Just one quick look at the kittens, and then we'd go back to Mormor's. It was fine. It was all going to be just fine.

This path was shorter than the one to Mormor's cottage, and we soon stepped out from the trees behind the large red barn with the two enormous doors standing wide open like a gaping mouth right in front of us. The main house somewhere up to the left wasn't a cottage, like Mormor's, but a large white house with tall windows on two floors. It looked strangely normal, with flowerbeds all along the side and pretty curtains in all the windows, but all I could think was that I had stepped straight into a nightmare, a confusing and scary nightmare that I was worried I would never wake up from. Part of my brain was in full-on panic mode, and the other part of it was chiding the first part for being such a baby. There was nothing going on; we were just going to look at some kittens, calm down.

But I couldn't. I was freaking out, and stepping inside the dark, cavernous barn onto an ice-cold concrete floor didn't help to calm me down. The Hunter hadn't said a word since we left the lake, and he didn't even look to see if we were following him as he strode on his long legs over to a ladder and started climbing it up into the darkness.

"Ellen, please," I pleaded. "Can't we just go home?"

But Ellen had already grabbed hold of the lowest rung she could reach and started climbing. "I just want a peek, Lisa. It'll only be a minute." She glanced at me over her shoulder. "Will you be able to manage the ladder?"

I wanted to say no, I couldn't manage it, we had to go home without seeing those precious kittens, sorry, but she wasn't really worried about me, that much was obvious, since she was already halfway up to what I now realized was a hayloft. I'd never been in a hayloft before. The strong smell of hay tickled my nose as I walked over to the ladder and closed my cold, numb fingers around a rung. But in my other hand was a bundle with my towel, my bathing suit, and my underpants, and I knew I couldn't climb with only one hand.

Looking around, I saw a metal bucket, upturned, over in a dark corner. I went and got it, carrying it out of the shadows into the middle of the floor where the light streamed in through the open doors. Then I placed my bundle on the bucket, extracting my underpants. They were cold and damp from being bundled up with my wet bathing suit, but I pulled them on anyway. When I looked up, Ellen had disappeared out of sight above me. The cold of the cotton fabric against my bum was nothing compared to the cold I felt within just from being here, in this strange and scary place.

Somehow, I made it up the ladder. Don't ask me how. But being alone down there in that cavernous barn was even worse than being up there, with him.

Upstairs in the hayloft, there was barely any light, only what came in through the cracks in the walls, but it was enough for me to make it over to where Ellen was sitting, hunched over, next to a large pile of hay bales. She was making cooing noises and didn't even look at me when I squatted down next to her. She was already reaching into the hollow between the bales where a large black cat with a white bib right under her chin was laying, a row of squirming kittens lined up along her large belly.

They were tiny. Probably the smallest cats I'd ever seen, but the only thing I could think about was the tall, dark shadow of a man standing somewhere over to the left, watching us.

"Very cute," I said. "Can we go now?"

But Ellen didn't seem to hear me. She moved in closer and picked up one of the squirming little things that honestly looked more like rats than cats. She held it up to me, and I saw its paws still moving in the same way as it had against its mommy's belly, and its closed, blind eyes.

"Do you want to hold it?"

I shook my head. "No. Can we just go, please?" I tried again, but Ellen wasn't listening. She put the kitten back and picked up another that had just left its mother and was crawling off to one side.

"No, you stay here with your mommy," Ellen said to the straying kitten in a soft, scolding voice, and how I wished I could be with my mommy right now, I would give anything to be with my mommy back in town, and not be here in this darkness, feeling the chill of the damp underpants against my butt, hoping they didn't leave an imprint on my sundress the way that Ellen's bikini top had done on hers. I did not want the Hunter to look at me that way, not ever.

I glanced over at him and felt a chill run along my spine when I saw the gleam in his eyes where a narrow ray of sunlight fell across his grim face.

I grabbed Ellen's arm and tugged it hard. "Ellen, come on now. You've seen the kittens; now let's go back." It was part pleading, part an order, part pure desperation and fear and panic and cold and so many emotions all at once.

She shook off my hand, glancing over at the Hunter. "Is it OK if we stay here for a while," she asked. "It looks as if they're going to sleep now. I'd love to just sit here and watch them."

The Hunter didn't reply, apart from another one of those grunts that could mean anything.

"Let the kittens sleep," I said. "Ellen, please, can we go?"

She turned and looked at me now, and the annoyance in her eyes was clear to see, even in the dim light. I had seen the same look in Astrid's eyes a million times. And Ellen didn't even have a little sister. She wasn't used to having to put up with someone always wanting to tag along. "I'm going to stay here for a while and watch them sleep," she said, and there was an edge to her voice that I'd never heard before. "If you want to go back to your grandma's, then go. You know the way."

Did I? I had no recollection of the way we'd walked through the woods when we were last here. I'd been following Astrid, who always seemed to know the way. But at the same time as I thought that, a mental map appeared in my brain, of the short path back to the lake and then the familiar path back to Mormor's. Yes. I *did* know the way. I *could* go alone.

"Fine," I mumbled, getting up and moving cautiously back to the ladder. It took me a while to figure out how to get back on the ladder from above, but then I climbed slowly back down on trembling legs. I grabbed my bundled towel from the bucket with such force that the bucket wobbled on the concrete floor, creating a loud racket that made the hairs on my arms and legs stand on end.

"You alright down there?" came that gravelly voice from above. The Hunter.

I didn't reply. Was I? I didn't think so.

But it wasn't until I was halfway along the short path to the lake that I stopped to wonder if Ellen would be alright up there? With him.

13

LISA

I HAD FORGOTTEN to draw the curtains and woke up a little after 5 AM when the sun came up. I had only slept in fits and starts all night anyway, but this time when I woke, I knew that I wouldn't be able to get back to sleep. The funeral wasn't until this afternoon, but I had a full day ahead of me.

My dreams had been even more confusing than usual, and I woke up with a tension headache unlike any I'd ever had before. Being here was either going to put my nightmares to rest or kill me.

Either way, all of this would end today.

After the funeral, I wouldn't be coming back here.

I would rather sleep at the cemetery, to be honest. No offense, Mormor.

I got out of bed and found some clean clothes and my washbag in my suitcase. Then I moved as quietly as possible over to the bathroom, where I brushed my teeth and washed up. Splashing some cold water on my face made the headache recede a little, and I felt marginally better as I returned to Mormor's room, leaving my dirty laundry on the chair by the door.

I refilled my empty Coke bottle in the kitchen, and then I left.

The cottage was still silent, but the outside was buzzing with bird song and insects when I stepped out through the kitchen door. It was weird. I was so used to traffic noise, but even though the cottage was far away from any major roads, it still wasn't quiet. It was just different sounds.

I moved across the yard, just as I had done so many times before, and onto the path down to the lake. It looked pretty much the same as I remembered it, but was much shorter than it had been when I was a girl. Still, it was hard work walking on the uneven ground, especially since I couldn't see where I put my feet. As a child, I had run down this path like the wind. Now, I became out of breath from just walking slowly. My head was still pounding, and my chest felt tight. And my belly … Oh, I couldn't remember the last time I'd been this hungry. My stomach was growling and writhing underneath the blubber, but I did my best to ignore it. I wasn't going to starve to death; I knew that much. I'd be the last person on earth that starved to death.

I was panting and sweating when I arrived at the lake and saw the pier jutting out into the reeds. The angles were off, and this had to be a different pier than the one I'd gone swimming from all those years ago; I knew that. But apart from that, it was pretty much as I remembered it. The small, deep lake surrounded by woods. Thick reeds lining the water's edge on my left and a small stretch of sand to my right. Our "beach". It wasn't wide enough for me to lay down on, but when I was little, it had been the Riviera, and I had built many sandcastles there.

Stepping out onto the pier and feeling the boards give a little under my weight, I struggled to remember the happy feelings from when I'd come here as a child. Any happiness I'd ever experienced was buried underneath so many other emotions, and I had trouble making out any details. I made my way out to the end of the dock, where there was a ladder down into the water. Not the one I'd used as a child, and that had given me the scar that was still visible on my leg to this day as a thin white line. That ladder had been on the side of the dock, on the beach side. But this one looked just the same, with metal handles reaching up to help you get into or out of the water. I sat down next to it, using the handles to ease myself down onto the boards. The pier was higher up than I remembered it, or perhaps the water levels in the lake had lowered over the years. My feet didn't reach the water, even though my legs were much longer now.

I leaned against the cold metal railing and glanced over at the reeds to my left. They were rustling in the wind, moving back and forth in a movement that mimicked the small waves on the water. It was a beautiful place. I had been happy here; I was sure of that. But now, all I could think about was death. Death in all shapes and forms. Drowning. Fire. Guns. Deep woods and loneliness. Hunters and prey. Fear. Most of all, fear.

I had been frightened here, frightened out of my mind. Just seeing the pier had made my heart beat faster, and I had to force myself to take deep, slow breaths. There was nothing to fear here now, no real threat, but I was still panicking, slowly. I wasn't a little girl anymore, but I still felt so very small.

I lay back on the wooden boards of the dock and stared up at the blue, blue sky. It had looked just like this, that morning. When Ellen and I had come down here for a swim.

I rolled over on one side and looked over at the small strip of sand. In the shallows over there was where I'd played for hours on end as a child.

I could picture myself now, searching through the pebbles on the bottom of the lake for a pearl. A mermaid pearl. I couldn't remember who had come up with the game, but I remembered the small stone I'd found, that Ellen had said was the missing pearl.

Whatever happened to that stone? I don't remember bringing it back home with me. I usually did, as a child. I was always collecting things. But of course, being a girl, most of my clothes didn't come with pockets. The pearl had probably been left behind here, somewhere. Gotten lost again. The poor little mermaids had never been able to return to their castle.

Ellen was swimming with the mermaids, the policeman had said, but I'd known even then that he'd been wrong. Ellen had gotten bored with the mermaid game. She'd gotten out of the water. She hadn't drowned. Astrid had believed that story, but I knew it wasn't true.

Using the handles for the ladder as support, I managed to get up from the pier and walked slowly back along the wooden boards, back onto land. Feeling the solid ground underneath my feet didn't calm me down. Instead, I felt the panic that I'd experienced here as a child. Standing here with Ellen and the Hunter. All I'd wanted had been to leave here, to run back to Mormor's cottage. But we had taken the other path, the one over there, that led to the barn. The Hunter's barn.

The one where the kittens had been. I could remember the little hollow in the hay where the mother cat had made her nest.

The skin on my arms was covered with goosebumps, but I still made myself walk over to the gap in the line of trees and started walking up that second path. The one that led to the Hunter's farm.

Even though the sun was shining bright, even though I was a grown-up now and not a helpless little girl, I still had to force myself to walk into the woods. It was darker among the trees and a lot colder, but that wasn't the only reason I had goosebumps as I moved along the path.

WHEN I REACHED the end of the path, I thought that I must be in the wrong place. Nothing looked as I remembered it. There was no barn there, just a wide-open yard. The house across the yard looked dilapidated and abandoned. There was a moment of relief as I realized that my fragmented memories were all wrong.

None of the scary things I'd thought I'd remembered had been true. It was all constructs made up of nightmares, movies, and my vivid childhood imagination. The relief washed over me like a bucket of ice-cold water. None of it had been real. Astrid had been right. It *was* all in my head. I had never been here. Ellen had never been here. It was all just false memories.

And then I saw the concrete slab that was once the

floor of that barn, and in a split second I was transported back to that dark and cavernous space. My chest constricted so hard that I thought I would throw up, and I had to force myself to take deeper and slower breaths so that I wouldn't pass out. I might do that anyway. The memories—and yes, they were *memories*, not fantasies—were coming at me so hard and fast that I didn't know what to do with them.

At the edge of the forest lay the remains of a fallen tree trunk, and I staggered over, collapsing on top of it, more than sitting down. I was just a few feet from the concrete slab that had once been the foundation of a large barn, and it was freaking me out. I didn't care what Astrid said; I *knew* that I had been here before. I *knew* that I had been inside that barn. And the kittens. They were real. I remembered them clearly, curled up in that little nest in the hay, Ellen fussing over them.

And then, they weren't there.

I frowned. Weird. I could remember the kittens being there, and I could remember them *not* being there. That didn't make any sense. It had to be either-or. It couldn't be both.

Just as Ellen couldn't have drowned and *not* drowned. Those things couldn't both be true. But my brain kept telling me that they were.

Perhaps Astrid was right. Perhaps I was just fabricating memories to make sense of something that couldn't ever make any proper sense. Because no matter how you spun it, little girls weren't supposed to die. And whatever happened to Ellen, if she drowned or didn't drown, she did die.

I sat there for a long time, staring at the concrete slab. It was cracked in places, and grass and weeds pushed up through the gaps in uneven tufts. In another thirty years, nature would have reclaimed this place completely. I wished I had waited that long to come back. My eyes wandered slowly across the yard and over to the large house up by the road. It was as large and intimidating as I remembered it from my childhood —the only thing in this weird place that hadn't shrunk —but it didn't look like the same house. I remembered it as being impressive and well kept, but this house looked neglected, and the flower beds had all gone to seed. One or two flowers were still in bloom, but most of the greenery were weeds, mostly dandelions. The white paint on the façade had gone gray and peeled off in flakes here and there. The windowpanes were grimy in the bright morning sun, and the curtains were drawn in almost every room. It didn't look as if anyone lived here, but there was a car parked on the side of the house, so it couldn't be completely deserted.

A movement in the corner of my eye drew my attention to a window upstairs. There was a narrow gap between the curtains there, and I could have sworn I saw something move. Was someone in there, watching me?

I suddenly became very aware of the fact that I had walked onto someone else's property. There was no way I could have explained what I was doing here if anyone should come outside and confront me. I staggered onto my feet and hurried back down to the lake. The back of my neck prickled as I set off down the path, as if someone was watching me leave.

Not the Hunter, though. It couldn't be him. He was dead. Astrid had said so.

And some part of me felt as if I already knew that.

But as with so many other things, I had no idea *how* I knew that.

Or if any of the things I knew were actually true.

14

CAROLINE

I PUT the teacup on the tray, straightened the napkin, and lifted the tea tray with both hands, walking slowly toward the kitchen door. I mustn't spill any of it. Mother would be able to tell. I wasn't sure how, since she'd been almost blind for more than ten years now, but she would be able to tell, and she would refuse to drink her weak tea from the sloppy tray, and she might even make a scene, knock the tray out of my hands if I didn't back away fast enough.

I did not intend to make that mistake twice. I never did. But despite my almost manic perfectionism, Mother never ran out of things to accuse me of, blame me for.

I stopped outside the door to my mother's drawing room and took a breath, steadying myself and checking the tray one last time. Everything was as it should be.

With the tray balanced on one hand, I knocked ever so lightly, pressed down on the door handle, and grabbed the tray with both hands before entering.

The room smelled of ammonia and near death.

The curtains were almost entirely drawn, with just a narrow gap where my mother kept pulling one of the heavy, dusty drapes back a few inches to be able to see outside. What she could make out with those almost completely grayed-out eyes, I didn't know, but she kept up a constant vigil, from the crack of dawn until long after nightfall, except for her midday nap.

"I've got your tea, Mother," I said softly, trying my best not to grimace at the stench. Mother must have wet herself again. It happened almost every day now, but the stubborn old woman still refused to wear the adult diapers that the county nurse had brought for her, and she even refused to sit on the seat protectors, tugging them from under her wide bottom as soon as I had left the room and throwing them crumpled into the corner, out of sight. I would have to burn that chair, I thought, and then immediately almost choked from the guilt. This was my mother. I must be respectful and under-standing and loving and ...

And I must never, ever tell my mother that she stank like hell.

The old woman would surely not be around for much longer, and once she was gone, I would be all alone in the world.

As much as I was longing for the day when all my time and energy wasn't needed to cope with my moth-er's care, it was also my biggest fear. Without my mother, what would I do? How would I ever be able to cope all alone in this big house?

I walked over to the small table by the window and put the tray down before my trembling hands made the China rattle and gave away my nerves. I forced myself to look up at Mother, steeling myself for her withering and critical stare, but my mother's eyes were glued to a spot across the yard, over by the trees, and she didn't give any sign that she had noticed me, or the tea, for that matter.

"Mother?" I tried to sound calm and unconcerned. "Would you like a change of clothes, Mother, before you drink your tea?"

Mother slowly pulled her eyes from the trees and toward me, her only daughter. "What on earth for?" she replied, her voice as gentle as icy razorblades, dripping with contempt. "Have you gone completely round the bend, girl? It's the middle of the afternoon. Why on earth would I want to change my clothes?"

I forced myself to stand up straight and not look away, even though my cheeks burned with embarrassment. "Your dress and underpants are all wet, Mother," I said quietly. "You must be cold. Let me fetch you a …"

The old woman who had just a moment ago sat hunched over, frail and crippled, flew up from her smelly chair and clipped me over the side of my face with the palm of her withered hand. The force behind the blow was impressive, and I staggered back.

"How dare you?" the old woman shrieked, and she was the epitome of a nasty and evil old witch, exactly the kind of wicked witch that all children had nightmares about after reading the classic fairy tales. But this was no fairy tale, I thought, and ducked to one side as the teacup came sailing against my head. Another couple of steps back toward the door, and I was out of range for the frail old woman's throws. The teacup shattered into sharp little pieces, but the saucer flew like a Frisbee across the room and landed with a rattle on the floorboards over by the door. I couldn't help myself. I bent down and picked it up and then hurried back to gather up the pieces of the teacup before Mother could hurt herself on them.

Or hurt her daughter with them, I thought, and was immediately assailed with guilt. What a thing to think of one's own mother. As if Mother would ever do anything to harm me. She was just confused, that was all. And frustrated with her clumsy and stupid daughter, who could never do anything right.

I found all the pieces and stood up, looking at my mother. She was right. I was a horrible daughter. The bane of my mother's existence.

Perhaps it would have been different if Father had lived.

I forced myself to walk over to the table and fetch the tray. I placed the saucer and the fragments of the teacup on the tray and picked it up. Mother didn't acknowledge my presence. Her eyes were once more fixed on the other side of the yard. I rested the tray on my hip and stepped a little to the side to see out through the gap in the curtains.

There was nothing there. Just an overgrown and cracked slab of concrete where once a barn had stood.

"I'll fetch you a new cup of tea," I murmured and walked away, forcing the nightmarish images of that barn in flames from my mind.

I couldn't think about that now. I had to think of a way to get Mother out of those wet clothes before she caught her death.

I stopped by the door, shifting the tray to one hand and glancing behind me as I twisted the door handle with my free hand.

My entire body was trembling from the stress and

tension that always came over me in my mother's presence.

I'd fetch my mother another cup of tea.

But perhaps not right away.

Back in the kitchen, I placed the tray next to the sink and just left it there, wandering over to the refrigerator. On one of the bottom shelves was a large black bag-in-box of red wine. I took a glass from the cabinet and poured myself a drink. Then I sat down at the kitchen table, clutching the glass in both hands. My cheek stung from the slap.

Mother hadn't done it on purpose. It had been a reflex. She was old and confused. She didn't know what she was doing half the time. She had never meant to hurt me. Dementia was a cruel disease, hurting the family members and caregivers as much as the patient.

I had lost track of all the times I'd sat here in this kitchen, telling myself all these things. When Mother had disappeared into the Alzheimer fog more than ten years ago, I had believed that the worst was behind me. Dementia had mellowed my strict and rigid mother at first. A lot of the time, she hadn't even recognized me, and she'd been polite and pleasant, as she'd always been with strangers.

And I had, of course, believed that the dementia meant that my mother was old, that she didn't have long.

But Mother still clung on, more than ten years later.

She refused to let go.

I couldn't understand why.

It was not as if the old woman had anything to live for.

All she ever did was sit there in that chair and stare

out of that window.

I glanced at the clock on the wall. A quarter to four. The home nurse would be here in forty-five minutes. I emptied the glass and walked over to the sink, washing it and drying it and putting it back in the cabinet before I left the kitchen. A stick of gum from the pack in the pocket of my cardigan would take care of the smell of alcohol on my breath. Besides, I thought, placing my hand on the door handle. The stench of my mother would mask all other smells.

I knocked briefly and opened the door.

"There you are," Mother said angrily. "How long am I supposed to wait for that cup of tea? I'm completely parched."

I forced a smile onto my lips and walked over to my mother. The warm feeling the wine had given me wrapped around me like a protective cloak. "You've had your tea already, Mother," I said. "Did you forget?"

I grabbed my mother's arm and lifted her up from the chair, fortified by the light buzz. "We need to get you out of these wet clothes before the nurse gets here," I said firmly. "Otherwise, she'll report back to her boss that I am unable to care for you, and then they'll put you in a home. You don't want that, do you?"

The old woman stared at me, confusion and anger intertwined in her eyes. "What are you talking about?"

"You've wet yourself, Mother. And if you keep throwing away the seat protectors, you'll have to sit on a hard chair. This one's all ruined," I said, wrinkling my nose as I looked down on the large, dark patch on the upholstered armchair. The wine might have dulled my anxieties and given me the courage to deal with Mother, but it hadn't dulled my sense of smell.

The old woman followed my eyes and jerked with disgust when she saw the stain. At first, I thought that she was going to have another fit. Perhaps accuse me of pouring the tea directly on the chair to make it look as if she was incontinent. But instead, the old woman withered in my arms, and she didn't protest as I led her into the bathroom.

Father had added the bathroom in the seventies, as a wedding gift to my mother, and the mustard yellow basin, toilet and bidet, and the plastic shower cubicle clashed pretty bad with the rest of the house. My mother had hated it and refused to use it, scolding Father for having ruined her childhood home for his own convenience. She had kept using the old bathroom downstairs and even covered up the door to the new bathroom with a large woven wall hanging.

Since she had lost her marbles, though, I was grateful for having the shower close at hand, and as long as I left the wall hanging in place, Mother didn't seem to have a problem with it.

When the nurse came to get Mother ready for bed, she was sitting in the downstairs drawing room, with windows facing the road. After I'd let the nurse in, I went back upstairs to Mother's drawing room, opened the windows wide, and pulled the curtains all the way back to air out the stench.

It was too hot outside and barely any wind. The curtains hung limp, and I leaned my forehead against the window frame, staring out at the spot where Mother had kept her eyes fixed, every day for as long as I could remember.

The spot where Father had died.

15

LISA

THE TINGLING SENSE at the back of my neck stayed with me all the way down the path to the lake. I tried to fight it, telling myself that I wasn't a little girl anymore and there wasn't anything here for me to be afraid of.

But I *was* afraid.

And as I stepped out into the sunlight just above the dock, it dawned on me. That was it. That was what I had been feeling all this time.

All my life.

Afraid.

I made my way over to the dock, walked slowly out to the end of it, staring down into the dark and murky water. There was no way to see anything down there, but I still stared, and then I turned and looked at the thick curtain of reeds that covered the edge of the lake on one side of the dock.

Somewhere at the back of my mind, a memory took shape. A man. The policeman. Sitting across from me, telling me something that I knew wasn't true.

I remembered the weird feeling of knowing something that an adult didn't. Up until that point, I had assumed that adults knew everything and kids knew very little. But that policeman had told me something about these reeds, and I had known that it wasn't true. It had been empowering and terrifying at the same time.

But what had I known? And *how* had I known? That part, I couldn't remember. I had been in the barn; I was pretty certain of that now. But had Ellen been there? I had no memory of her there. Just the kittens. And then … no kittens.

I buried my face in my hands and bit my lip to keep myself from screaming. It was so frustrating. Every fragment of memory was like a piece of soap in the bath. Just when I thought I knew something, it slipped between my fingers and was gone again.

But I knew this. Ellen didn't drown.

I had no idea what had happened to her, but I was certain of this. The policeman had said something about the reeds. I forced my hands from my face and stared at the green stalks that moved back and forth in a wave pattern. Was that where they had found her?

It didn't make any sense. We had gotten out of the water. I remembered that, because of the scar on my leg. We had been mermaids, and then we had gotten out.

We had gone to see the kittens.

And then … Darkness.

Something had happened to Ellen, but I didn't know what.

I never saw what happened. I wasn't there.

Of all the conflicting information that was crammed into the dark recesses at the back of my mind, that was one gleaming fragment that I felt pretty certain of.

Whatever happened to Ellen, it happened when I wasn't there.

But then … where was I?

I SLOWLY MADE my way back to Mormor's cottage. The woods were dark and still on both sides of the path, but just as I was about halfway there, a large bird spooked up out of the undergrowth and flapped its wings frenetically in the shadows just to the left of me. My heart pounded so fast that I felt certain that the heart attack that my doctor had been warning me about was imminent, and I stared into the darkness. There was something about that sound, something about the smells and shadows, the racing heart, and the short hairs at the back of my neck standing up straight … Everything about this situation was so familiar.

Well, duh, the voice in the back of my head said. You used to play in these woods all the time when you were little.

Yes. But that wasn't what made this so familiar.

I had been *terrified* in these woods.

That was what I was remembering.

LITTLE LISA

THE TALL, dark trees shut out all the light as I hurried down the path from the Hunter's barn, and my heart was in my throat, pounding fast. When I could glimpse the lake ahead of me glittering in the late morning sun, my steps faltered and I slowed to a halt. The slight relief I'd felt when I slipped away from the uncomfortable situation up in the hayloft was completely overshadowed by the fear that had crept up on me during the last half hour or so. I remembered those helpless kittens squirming into their mommy's fur and felt sick to my stomach. I wanted my mommy too! Ellen, stupid, stupid Ellen, had told me to go. To leave her there and walk all by myself through the dark woods. Anything could happen.

But as frightened as I was for myself out here all alone, I was more worried about Ellen. I felt guilty about leaving her there, all alone.

Don't be silly, I could hear Astrid say, in that patronizing voice she always used only with me. Ellen is fine. There's nothing to be afraid of. It's all in your head, stupid. The Hunter, he's just some man, some boring old farmer. You've been watching too much TV. I'm going to tell Mom, and she'll cut your TV time.

I forced my legs to keep walking toward the light, toward the sun, toward the warmth that was the complete opposite of the chill here in among the trees. As I stepped out into the sunlight, I turned my face toward the sun, keeping my eyes shut tightly. The glowing orb was still visible through my eyelids, and the warmth from the intense sunlight started to spread throughout my body. Perhaps it *was* just my imagination. It had played tricks on me before, and I often had to remind myself that the stuff on TV and in movies didn't actually happen in real life. Especially at night. Especially in the dark.

But it was day now. And the sun was out.

There was nothing to be afraid of.

So then, why was I trembling?

I cast a final glance behind me, back the way I'd come, hoping to see Ellen coming along the path, but there was no one there. How long were those kittens going to sleep? A while, probably. And Ellen was going to stay there and watch them sleep, and then she would come straight home.

Everything was going to be fine, I told myself. And Ellen and Astrid would never let me hear the end of it if I caused a scene over nothing. They'd never let me play with them again. Lisa is such a baby, they would say. She's so weird. Afraid of her own shadow, that one!

I shook off the last of the cold chills and hurried over to the path that led back to Mormor's. I was feeling better now, and had almost managed to convince myself that it had all been my vivid imagination running wild. Almost.

Then a branch snapped somewhere in between the trees on my left, and I jumped almost straight out of my skin, shrieking loudly. A violent flapping noise followed, and as I turned my head I saw a large bird disappearing away from me into the darkness. My heart was beating so fast it made my chest hurt, and I realized that I hadn't been fine at all. I'd been so tense that I'd almost snapped when that branch did.

This fear was not my imagination. I was truly and honestly afraid for Ellen.

Then why did you leave her there, with that scary man? the cruel voice at the back of my head said. *How could you, if you thought she was in danger?*

Yeah, how could I?

I turned and looked behind me. I was almost back at Mormor's cottage and couldn't see the lake from here. But no Ellen was coming along the path behind me. She wasn't coming.

What if she never came?

You have to go and get her, the cruel voice said.

But I'm too scared, I whimpered in reply.

Then go back to Mormor's cottage and fetch someone to go with you, the voice said. *Tell your grandmother and your sister that you are too afraid to walk through the forest alone, and fetch Astrid's friend from the kind neighbor with the cute kittens, where Ellen may or may not be in mortal danger.*

The cruel voice's melodrama was the kicker. No way was I going to ask Mormor to come with me. No way was I ever going to admit to Astrid that I was too scared to do something.

Never ever.

My feet felt like lead when I started back along the path toward the lake. But I did it. I went back. I went back to fetch Ellen.

I was halfway up the path to the barn with the kittens when I saw something move on the trail up ahead. At first, my heart lifted because I assumed it was Ellen coming, finally. Then I realized that it couldn't be her. It was a much taller person moving heavily in the shadows up ahead. I ducked in behind a fallen tree a short distance from the path. The roots had come up out of the ground and pulled a lot of soil with it, a large gnarly lump, big enough for me to be hidden completely from sight. I held my breath and waited.

The heavy steps came closer and I pushed myself against the tree trunk. As the steps seemed to pass me, I leaned forward to peek out at whoever it might be.

It was the Hunter. I recognized the green trousers and the heavy boots. But there was something strange about his head. I leaned a little bit further out from the root lump as he disappeared out of sight behind a thick tree trunk. As he came into view again, I gasped. He was carrying something over his shoulder; that's what made his head look so weird. But whatever it was he was carrying seemed so familiar. I knew what that was. I just couldn't …

I leaned a little further, and the root that I was holding on to came loose with a dry snap that echoed through the silent forest. The Hunter stopped and turned toward me. I pushed back against the tree, hoping that it was too dark in here where I was hiding for him to be able to see me. He had stopped in a narrow strip of sunlight, sneaking in between the thick branches above. It was like a spotlight, highlighting him, making him stand out even more from the brown trees around him. The thing he was carrying over his shoulder looked so familiar. So pretty. Delicate little flowers on a pale-yellow background. I knew that fabric. I knew that dress. I had wanted one just like it for weeks. Ever since I saw Ellen wearing it for the first time.

Still, my brain didn't make the connection. That couldn't be Ellen there, dangling over the Hunter's shoulder, like a sack of something. It just couldn't. It couldn't even be a person.

The Hunter turned his back to me again and kept walking toward the lake. As he turned, two long, tanned arms swung into view, dangling down his back. Completely limp, like a rag doll.

Ellen couldn't be a rag doll.

She was watching the kittens sleep.

She was fine.

She had to be.

She was *not* a rag doll.

She could be a Sioux girl. A mermaid. Anything she wanted to be.

But not a rag doll.

Please, not a rag doll.

I stumbled out from behind the tree and over to the path, staring wildly in first one direction and then the other. I couldn't follow the Hunter and his weird Ellen rag doll. And I couldn't go back to the Hunter's farm. Where could I go? He might be back any minute. My head spun back and forth, and then a bird chirped, and I bolted straight into the forest ahead of me and ran as fast as I could, straight into the darkness.

I stumbled through the thick, dark forest, being

slapped and ripped by undergrowth and low-hanging branches as I pushed blindly ahead. I had no idea where I was or where I was going; I just knew that I had to get away. I could barely see where to put my feet for all the images that flashed on my retinas, helpless mewling kittens, limp, dangling, rag doll arms, underwater monsters, tugging at my feet, trolls and goblins lurking in the shadows around me, just waiting for me to fall before they would pounce on me and drag me with them down to the Netherworld. I didn't realize I was crying, but when I stumbled out onto a narrow path and stopped to rub my cheek where a branch had whipped me hard, my fingers came away wet. At first, I thought it was blood, but my fingers weren't red. Just wet. Wet, and pale and trembling. I stared both ways on the path and immediately recognized a gnarled tree on the other side, bending over a large boulder. I knew that tree. I knew that boulder. It was on the path to Mormor's cottage.

I staggered past the boulder and tree, continuing along the familiar path. It was just another minute or so before I staggered out into the yard, into the unreal sunlight that blinded me after the darkness in the forest. It felt so unreal, less like reality than the nightmare images that my brain bombarded me with. I couldn't feel my legs when I crossed the yard and wobbled up the steps to the kitchen door, but instead of reaching for the door handle, I just stood there. I couldn't move, my arms hanging limply down my sides as if I too was a rag doll.

For what felt like an eternity, I just stood there on the stone steps, unable to open the door.

After a while, the door opened anyway. Mormor was

standing in the doorway. I couldn't lift my eyes to meet hers, just stared straight ahead into her stomach, into the flowery fabric of her dress and the buttons, shimmering in the sun. *Mother-of-pearl*, I heard Astrid's voice, the know-it-all, patronizing voice of hers that she only ever used with me. Her Lisa voice.

"I was just coming to look for you," Mormor said. "You've been gone ages." She paused for a while. "Where's Ellen then?" And when I didn't reply, "Lisa? Honey? What's wrong?"

That was it. The softness in her voice when she said that. The love and warmth that usually enveloped me so completely whenever I was with her but now repulsed me. Because I knew she'd never look at me like that again. She'd never speak to me like that. Never again.

Everything was so wrong and nothing could ever make it right again. Nothing could ever turn me back into a real girl. I was a rag doll now.

It was all over.

The summer.

My life.

Everything.

I felt Mormor grab my chin and started to tilt my face up toward her. But before my eyes met hers, everything went black.

LISA

THE ONSLAUGHT of memories almost brought me to my knees. I stood there on the path staring into the darkness in between the trees as it all came back to me. Running alone through the woods, stumbling on roots, branches whipping my face. The monsters, trolls, and goblins that I had feared. And the real monster. The Hunter and the limp rag doll over his shoulder.

Oh my god. Ellen.

There was no air in my lungs, and I couldn't remember what to do to fill them again.

Ellen.

I had seen her, dead.

And the Hunter carrying her back down to the lake.

Where she'd been found.

Puzzle pieces that had rattled around inside of my head for so long suddenly clicked into place.

Ellen didn't drown.

We went to see the kittens.

Ellen was found among the reeds, and the policeman

said that she would be swimming with the mermaids forever.

It hadn't just been in my head. Sure, I had been watching too much television, but that wasn't why I'd freaked out that day.

The terror had been real, and it had been so intense that I hadn't been able to take it in. But now I was a grown woman, not a helpless little girl, and there was nothing to fear here, now.

The Hunter was dead.

Again, those haunting images of sparks against a pitch-black night sky.

He had died in a fire. And whatever he had done to Ellen, he couldn't ever have done to anyone else ever again.

There was nothing to fear here.

All the horrible things that happened, they happened in the distant past. But this was now.

I took a deep, rasping breath and felt the dizziness start to abate. One more breath. You can do it, I told myself.

You are safe.

I had no idea what to do with all of this. But this had to be what all of my therapists would call a break-through. I was remembering some truly important shit, and surely, that had to lead to some kind of change. Somehow.

But as I slowly made my way back to Mormor's cottage, I felt just as sick and helpless as I had then.

THEY WERE ALL UP. Of course.

I could hear them as I crossed the yard, talking animatedly to each other in the kitchen. The door was wide open and hooked to the railing with a piece of frayed string. I stopped and stared at the cottage. The familiar red walls with crisp white trimmings. The small window upstairs to the room where Astrid and I always slept when we visited.

I had been happy here. So very happy.

And then as miserable as I'd ever been.

When I had left here, I had somehow managed to leave some of that misery behind, along with the worst of the memories. That was why I had never wanted to come back. Why I had freaked out whenever anyone mentioned Mormor or this place. Because I hadn't been able to deal with it all.

Standing here now, I could understand it, on some level. But the most overwhelming feeling as I was standing there—with the sunlight warming my back, listening to those happy children's voices coming from inside—was grief. Grief for the child I'd been.

Ellen wasn't the only little girl who died that day.

I saw her. I saw what the Hunter had done to her, a thin voice at the back of my mind whimpered. My voice as a five-year-old. My knees felt as if they would buckle under me, but I stayed standing. Remembering was good. As sick as it was making me, I had bottled all of this up for way too long.

The little girl I had been up until that day was gone, long gone. But perhaps I could reclaim some little part of my life if I could just find a way to deal with these memories.

Astrid appeared in the doorway. When she spotted me, her look of worry was replaced with relief, but just for a moment. Then the worry reappeared. She came out onto the back stairs, stepped into a pair of wooden clogs that stood outside the door, and came toward me across the yard.

"Lisa! Where on earth have you been?" She frowned at me. "I didn't hear you leave and I've been awake for hours." She stopped right in front of me, searching my face. "Are you all right?"

I nodded. Then I shook my head. Was I? I had no idea. This was all too much, but I had to deal with it. It had been buried for way too long.

Buried. Oh god. Poor Ellen.

And poor Mormor.

Perhaps even … poor little me.

"Lisa?" Astrid reached out a hand and placed it on my fat shoulder.

A violent sob tore through my body. It was such a tiny gesture, but no one ever touched me of their own volition to demonstrate concern. The only ones who touched me were doctors, and even though they were very professional about it and their faces never revealed any disgust or repulsion, there was also never any real care or affection in their hands on my bulk. They never saw me as a person, as a woman. Just as a poor specimen of humanity, in need of their clinical skills.

"Oh honey," she said, and her voice sounded just like Mom's.

I pulled back. I couldn't stand the intimacy right now. I needed to be strong to deal with this, and too much emotion was only going to weaken me.

Bracing myself, I looked her in the eyes. "I remember," I said, and even though I felt as certain as I'd ever been about anything in my life, my voice still quavered. "I remember what happened to Ellen."

Astrid bit her lip. A quick glance over at the wide-open kitchen door. Then she looked at me. "Where have you been?" she said.

"The pier," I said. "And the Hunter's place. Where it happened."

She bit her lip. "Are you all right?"

I shook my head. "No. But I will be. Because I remember now."

THE LOOK on Astrid's face was of incredulity and fear, but there was still some concern there, and I clung to that. The relief was immense. My sister would believe me, if she knew. If I could somehow explain it all. If I could just find the words.

Then the healing could finally start.

But where to begin?

Astrid glanced back at the cottage again, back at the sound of children's voices. Her family. Her happy little family at her happy place.

I felt like a monster, ruining that for her.

Maybe, if I could bottle it all up and take it with me back home, I didn't have to do that. The question was, could I carry all of this on my own?

Yes, if I could just be certain that those kids were safe.

That terrible thing that happened had taken Ellen's life, and ruined mine, but it didn't have to ruin Astrid's.

And those darling little kids. Their light voices carried out to me, completely void of worries or fears. They were happy here.

And if the Hunter was dead, they were safe here.

The danger was no more.

There was no need to destroy their summer paradise, bringing up a bunch of nightmares from the past. These were my nightmares. What right did I have to impose them on my sister and her beautiful family?

Another peel of laughter from within the little cottage, and my resolve to tell Astrid everything weakened further.

She turned toward me, once again placing her hand on my arm.

"Tell me, Lisa. What are you remembering?"

Her concern was sincere, but there was also a hesitation there. She wanted to know, for my sake, but she also didn't want to know. To protect her family, she needed to keep me and my nightmares away.

An infinite sadness came over me as I realized that this was it. My sister, the last of my family to reach out to me, didn't really want to know what had happened. What had made me this way.

Forcing myself to look her in the eyes, I saw the truth there. She was afraid of what I was going to say. Of what my truth would mean to her and her family. The people she loved.

Me, I wasn't a part of that group any longer.

I slowly shook my head, brought up one hand and rubbed my face. "It doesn't matter. It was a long time ago." I glanced over my shoulder toward the path into the woods. "Time to let it go."

My voice sounded dull and unconvincing to my own ears, but Astrid smiled. "Perhaps it was good for you to come back here, after all," she said. "I know you didn't want to, but running away from your fears is never a good idea."

Images of the Hunter moving through the forest flashed through my mind, and I thought that Ellen would have been fine if she had only run away from my fears. But I didn't say anything. I forced a weak smile to my lips. "Perhaps you're right."

Astrid put her arm around my shoulders. "Come. Have some breakfast." She steered me toward the kitchen steps, and I let her, steeling myself for what was waiting inside.

Astrid's family sat around Mormor's old kitchen table. Fredrik had just started to put the lids back on the jam jars and the butter, but he stopped when he saw us at the door and put down the lid he was holding.

"Lisa," he said, and it almost sounded as if he was glad to see me. "Just in time. Would you like coffee or tea with your breakfast?"

Two liters of Coke, I thought, but I pushed that idea from my head. I didn't have a drop left, and there hadn't been any soda in Mormor's fridge. "Eh, coffee, please."

Fredrik bounced up from his chair and grabbed a mug from the cabinet above the small sink. Astrid pulled out the chair closest to us and I sank down onto it, feeling the stares from the two children on the kitchen sofa on my right. I glanced over at them with a little fake smile.

"Good morning," I mumbled.

Jonas had his mouth full but still replied. Elinor just nodded. She looked so much like Astrid at that age, it wasn't even funny.

I looked over at Astrid, who had squeezed down on

the kitchen sofa next to Jonas. "She looks just like you," I said, nodding over at Elinor.

Astrid reached out a hand behind Jonas's back and patted Elinor on the shoulder. "Really? You think so?" She smiled, pleased. "Perhaps a little."

Elinor pushed a strand of hair from her face with exactly the same gesture that Astrid had always used, and I felt myself shrinking. How many times had I sat here, in this kitchen, eating breakfast with Astrid and Mormor? Everything was so familiar, but different at the same time. The bread in the basket was store-bought, and the jams were from a factory somewhere, not Mormor's homemade. The wood-burning stove was the same, but there was a microwave on the counter and a small coffee maker instead of the filter Mormor used.

I was hesitant to eat in front of these people, but I took a piece of bread and made myself a sandwich, careful not to slather on too much butter or jam. Then I took a bite and forced myself to put the sandwich down on my plate while I chewed slowly, looking around the small kitchen. Time hadn't exactly stood still, but there were a lot of things that I remembered.

Fredrik had finished the coffee and placed a mug in front of me. It was handmade, probably bought at a craft fair somewhere around here, many, many years ago. Mormor had served me hot cocoa in it, last time I was here. Large daisies with chunky leaves. I placed my index finger on the petals and traced them. I knew this mug, but there was something wrong. It took a while before I figured out what it was.

"These used to be in different colors," I said, my voice fractured and weak. I could see it clearly in my memories.

"That's right," Astrid said, reaching across the table for her teacup. "They washed off, over the years. I had forgotten about that."

Wrapping my hands around the warm mug, I did my best to forget, but the floodgates to my memories were wide open now, and it all kept coming.

18

LITTLE LISA

THE NEXT THING I KNEW, I was in bed, upstairs in the loft. Somewhere far away, below, I could hear voices. No, just the one voice. Mormor's voice. She sounded worried. There were long pauses, and then she'd start speaking again. I lay completely still for as long as I could, but after a while, I really needed to rub my eyes. They felt sticky and filled with sand.

When I raised my hand, I heard a voice from just across the room. Astrid was sitting on her bed, looking at me.

"Where's Ellen, Lisa?" she said, and there was no worry in her voice. Just anger. Annoyance. As if I had borrowed one of her toys and broken it.

But I didn't break Ellen. I didn't make her into a rag doll. It wasn't me. It wasn't my fault.

Or was it?

I rubbed my face hard, but didn't look her way, just stared up at the sloping ceiling right above me, at the familiar wood grain patterns and gnarls. Everything

143

was just as when I'd woken up this morning, and at the same time, everything had changed.

Or perhaps it was just me.

"Mormor!" Astrid shouted.

I heard steps coming toward the stairs. "Yes, dear?"

"Lisa's awake."

The steps hurried up the staircase. Mormor hardly ever came up here. She said that the stairs were too steep for her old legs. But now, she hurried up them, and her gray-haired head appeared at the top of the stairs. "Lisa, dear, what on earth is the matter?" She came over and sat down on the side of the narrow bed. "Are you alright? Where is Ellen?" Her warm hand rested on my forehead, stroking it gently. It felt like a slap. "And what happened to your face. You look like you've been horsewhipped."

I forced myself to look at her, but as soon as I saw her face peering down at me with concern in her eyes, mine filled with tears and she disappeared in the blur.

"Oh, Lisa, dearest child, please just talk to me. Did you and Ellen have a fight?"

Somehow I managed to shake my head.

"Do you know where she is?"

Another shake.

"Oh …" She was silent for a short while, and then: "Astrid, I know you're not feeling well, but I need you to look after your sister for a little while, while I go and see where Ellen has got to."

There was a groan. "Alright," Astrid said reluctantly.

"I won't be long. I need to start making some lunch, but I'm honestly worried about Ellen."

"Don't be," said Astrid. "Lisa probably just got on her

nerves, so she took off for a while to get some peace and quiet. She'll be back soon."

"All the same," Mormor said. "I'll just walk down to the lake and see if she's there. I don't like the idea of her swimming on her own."

She got up and disappeared down the stairs. I heard her putter around downstairs, and then the kitchen door opened and closed.

"Way to go, you little pest," came Astrid's voice from the other bed. "Ellen is never going to want to come with me here, ever again. Why do you have to be such a nuisance all the time?"

I turned my back to her and stared into the wall.

After a while, I heard Astrid get up and walk over to the window. Then her footsteps moved across the room and down the stairs. The kitchen door opened, and I heard her voice. "Didn't you find her?"

"No, I don't understand where she can have got to," said Mormor.

"She wasn't at the lake?" Astrid's voice shifted from annoyed to worried. "But … where is she?"

"I don't know. Do you have a place that you go to and play, perhaps? Did you build a hut or something for one of your games?"

Astrid didn't reply. Perhaps she shook her head.

Then Mormor's voice again. "I'm going to call around to the neighbors to hear if they've seen her."

She made a few phone calls, and every time she put the phone down, her sighs became heavier. My duvet became heavier as well, with every sigh. How could I just lay here? But what else could I do? I couldn't do anything. I couldn't tell them anything. It was all I could do, just to keep breathing, to keep existing with all the horrible images that kept popping into my head.

Then Mormor made one final phone call. "Hello, could you put me through to the police, please? I'd like to report a missing child."

HOURS LATER, just as it was beginning to go dark, I heard cars coming, one by one. Voices, many, right outside, in Mormor's yard. Mormor had been up to check on me a couple of times, but I'd pretended to sleep. I just couldn't look at her. Couldn't speak to her. Couldn't anything.

It was dark up in the attic, all shapes and shadows when I finally turned my head away from the wall to look around. Lights were dancing on the ceiling now and then, sweeping from side to side. I pushed the heavy duvet off me and crawled out of bed. I was still in my sundress, and it felt sticky and chafing against my clammy skin. As soon as I left the warmth underneath the duvet, goosebumps spread across my arms and legs, but I kept moving over toward the window.

The yard was filled with people, and more kept coming along the driveway from the big road. Most of them had flashlights, and when they turned and moved and gesticulated this way and that, the beams hit my attic window and lit up the small room, just for a moment. Mormor was out there, pulling her big, warm cardigan close around her and talking to the people who came. Another car pulled into the yard, a police car with a blue light flashing on the roof. It lit up the entire yard and made the grass look weird and blue. A man stepped out, grabbing a jacket from the trunk and pulling it on as he moved toward Mormor.

I couldn't hear what he said, but he only spoke to her for a moment. Then he walked over to another car that was parked nearby, where someone had spread out a map over the hood. Lots of pointing and shaking of heads. Then people set off in smaller groups, in different directions. A search party. I didn't know where I'd heard that word before, but I thought it was strange. I'd never seen anything that looked less like a party.

The policeman came back over to Mormor, put his hand on her shoulder and said something. Then his head turned slightly and his eyes moved up to where I was standing.

Perhaps I should have ducked out of sight, but I couldn't move. His eyes met mine. They looked kind, but I didn't know anymore. How could one tell? I didn't know what to believe anymore.

Then someone came walking out of the forest by the path to the lake. I'd thought I was cold before, but now I froze entirely.

The Hunter.

Still in his green hunting clothes and carrying a large flashlight that lit up the whole cottage when he turned toward it. I felt the beam hit my face and my eyes watered, but I couldn't close them, couldn't look away.

The Hunter walked straight up to the policeman. I felt faint. I wanted to open the window, wanted to scream to the policeman with the kind eyes, *Ask him where Ellen is, ask him what he did to her, ask him about the rag doll, ask him.*

But I couldn't move. Couldn't say a word.

And then the policeman reached out his big hand and shook hands with the Hunter, as if they were old friends, patting his shoulder, friendly, entirely without suspicion or mistrust.

I knew then that I could never tell the policeman what I had seen. Because he would never believe me. Not when the Hunter was a friend of his.

The Hunter pointed in the direction of the path behind him and then set off back in that direction again. A group of men and women followed him. The policeman and Mormor walked toward the cottage, and I heard the kitchen door open below.

Mormor came up the stairs, groaning a little with every step. Poor Mormor. How many times had she gone up and down that steep staircase today? Her poor knees.

"Lisa, honey." She came over to me, put her hand on my arm, and then, "Oh, honey, you're freezing. Let's get you some warmer clothes."

I let her guide me back over to the bed, pull out my small suitcase from under the bed and find my jeans and a sweater. When I didn't move, she pulled the sundress over my head and dressed me as if I was a helpless baby. No, not a baby. I was a rag doll. Just like Ellen. When I was dressed, she took the hairbrush from Astrid's bedstand and started to untangle my hair. Astrid wasn't going to like that, I thought, but I didn't say anything. What did it matter, now? I wasn't her annoying little sister anymore. Just a rag doll. Nothing more. No one could get annoyed with a rag doll, surely?

She braided my hair quickly into a loose braid down my back and fastened it with one of Astrid's pink hair ties. "Now, Lisa. There's a policeman downstairs who wants to talk to you." She patted my cheek and bent down to look into my eyes. I flinched and looked away. "You need to tell him what happened today, Lisa," she said sternly. "So that he can find Ellen before something bad happens to her."

I wanted to tell her. I really did. But the words wouldn't budge from the back of my tongue.

Mormor led me down the stairs and into the kitchen. The policeman was sitting in one of the chairs at the kitchen table, and Mormor led me over to the sofa on the other side.

"You must be hungry, poor child," she muttered. "You've eaten nothing all day."

And then she busied herself over by the pantry and the refrigerator while I sat there opposite the policeman. He rested his underarms on the table, with his hands clasped as in prayer. They were huge and looked remarkably soft, but all I could think about was how he'd shook hands with the Hunter a moment ago, right outside. His buddy, the Hunter, who turned little girls into rag dolls.

"Hi there, Lisa," he said. "I'm Robert. And I'm here to try and find your friend, Ellen. But in order to do that, I need you to tell me what happened today, down by the lake."

I couldn't look at his face, just stared at those huge hands, wondering if they also made little girls into rag dolls. It looked as if they could, easily.

"Lisa, honey, please talk to the policeman," said Mormor and put a plate in front of me with a large bread roll, cut in half and spread with butter and jam. My favorite. But I couldn't face a single bite. Rag dolls didn't eat. They didn't even have proper mouths.

Mormor returned to the refrigerator and came back with a tall glass of milk. "Try and eat a little," she said. "You'll feel a lot better if you do."

Somehow I doubted that. I couldn't imagine that I would ever feel better. This was what my life was like now. Nightmares in my head, all the time, night and day. And everyone was a monster, even the ones that looked kind.

"Lisa, your grandma told me that you and Ellen went off for a swim at the lake. Did something happen while you were there? Did you have a fight?"

I mustered up all my energy and managed a slight shake of my head. Then I forced myself to pick up one of the pieces of bread and bring it to my lips. I took a bite. The bread was soft and the jam was my favorite kind, but it tasted of nothing at all. I chewed and chewed, but the bite just grew and grew in my mouth until I thought it was going to choke me. I swallowed it, bit by bit, and washed it down with milk. Mormor had been wrong. I didn't feel better. Not at all.

"You didn't have a fight? What then? Did Ellen run away? Was she unhappy here?"

Another minuscule head shake. Another bite of the roll. A smaller bite, this time, but it was just as hard to swallow.

"Where is she then?" The policeman leaned over the table, looking me straight in the eyes. "Do you have any idea, Lisa, any idea at all, where Ellen is right now?"

I didn't. I hadn't the slightest clue. Another shake. Another bite.

The policeman frowned, but then he forced a smile onto his lips. "I don't want you to worry now," he said. "There are so many people out looking for your friend, and I'm sure they'll find her soon. She couldn't have gotten too far." He looked up at Mormor. "I understand that this is the first time she's been here, so she's not too familiar with the surroundings?"

Mormor nodded.

"Then I'm sure she's just wandered off into the woods for a pee or something and gotten turned around." He glanced over at the window. "It's a bit chilly now that the sun has set, but she won't freeze, not tonight. We've got people out in all directions. I'm sure they'll find her soon."

He turned toward me again. Another fake smile. "Don't worry, Lisa. You'll soon be able to play with your little friend again."

The bread roll swelled in my stomach and forced itself up my throat, exploding out over the table in a flood of chewed bread and milk. The policeman pushed his chair back and stepped away from the table before the mess reached him. Mormor tutted and fussed, cleaned me up with a kitchen towel, and helped me back up the steep stairs to put on a clean nightgown and crawl back into bed.

I lay there in the darkness, all alone. Astrid was downstairs, whining and complaining to Mormor about something, but I couldn't make out the words. I rolled over and stared into the wall again. Everything was a mess in my head right now. I didn't know what had happened to Ellen, but I was pretty certain that the policeman had been wrong. She wouldn't come back. Once a little girl has turned into a rag doll, she could never turn back into a little girl again. It was not like being a mermaid, where you got legs when you were on land and a fin when you were underwater.

151

After a while, there was a knock on the door downstairs. A man's voice, and Mormor saying "Oh no, oh, please no" and then steps on the stairs. Heavy steps. Not Mormor, this time.

"Lisa." It was the policeman. "Lisa, are you awake?"

I didn't move, but he put a hand on my shoulder and turned me over so that I was forced to look at him. He found the switch to the small lamp on my nightstand and turned it on. He looked grim. But not angry or annoyed like before. Just … grim. From downstairs, I could hear howling. It was Astrid, crying, wailing even. Mormor was trying to calm her down.

"Lisa, I'm sorry to have to tell you that we've found your friend," the policeman said. He took a step back and sat down on the edge of Astrid's bed, across the small space. He had to lean forward a bit to not bang his head on the ceiling. He rubbed his hand over his face and looked at me again. "I understand that it must have been horrible for you, but I want you to know that it wasn't your fault."

My fault? Why should it be my fault?

"Accidents happen sometimes, Lisa," he said. Another face rub. "And when it happens to little children, it's … It's just dreadful. But I don't want you to feel bad for Ellen. She's in a better place now."

She was? Where?

Downstairs, Astrid's distraught crying slowly subsided into heart-wrenching sobs. I didn't cry. I didn't have any tears. I didn't have any feelings. The taste of vomit was still faint in my mouth, and my stomach felt strange. So empty. Completely hollow. I could picture my insides as a large void. Nothing in my stomach. Nothing where my heart should be.

What kind of monster was I that didn't cry when a little girl had died? Everyone was so upset, and I just lay here.

The policeman looked over at the window, at the dark night sky outside. And then he told me that a group from the search party had found Ellen, in among the reeds at the edge of the lake. Her dress and towel had also been found in the water, underneath the pier. They must have blown off, and that's why Mormor hadn't seen them when she went and looked for Ellen earlier.

"From the looks of it, your friend hit her head on the ladder to the pier," he said. "Apparently, it had very sharp edges. I understand that it must have been scary to see that. The coroner will have to take a closer look, but he said that she was probably dead when she fell in the water, or at least unconscious. She wouldn't have suffered, he told me to tell you. It wouldn't have made a difference if we'd found her sooner. There was nothing you could have done."

I didn't understand. Ellen hadn't hurt herself on the ladder; that was me. And of course, there was something I could have done. I shouldn't have left her there with the Hunter. She hadn't understood how dangerous he was. I had. This was all my fault.

"She'll always be with you, in spirit. And if it helps you, you could think of her as forever swimming with the mermaids at the bottom of the lake."

I wanted to tell him that he was wrong. That she wasn't a mermaid. That she was a rag doll. And his friend had made her into one.

Just because she wanted to look at those stupid kittens.

"No," I croaked. "She wasn't swimming ..." But then I couldn't think of the words to explain any of it. Everything was such a jumble. How could her dress have been on the pier? She had gotten out of the lake. She had been wearing her dress. The pretty yellow one with the flowers. She hadn't hurt herself on the ladder, I had.

This didn't make any sense. I was so confused.

He leaned over and patted my arm. "I understand that it must have been a terrifying experience for you, but I want you to know that no one is blaming you for what happened." He sat up again. "Perhaps you shouldn't have been at the lake without adult supervision, but under the circumstances, it wouldn't have made any difference. This was a dreadful accident, and accidents happen sometimes. There was nothing you could have done differently."

I turned my head and stared at the wall. I didn't understand any of this, but I knew that he was wrong.

I knew that this was the Hunter's fault.

Mine as well, but mostly the Hunter's.

19

LISA

I COULD ALMOST TASTE the vomit as I sat there at the kitchen table, remembering the policeman up in the loft, telling me about Ellen. It had been the first time I'd realized that adults didn't know everything. It had felt strange. Frightening, mostly, but also empowering, in some ways. The fact that I knew something that he didn't. And I was just a little girl.

That he had been a friend of the Hunter's must surely have been a factor in why I never told him what happened, but it was never a decision I'd made. I never *decided* not to tell anyone. I would have told, if I could have just found the words. If I could just have made sense of it all, enough to know what to tell them.

But it never made any sense. The confusion just grew, and the guilt. Because regardless of what the policeman had said, it *had* been all my fault. Not because I couldn't save Ellen from drowning, but because I had left her there, with the kittens and the Hunter.

I still felt the shame burning inside me over that decision. I had been afraid, and I had run away.

Of course, I had no idea what might have happened if I had stayed. The nasty part of my brain thought that nothing would have happened. That we would have watched the kittens in the hay for a while and then gone back home to Mormor's, and everything would have been fine.

Another part of my brain could easily picture another rag doll slung over the Hunter's back as he walked down to the lake. A rag doll bearing a striking resemblance to five-year-old me.

I didn't know if I had been in any danger that day, but even if I had, it didn't help to think about what I'd done as saving myself. Because, honestly, wouldn't it have been better for everyone involved if I had died and Ellen had come back home?

After all, my parents had two daughters, and Ellen had been an only child.

And Ellen had been … well, Ellen. And I was just me.

I picked up the sandwich but then put it down again without taking a bite. I felt sick and confused and was afraid of embarrassing myself, again, in front of Astrid's family. I wouldn't be able to push past Fredrik and get to the bathroom in time if my stomach decided it didn't want any breakfast after all. I took a tiny sip of coffee instead. It was amazingly strong. I had forgotten what coffee used to taste like but was grateful for the punch. I needed it.

The children had finished eating, and Jonas was studying me unashamedly. Elinor more discreetly. I ventured a smile but didn't think I could pull it off.

"What do you do for a living?" the boy asked suddenly.

I didn't know what to say. I'd been on disability for so long, but since I'd lost my benefits, I'd been more or less living in denial. The money had been running out steadily, and for the last couple of months, I'd been living off a credit card that was almost maxed out. "I'm not working right now," I said, smiling apologetically.

"Do you have any children?" he asked again, not in the least fazed by my answer.

I almost laughed out loud at that one. "No," I said.

"A husband?"

I didn't even answer, just shook my head. This was so weird. As if he thought I was ... just a normal person, living a normal life. With a job and a family.

I couldn't remember the last time anyone had seen me as a normal person. It was disturbing.

"I'm starting school in a couple of weeks," Jonas said.

"Oh," I said. "Are you looking forward to it?"

His grin told me that his first day of school was going to be very different from mine. I had been shell-shocked from what had happened with Ellen. More or less mute, jumpy and terrified of everyone and everything. Not a great way to fit in and make new friends. I had been the weird one at the back of the classroom for ten long years.

"My teachers are Anders and Marianne," he said. "Anders has a beard."

I nodded. "And Marianne doesn't?"

He stared at me for a moment, then burst out laughing. It was the most wonderful sound, but Elinor rolled her eyes.

"You talk funny," Jonas said. "Why is that?"

Fredrik looked embarrassed and Astrid muttered "Jonas!" under her breath.

I smiled at him. "I haven't spoken Swedish in almost twenty years," I explained. "After a while, you forget how to do it."

He didn't look convinced. "Don't you have anyone to talk to, over there?"

He meant talk Swedish, but as I shook my head in reply, the truth was that I didn't have anyone at all. To talk to or anything else.

"Why haven't you come to see us before?" he asked, and I saw in the corner of my eye that Astrid gave Fredrik a look, pleading with her husband to please distract the child, please shut him up.

"I live really far away," I said. "The plane ride was sixteen hours." Not the whole truth, and not the reason *why* at all. But Jonas accepted it.

"When are you going back?" he asked.

I glanced at Astrid. "After the funeral," I said vaguely and felt the anxiety levels start to rise even further. We hadn't talked about it, and I was suddenly gripped by a fear that perhaps Astrid wouldn't want to get me a ticket back, at least not right away, as I had planned. I didn't have enough money to get my own ticket. The last of my credit cards was almost maxed out. The helplessness of the situation, of being stuck here, of not being able to leave, made me feel nauseated, and I pushed the plate away.

Jonas looked disappointed. "Aren't you coming back to our place?"

I shook my head. "I don't think so. Some other time, perhaps."

The boy slumped back against the carved backrest,

and Fredrik stood up across the table, starting to clear away the breakfast. "We've got time for a quick swim before the funeral," he said cheerfully. "Who wants to come?"

"I do," Elinor said quickly.

Jonas perked up. "Yes," he said, sliding out through the narrow gap between the kitchen sofa and the heavy table. "I'll go and get my goggles."

Both kids disappeared up the stairs to the loft to get ready. Astrid sighed. "I'm sorry," she mumbled as she put the rest of the bread back in the plastic bag.

I shrugged. "It's fine." That was a lie, of course. Nothing about this was fine. I shouldn't have come here. I should have stood my ground.

We sat there in silence for a while, while Fredrik cleared away everything and started to fill the sink.

"I'll do the dishes," Astrid said to him. "You and the kids should go now if you want to swim. There isn't much time before we have to get ready."

"Are you sure?" Fredrik said. Astrid smiled at him. "All right." He started pulling towels and bathing suits from the drying rack above the stove and put them in a large crinkly shopping tote that stood by the door. When the kids came thundering down the stairs again, he followed them outside. Astrid looked out the door until they must have disappeared out of sight. Then she got up and walked over to the sink, burying her hands in the sudsy water.

"You don't have to go back right away," she said, not looking at me.

I didn't reply. Oh, yes, I did. I should never have come here in the first place. This had all been disturbing for everyone involved, and for what? So that I could stand there next to Astrid and her perfect little family at the funeral this afternoon? She didn't need me here. That had all been a lie. She had her husband and her kids.

Astrid rinsed a couple of plates and put them in the drying rack. Then she turned toward me, her hands still in the water. "In fact, you don't have to go back at all."

My chest started to constrict. Oh no. Please don't. I opened my mouth to protest but she beat me to it.

"What do you have to go back to?" she asked. "You have no job, no place to live."

"I … it's where I live," I said faintly.

"But it doesn't have to be," she said. "People move." She grabbed a glass and scrubbed it with a sponge. "Wouldn't it be better to move back here? Start fresh. Get a new place. A job." She glanced over at me. "I could help you."

I didn't know what to say. Didn't know how I felt about it, even. Moving back to Sweden had never even been an option, as far as I was concerned. I'd swore I'd never set foot here again.

But Astrid was right. I had no life to go back to.

And the Hunter was dead. Wasn't he the reason I'd run away?

No, not the only reason.

As soon as I even considered the idea, all kinds of objections started to pop into my head. I couldn't just start over. I couldn't imagine getting a job, going to work every day with other people. Other people were exhausting, and I wouldn't be able to keep it up. I didn't know what options there were for someone like me over here, but I couldn't imagine any landlord who would want to rent an apartment to someone like me who didn't have a job and didn't have any references.

It was too much. Too difficult.

I'd be completely dependent on Astrid and her family. It would be awkward. Humiliating.

Even though I knew that it would be difficult back home, with the eviction and everything, that still felt like the least unsettling option, weirdly enough. I could picture what was going to happen to me there. I'd only have myself to worry about. Whatever hardship was looming up ahead, it would be just for me. It wouldn't affect anyone else.

I couldn't picture a future for myself here. If I could picture a future at all that didn't make me want to scream, it would be me on my sagging sofa with my hand in a bag of Doritos and a large pizza with everything on it slowly cooling on the table in front of me. Oh, pizza. What I wouldn't give for a pizza right now. I hadn't eaten anything in forever and didn't think I'd be able to, as long as there were people around. My sandwich, with one bite taken out of it, still lay on the plate in front of me. A bowl of fruit stood in the middle of the table.

Pushing away from the table, I stood up. "I need a shower before the funeral," I mumbled. Then I grabbed an apple and the rest of my sandwich and pushed past Astrid out into the hallway.

Astrid sounded disappointed when she called out after me. "Think about it. Please just … think about it."

I slipped inside Mormor's room. "I will," I mumbled and then slammed the door shut.

I didn't think I'd be able to think about anything else.

Staggering across the tiny room, I collapsed on the unmade bed, clutching the sandwich and the apple. My stomach growled like a lion, but this was all I had.

Placing the apple on the bedstand, I took a tiny bite of the bread and chewed it until it had completely dissolved. Then I swallowed and made myself count to ten before I took another bite. I must have sat there for at least ten minutes, slowly eating my sandwich. Then I forced myself to get up, take out the dress I'd bought for the funeral and my wash bag, and go across into the bathroom and take a shower.

I'd eat the apple when I was dressed and ready.

ONCE I'D SHOWERED and gotten ready, I went back into Mormor's room. I made up the bed and put away my things neatly in the suitcase. I did not intend to come back here, so I needed to make sure that I had everything with me to the church. Surely, there had to be a bus stop or something in the village? I could find my way back to the airport, somehow. All Astrid had to do was to get me the plane ticket. I'd sign any paper she put in front of me. I didn't even care about the money or Mormor's cottage anymore. She could have it all. I just had to get home, get away from this place and everything that had happened here. Get as far away from the person I'd been here as I could.

The fact that Astrid wanted me to stay scared me. She *had* to buy me that ticket. I couldn't do it myself.

I hadn't even asked her about the money for the cottage; I had no idea how much money we were talking about. Looking around, I couldn't even begin to guess what a cottage like this might be worth. It was far away from everything, and I had no clue about the Swedish housing market. I'd been carefully avoiding all news from "back home" ever since I'd gotten to the States. Hadn't wanted to know. Hadn't wanted to be reminded.

When everything was packed and tidied, I sat on the bed. The kids and Fredrik had come back from their swim and were getting ready, bouncing up and down the stairs right outside the door. I plugged in my headphones and started another YouTube video. Then I leaned back against the headrest and picked up the apple. I didn't take a bite, just held it, turning it over in my hands. It was a large apple, but there wasn't an apple large enough in the world to fill me up right now. I needed fat and sugar. Chocolate and potato chips and … Coke. Gallons and gallons of Coke.

Glancing over at the bag of trash by the door, I could almost taste the panini from yesterday. It had been dreadful, but I still wished I had some more right now. Anything.

With a sigh, I placed the apple on the bed stand. It was best not to eat it until I absolutely had to. Hopefully, I'd get an opportunity to slip away from Astrid and her family before the funeral. I couldn't remember if there was a shop in the village where the church was. Part of me thought that there might not be. That the closest shop was at the mall we'd driven past yesterday. That was in the other direction. But there had to be something. A pizzeria. A gas station. A tobacconist. A newspaper stand. A roadside stand. A farmer's market.

There had to be something to eat around here. There just had to be.

And even if there wasn't, I'd be on my way back home in just a few more hours.

Clutching my phone to my chest, I stared at the apple and blinked to keep back the tears.

Just a few more hours. I could do this.

Couldn't I?

AFTER TWO AND a half episodes of an old sitcom, Astrid knocked on the door. It was time to leave. Stepping out into the hallway, I saw that she was dressed in a serious black outfit that fit her slim figure like a glove. She looked amazing, with impeccable makeup and her hair looking as if she'd just come from a high-end salon, but her eyes were a little red, and she kept hugging and touching her children.

I hadn't shed a tear for Mormor yet and didn't know if I ever would.

Everyone crammed into the car. I sat in the passenger seat in front. Fredrik, dressed in a smart black suit, was in the driver's seat, and Astrid and the kids were in the back. I kept my eyes open for a shop or a gas station but didn't know how I'd convince everyone I needed to go shopping right now. They were all somber, the boisterousness from this morning gone. Jonas was sad and said so. Elinor was silent. She was sitting right behind me, so I couldn't see her face, but I could picture her staring out the window, remembering her great-grandmother.

The church was only a few minutes away. As Fredrik parked the car, I noticed that the small car park was almost full, and there were cars parked along the road as well. I felt like an idiot. Somehow I'd expected it to be just us, but all along the path up to the church and outside the large doors were people. Lots and lots of people. Mostly old people, but there were some families as well, with children of all sizes, from cuties in smart pushchairs to awkward teenagers tugging at the collar of their funeral outfits. Of course. Mormor had lived here all her life. Everyone knew her. Everyone would want to pay their respects.

My feet felt like lead and I could barely lift them, but somehow I managed to follow Astrid and her family over to the church. Everyone around us wanted to say hello, offer their condolences, shake our hands. Not just Astrid and Fredrik, but me as well. I had hoped that no one would know who I was, but of course, they did. Not because they recognized me, but because I was there with Astrid, I had to be the long-lost granddaughter. I didn't have to look around me to know that they were all staring at me. If I could have swapped places with Mormor at this moment, I would happily have done so. The solitude in that casket would be a haven, compared to this.

And Mormor would have loved to see all of these people who'd come just for her.

I shook so many hands on my way over to the church, mumbled "Thank you for coming" a million times to one stranger after the other. This was more people than I'd met over the past ten years, all in one go. I was starting to panic, but then the priest came out to greet us, and after his firm handshake we were finally ushered inside, away from the crowds.

The church was cool and echoey, even though it wasn't very big. It was plain and sparse in its decorations, compared to most other churches I'd seen, but it was pretty and I thought that Mormor would have liked the service. Great turnout. Great music. I clutched the hymnal and was immensely relieved that I wasn't expected to get up in front of all these people and say something. It was a short ceremony. The priest said a few words. We sang a couple of hymns. I mimed along since I didn't know the melody.

Afterward, we all filed past the casket. I kept my head down and avoided looking at all the people in line after us. Staring at the white casket, I couldn't wrap my head around the fact that Mormor was in there. I'd done my best not to think about her, about this place or anything to do with my childhood, in all the years since I'd last seen her, but if she had crossed my mind, I had assumed that she was living her life here exactly as she'd always done. That she puttered around in her little cottage, happy in her solitude.

The fact that her life might have been in some way affected by my absence had never occurred to me, at least not in any negative way. Astrid had said that she had been sad and confused at the end, asking for me, and that stung, but I needed to be strong now. I needed to keep my cool, somehow. The funeral was almost over. I could practically taste the freedom.

When we finally left the church, I set off toward the car, but Astrid called me back. She and her family had stopped right outside the door, and as the other funeral guests started to file out, we had to shake everyone's hand again. This was torture. I felt exhausted and considered leaning up against the cold brick wall of the church just to stay on my feet. Why couldn't everyone just leave?

But no. They all stayed on the graveled court in

front of the church, standing in small groups, chatting. And once the church was empty, the priest led his congregation over to a low, yellow building across the road. I looked around in all directions, but there was nowhere to go, nowhere to run.

And nowhere to buy something to eat.

Astrid put her arm around me and more or less dragged me across the narrow road.

Inside the yellow community hall, a buffet was set up, with cakes and cookies, lemonade in large plastic jugs, and two huge coffee urns. Somehow I ended up at one of the round tables that were scattered around the space, with a cup of black coffee in front of me.

"Would you like something with your coffee?" Fredrik asked. "Some cake? Or a sandwich?"

I shook my head mutely. I wasn't sure how I was still alive after this prolonged fast, but there was no way I was going to eat anything in front of this audience of curious onlookers.

Fredrik and the children went off to raid the cookie platters. Astrid put her arm around me again and gave me a sideways hug.

"Thank you for coming," she said. "It really meant a lot to me."

I couldn't even look at her. It almost sounded as if she meant it, but I couldn't imagine that it was true. Look at all these people. And her family, her husband, and those children. She had made it sound as if she'd be all alone at the funeral, but the community hall was packed. She hadn't needed me here. And judging by the looks I was getting from all directions, I was nothing but an embarrassment to her.

Oh, people would be talking about this for weeks

and months, about the dreadful granddaughter who had abandoned her family and only showed up at Britta's funeral. I didn't want to think about what they might say about me, but I felt bad about how it would all reflect badly on Astrid, who planned to keep coming back here.

People kept coming up to us to say a few words, kind words about Mormor, about the service, and then some badly hidden curiosities about Astrid's and my plans for the cottage.

"We're keeping it," Astrid said to one woman who had asked more or less straight out. "The cottage will be our summer home."

The woman smiled politely. "How lovely for you," she said, and then quickly made her excuses and disappeared to a table in the corner where she promptly passed on the information to some other women. I could just see them in the corner of my eye, but it was obvious that they weren't happy about it. Astrid and Fredrik exchanged a look but didn't say anything.

At the table next to us, an old woman sat alone, staring blindly into the room in front of her. She must be a hundred if she was a day. Her face was nothing but wrinkles, her hair a cloud of white cotton candy that did a poor job of covering her round skull. She was muttering to herself, a cranky tirade of words that didn't quite carry over to our table. A frazzled middle-aged woman hurried over to her with a cup of coffee in each hand.

"Here you go, Mother," she said, glancing over at our table and nodding at Astrid and me before she placed one of the cups in front of the ancient woman. "Would you like a biscuit as well? Something sweet?"

The old woman turned her head and stared at her daughter with unseeing eyes. "Useless," she said, and now, suddenly, her voice carried all around the room. I could see people's heads turning all the way over to the buffet. "Stupid, useless girl!"

The daughter hurried back to the cake platters, leaving her mother, who returned to her previous muttering state. I clutched the small coffee cup, feeling the warmth against the palms of my hands. This was hell. Stuck in a space filled with strangers, who all kept staring at me. If I survived this, I'd never leave the apartment again.

The frazzled daughter returned and sat down in the chair closest to me, with her back toward our table. The old woman ignored the cookies on the plate that appeared in front of her. Her head swiveled around the room, peering at all the people. "Why are we here?" she asked loudly. "I want to go home."

Her daughter leaned closer, speaking to her mother in a soft voice. "Please, Mother," she said. "We're going soon. We just need to pay our respects. Please keep your voice down."

"Why are we here?" the old woman repeated. "I want to leave."

Her daughter hushed her, pushing the cookies closer. "This is Britta's funeral, Mother. We just need to stay here a while longer. We're leaving soon. Have a cookie."

"Britta is dead?" the old woman said, incredulously and loudly. Everyone was looking at her again. "What happened to her?"

I could see the daughter's back stiffen with embarrassment. "Please, Mother," she pleaded. "Could you please keep your voice down?"

The old woman went from demented confusion to full-on rage in a split second, and the plate of cookies flew across the table in a high arch before crashing onto the floor in the middle of the room. The sturdy plate didn't break, but the cookies fragmented in a million sweet little crumbs that scattered across the room. Someone had a small dog with them, and it scrambled out from under the table and started to lick the floor. The old woman stood up, pulling herself tall. "Stupid, useless girl," she said, her voice dripping with contempt. "Don't you dare tell me what to do! I want to leave, so we're leaving."

She pushed away a chair that was blocking her path to the door, and suddenly I was right in her line of vision. She was a frightening sight, like something out of a nightmarish fairy tale, her eyes almost completely clouded over. She still seemed to see me, though, because her eyes fixed on my face. They wandered downward, taking in my size.

The old woman raised a trembling finger, pointing it straight at my nose. "And you stay out of my yard," she said threateningly. "If I ever see you there again, I'm getting the shotgun."

"Mother!" the daughter exclaimed, grabbing her mother by the arm. "I'm so sorry," she said, more to Astrid than to me. "She doesn't know what she's saying. She gets confused," she said and steered her mother toward the door while rattling off a bunch of apologies directed to no one in particular at our table. "I think it's best that I get her home. Lovely service. My condolences. Your grandmother was a lovely lady."

I was more confused than intimidated by the old woman's outburst. Despite her flab, she was a tiny little thing, and she was obviously too frail to hurt a fly. Astrid placed a hand on my arm and I glanced over at her, arching an eyebrow in a silent question.

The question I'd intended to pose was, "Can we leave soon?" but Astrid replied to a completely different query.

"That is the wife of the man you called the Hunter," she mumbled, squeezing my arm again.

THE HUNTER'S WIFE?

I stared at the entrance where the two women were struggling to navigate the double doors of the air-locked entryway. The Hunter had had a wife.

I think I knew that, on some level.

And then I flashed back to that time at the mall, when Mormor took us to the movies. That weird family. The scary Hunter, his fat little wife.

And their weird daughter.

There were no similarities between the timid girl in an old-fashioned outfit that I'd seen at the mall and the middle-aged woman who was struggling to get her elderly mother out to the car, but I knew it had to be the same person.

The Hunter had had a daughter.

A girl my age, or Astrid's, perhaps.

This woman had been much older than that, surely? She'd been hollow-eyed and gray-skinned.

Old before her time?

I remembered being amazed at her having a mother whose hair had been white, like Mormor's.

And then …

Stay out of my yard, the old woman had said.

"Does she still live there, at the farm?" I asked Astrid, trying to sound indifferent, but in reality I was trembling inside. The twitching curtain. Had she seen me? Surely not. She must be almost entirely blind.

But still …

Astrid nodded, taking another sip of her coffee. "Yes, she's still there. I can't imagine wanting to stay in that house after what happened to her husband. It is her childhood home, but still." She shook her head a little, put her cup down, and straightened the collar on Jonas's shirt. "It's tragic, really. That house used to be so grand, and now it's just … dilapidated. The two of them, rattling around in that big house." She shook her head again and sighed.

"The two of them? The daughter lives there too?" I glanced at the door, but the women were gone. That explained it. The daughter could have seen me and told her mother. My cheeks burned with shame over being caught. I didn't know what I'd been thinking, just walking onto their property. I wasn't a kid anymore. I was supposed to know better.

Astrid nodded. "Yes. By the time she was grown, her mother was getting old, so she stayed to care for her." Another sip of coffee. "They were always a tight-knit family, mostly keeping to themselves, or at least, that's what Mormor used to say. But after the death of her husband, the woman broke off all outside contacts. They've kept to themselves all these years. The district nurse comes by now and then, but the word on the street is that they barely let her in the house." She leaned closer, lowering her voice. "Apparently, the house is literally falling apart."

I didn't know what to think. On the one hand, it seemed to be a tragedy. That poor woman, losing her father at such a young age and then having to care for her elderly mother. It must be awful, being stuck in that old house with a demented and blind old woman who called you stupid and useless.

On the other hand, losing a father like the Hunter might have been less of a trauma than one might think.

I didn't know what had happened in the barn after I'd left Ellen there, but looking back at the events now, with adult eyes, I could imagine. All that stuff about rag dolls and mermaids aside, he had probably … done something to her.

I shivered, even though the room was clammy and stifling.

The Hunter had been a predator, taking advantage of being alone with a little girl.

Something had gone wrong. Perhaps Ellen had screamed or threatened to tell on him. And he'd killed her.

Staring at the door, I thought that losing a father like that at a young age might have been a blessing. Yes, he had been her father. But he had been a monster.

And he had gotten exactly what he deserved.

Again, those images of sparks against the night sky. The feeling of warmth against my face. The deafening roar of the fire.

Where did those memories come from? Was that another movie, one that I didn't remember seeing?

It just felt so real.

I glanced over at Astrid, who was exchanging pleas-

173

antries with a woman who stood behind her, with one hand on her shoulder. My sister was so at ease, even surrounded by all these people. Perhaps she knew them. I didn't recognize anyone, but it had been so long.

The woman left, and Astrid turned toward me.

"I should get going," I said, clutching my coffee cup to hide the fact that my hands were trembling. I felt disgusted by the helplessness, by being completely dependent on my sister to be able to get back home. I didn't want to ask her about the ticket. What if she said no?

Astrid had a smile on her face, the remnants of the polite smile she'd given the woman she'd just spoken to, but now it vanished. "Please don't," she said. "You've only just got here."

I was on my very last dregs of energy. "You wanted me to come for the funeral," I said quietly. "The funeral is over."

She glanced down at her coffee cup. It was empty. She pushed it away. "We still have the paperwork to deal with," she said, not looking at me. "If you still want me to buy you out."

"Of course I do," I said. "I need the money. And it's not as if I'm ever coming back here again."

She looked up at me, and she almost looked sad. "I thought that you might have changed your mind."

I stared at her. "Why would I have changed my mind?"

She looked down. "I thought you might want to stay."

Every part of me wanted to scream. "I have to go," I said, feeling the weight of it all pressing down on me. "I need to go back home."

Astrid looked annoyed. "You don't have a home," she said. "Not for much longer, anyway. Why not stay here? I can help you get an apartment. Somewhere nice."

I pressed my lips together to keep from embarrassing myself even further in front of all these people.

Astrid pulled herself up. "Just for a few days," she continued calmly. "You've only just got here, and you've already been remembering things; you said so. We could talk about it, clear some things out. You'll feel better afterward, I promise."

Somehow I doubted it. Going back to Mormor's cottage was *not* the plan.

Astrid placed one hand on my clammy arm and squeezed gently. "Just another day or two?" she said pleadingly. "I'll sort out all the paperwork, and you can get the money before you leave. If you still want to."

It took all of my self-restraint not to groan out loud. I was never going to want to stay here. That was never going to happen. Another day at the cottage? I thought about the apple on Mormor's bedstand. About that tiny room where all the scary thoughts came out of their hiding places. And then the Hunter. He was gone. There was no monster in the woods anymore.

"Fine," I muttered. "Just one more day. But I'll need to do some shopping before we go back."

Astrid smiled. "Great. What do you need?"

I looked down at my hands, clutching the coffee mug. "Just some snacks," I mumbled.

"Oh, there's no need for that," she said. "There's plenty of food in the kitchen. Help yourself to whatever you like."

I snorted, then looked away toward the window. "Is there a shop around here?" I asked.

"No," Astrid said. "Not anymore. It closed. Everyone does their shopping at the mall."

Feeling myself slipping even further into that helpless, despondent place, I pushed the chair back and stood up. I could feel everyone's eyes on me. "I need some fresh air," I mumbled.

Astrid started to push her own chair back. "I'll come with you."

"No!" I exclaimed. "I need to be alone."

Thankfully, she sat back down. "All right. We'll be here for another twenty minutes or so. Maybe half an hour?"

An eternity, as far as I was concerned. I nodded and made my way outside.

THERE WERE PEOPLE EVERYWHERE, all staring at me as I made my way to the door. Outside, more people were standing around, some of them smoking. Others were just chatting about who knows what.

Everyone turned and stared at me when I appeared. I just nodded at them and kept walking. I had no idea of where I was going; I just had to get away. Being surrounded by people all the time was such a strain, I couldn't take much more.

The church across the road looked depressing, even in the afternoon sun. I turned away from it and followed a path around the corner of the community hall. There were some garbage cans on wheels and a couple of parked bicycles. I kept going. I could still hear the voices of the people by the door. Someone laughed and I felt the hairs on the back of my neck stand up.

They might not be laughing at me; I knew that. But that was always my default assumption.

Turning another corner, I saw a loading dock and a gravel yard, large enough for a truck to back into. I walked over to the concrete ledge and leaned against it. It was too high for me to jump up and sit on, but there was nothing else. No bench or anything. A metal staircase was bolted to the wall on the other side, and I climbed it halfway, sitting down on the top step. The back of the building was in shadow, and the concrete was cold and damp, but I breathed a sigh of relief. Finally, a moment to myself.

Burying my face in my hands, I groaned. How could all of this be happening, and what was I supposed to do now? It didn't feel as if I had any control over anything at all at this moment, and I hated that feeling. Taking a deep breath, I pulled myself up and stared at the stone wall that lined the property. It was old and covered in moss here and there. Probably filled with snakes and other creepy crawlies.

Looking around the loading dock, I saw a stack of soda crates and some boxes with the familiar logo of a bread company by the back door. They were probably empty. I knew that. Otherwise, why would they have left them outside?

But just seeing them made my mouth water, and I struggled up from the steps, moving across the dark concrete. When I saw the caps on the soda bottles, I almost cried. Fishing one of them out of the crate, I stared at the familiar label. Sockerdricka. I hadn't had that since my teens. But I didn't have a bottle opener.

Lifting the lid on the bread boxes, I gasped. The boxes weren't empty, but they didn't contain bread either. Instead, the top box was filled with large round chocolate sponge cakes with disturbingly pink icing. Six of them, packed neatly into the box.

I just stood there, staring at them, feeling the saliva slowly filling my mouth. Then I looked around me. There was no one else here. Pulling one of the cakes out of the box, the plastic wrapping crinkled and I froze, half expecting the back door to open. But no one came. The voices on the other side of the building could be heard in the distance. Someone laughed again, and before I knew it, I had torn the wrapping open and slid the cake out a bit. I broke off a small piece of the cake and slipped it in my mouth.

The sugar rush was immediate and glorious. The cake was factory-made and probably full of additives and preservatives, but I didn't care. It was the most amazing thing I'd ever tasted. The chocolate sponge dissolved on my tongue, and the pink icing tasted of nothing but sugar and additives. I took another piece and another. Before I knew that had happened, I stood there with the empty cardboard tray in my hand and chocolate crumbles all down my front.

Taking a deep breath, I felt some of the tension start to fade. I wasn't fine, not by a long shot, but I could get through this. The worst of it all was behind me. Coming back here, meeting Astrid and her family. That had been so hard, but I'd done it. All the memories. The funeral and all the stares. All of that was done now. The Hunter was dead, and I was still standing.

For the first time in as long as I could remember, I thought that perhaps I was going to be fine.

Or, if not fine, then perhaps better, at least?

Staring down at the five cakes in the box, I shook my head. Who was I kidding? No one, that's who.

Lifting another cake from the box, I brought it and a bottle of soda over to the stairs. Holding the bottle cap against the edge of the metal steps, I hit the bottle hard from above, and the cap came off. There was something I'd forgotten that I knew how to do. I'd never actually done it myself, but I'd seen the boys at school do it and thought that it looked so cool.

Lifting the bottle to my lips, I let the carbonated sugar water rinse all the crumbs from my mouth and slowly started to feel like myself again.

Once the other cake was gone as well, I walked over to the garbage cans and threw away the wrappings. Then I climbed the stairs again and placed the empty soda bottle back in the crate.

My purse fit two of those cakes and two soda bottles, but it was a bit of a squeeze. The purse barely closed, and it would be obvious to anyone that saw me that I was carrying around much more than I'd done at the funeral. I would have taken more if I'd only had room for more, but this would have to do. Lifting the top box of cakes, I saw that the second box contained smaller pastries, snack-sized. I took four and filled my pockets. Then I walked along the gravel road that led back to the road. Crossing it, I found Astrid's car in the church car park and sat on the wall behind it, hiding my purse away out of sight as I waited for my sister and her family.

People were slowly emerging from the community hall, and after a while, I saw Astrid and Fredrik and the kids come out. Another round of handshakes. I could see Astrid looking around—looking for me—and spotting me at last. Even from this distance, I could tell that she was frowning. I should be there, she thought, standing next to her, thanking everyone again for coming.

But there was nothing in the world that could make me cross that road again.

My purse leaned heavily against my leg, and I could taste pink icing on my lips.

I was done pretending to be normal.

20

CAROLINE

MOTHER WAS MUTTERING and raging all the way back to the car. My cheeks burned with shame as I hustled her past all the people standing around outside the church hall, smoking. They greeted us politely, but as soon as we'd walked past them, I could hear their under-their-breath comments.

I knew they talked about us. They always had.

Whenever I went to the shops or to the local health center, I had to endure their stares. It was agony, so I didn't go anywhere unless I really had to. Nowadays, you could order almost anything online, and the postman dropped the packages off on his round, so I didn't even have to go and collect them. We lived too far from the city for grocery deliveries, though, so about once a month, I had to go to the mall for supplies.

It was just as well. The meager sum I received from the government for being my mother's primary care-giver twenty-four seven didn't allow for any spending sprees. There was never enough for any of the maintenance the large house required. Never enough for anything … fun.

As if I knew what that was.

Mother didn't believe in fun. She thought it was frivolous and sinful to do things just for fun. When I was a child, I had longed to go to school and meet other children. Perhaps even make a friend. But my mother wouldn't hear of it. Instead, she claimed to homeschool me whenever the authorities inquired about why I hadn't been in school.

She never did, though.

Father had taught me to read, at least well enough for me to figure the rest of it out for myself. After what happened, Mother had insisted that she needed me at home, and I'd never been allowed to go anywhere except to church.

You would think that coffee at the church hall every Sunday would be compulsory for a woman who was so fiercely religious, but we only ever went there after funerals. Any other service—weddings, christenings, communions, etc.—we always went straight home afterward.

I'd come to look forward to people dying. At least, then I'd get to be around other people.

When I was little, I'd been excited about that.

Now, not so much.

Especially not when Mother behaved the way she'd done today.

"You mustn't do that," I scolded her as I helped her into the passenger seat. "What were you thinking, yelling at poor Britta's granddaughter like that?"

Mother swatted at my hands, struggling with the seatbelt. Fine. No seatbelt. I let it go and closed the door. Maybe I'd do us both a favor and drive into ongoing traffic. That would solve all of our problems.

I leaned against the car for a moment before opening the door and getting in behind the steering wheel. The car wouldn't start at first; it just kept turning over and over. I had to stop trying for a while so that I didn't flood the engine, and I could feel the last of my strength seeping out of me.

In the passenger seat, Mother continued with her tirade, but her muttering was so inarticulate that I couldn't make out most of the words. I only caught snippets here and there, and they made no sense. "Not her granddaughter." And something about kittens being vermin.

I glanced in the rearview mirror. People were still standing around outside the church hall, but there were more of them now. That usually meant that the gathering was breaking up, and soon the car park would be filled with people.

I gritted my teeth and held my breath as I made another attempt to start the car. Please, please, please just work, I pleaded with the rusty old clunker, and for once, something went my way. The engine spurted to life just as Mother burst out into another tirade, raising one hand in an accusing gesture. "All your fault for being so useless," she scolded, and I felt myself go weary. How many times had I heard those words? So many that they didn't really hurt anymore. I knew they were true. Had accepted it.

But as I loosened the handbrake and backed out of the parking space, Mother's voice took on an even shriller pitch. "You useless, good-for-nothing man," she cried out, clenching her bony old hand into a skeletal fist. "Now look what you made me do."

I sighed, checked all the mirrors, and looked both ways before driving out onto the road. I wasn't a confident driver. Why would I be? I wasn't a confident anything.

I accelerated along the road toward home, and the old engine almost completely drowned out the sound of Mother's tirade. A few words made it through, though, and what I heard made me sick.

"Look what you've done," she repeated. "It's *your* fault that the wench is dead."

21

LISA

THE DRIVE back to the cottage was awkward but short. Fredrik drove fast but with ease, one hand resting casually on the steering wheel, humming to himself silently. I didn't recognize the song. He smelled nice.

I could still taste the pink icing, and it felt reassuring, somehow. My stomach wasn't altogether happy about the fact that I'd eaten two whole cakes on an empty stomach, though. It felt like a nest of snakes writhing and moving about in my belly. I swallowed and stared out the window. The sun was still shining. It was a beautiful day, but I couldn't enjoy it.

I thought about Mormor there in the white casket. How she had never known the real reason for me refusing to visit her again. The snakes writhed some more as the guilt enveloped me. It hadn't been her fault. None of it had. But since I hadn't been able to deal with what had happened, I'd been forced to shut her out.

Shut all of them out.

Mormor.

Astrid.

185

Mom and Dad.

Every single person I ever met.

It was so much easier that way.

Just another day or two, I thought. Then Astrid will have sorted out all the paperwork, and I'll be able to go back home with some money in the bank. Just think how much easier everything will be then.

I wasn't sure that half the money for a small cottage would buy as much as a dog house in the city where I lived, but I'd be happy to relocate if it meant that I got my own place. It was not as if I'd be moving away from my friends or a job.

Maybe things would be easier in a completely new place.

Maybe I'd be able to start going out a bit more.

Lose a little weight. Maybe even get a job.

Just thinking about it made the cake snakes in my belly writhe even more. This was nothing new. My emotions always had a physical component to them.

Fredrik parked the car outside of the cottage, and I was out of the passenger seat before the engine was even switched off. A cold sweat had spread over my neck and back, and I almost felt cold in the light summer breeze, even though it was a beautiful summer day. I shivered and moved away from the car, hearing the other doors open behind me.

"Lisa?" Astrid said somewhere behind me, but I kept walking, mumbling something about needing a minute to myself.

Crossing the yard, I spotted a bench under the apple trees and walked over to it. It hadn't been there in Mormor's day, but it wasn't entirely new either. I eyed it warily. Would it hold me? It was uncertain, but my legs didn't feel as though they would carry me much further, so I didn't have a choice.

I gingerly sat down, more or less expecting the bench to give way, but although it creaked ominously, it didn't break. Rubbing my face with both hands, I forced myself to take deep breaths to calm myself and the snakes. It felt as if I was going to be sick, but I managed to keep it in.

When I had finally pulled myself together enough to look up again, I was alone. The kitchen door was open, held back with the frayed piece of string, and I could hear voices from inside. Completely normal, everyday voices. Completely normal people, going about their completely normal everyday lives.

So that's what that sounded like?

I had felt like a freak for as long as I could remember, but being here, this close to normal people, made it so much more obvious how much was wrong with me. I was used to feeling bad about that, but now, for the first time, it also made me feel sad, and I had to blink to keep the tears back.

The little red cottage was so beautiful where it lay, nestled in this clearing surrounded by tall, imposing trees. So peaceful. And the people inside were also beautiful. Well dressed. Slim. Happy. Heck, they even smelled nice.

The realization that I would never have a husband like Fredrik or children like Jonas and Elinor was surprisingly painful, considering that I'd never wanted a family. It was just that I could see the point of it all now, seeing it from the outside this close up. It was *the* point. Reproducing and passing on your genes to the next generation.

But that was only for those who had genes worthy of replicating, of course.

Glancing down at my bulk, I wondered, like I'd done so many times before, what had been the point of me? Why was I even here, after all this time? No one needed me here. I didn't do anything. I wasn't important to anyone.

All I did was upset people and make them sad or worried or uncomfortable. I could see it in their eyes. That's why I didn't like looking people in the eye. That's where I saw the true reflection of myself, and it was not a pretty sight.

Astrid came out onto the kitchen stairs and held up her hand to shade her eyes as she looked over toward me. After a moment's pause, she came over. She had changed out of her funeral garb and had on a sundress. It fluttered in the breeze, and she wrapped her arms around her as she stepped into the shade under the apple trees.

"Are you all right?" she asked.

I didn't know what to say, so I just nodded.

"We're going for a swim before dinner," she continued. "Would you like to come?"

My instinctive reaction was to say no, but there was something in Astrid's eyes that made me hesitate. "You go ahead," I said. "I need to change and stuff. I'll join you in a little while."

She smiled but her eyes still looked worried. "Great. We'll see you in a minute then?"

I nodded again. It would probably be a little more than a minute.

I stayed under the apple trees until the whole family had disappeared out of sight. Then I slowly got up from the bench and made my way back to the cottage. When I saw the car parked around the corner, I realized that I'd left my purse in there, and my heart began to pound again. Hurrying over to the car, I tugged on the handle to the passenger seat, only to have my fears confirmed. The car was locked. Of course. And my cakes were in there.

Holding up my hands around my face to block out the sun, I peered inside, but I couldn't see my bag. My racing heart shifted into an even higher gear. Had I left it at the church? No, surely not!

I turned and hurried inside, looking around the kitchen, but my purse wasn't there either. I must have forgotten it at the church. Completely deflated, I made my way past the kitchen table and out into the hallway. The door to Mormor's room was ajar. I was certain that I had closed it when we left for the funeral. With my heart in my throat, I pushed the door open, and there, on the bed, was my purse.

Someone had brought it in from the car.

I stared at it. Its bulging sides and weight must have made it obvious to whoever carried it that I was lugging around so much more than just some Kleenex and a Chapstick. I wondered who had brought it in. Astrid? Fredrik? What had they thought when they picked it up?

I walked over to the bed and looked down at the bag. Had they opened it? I reached out one hand and unclasped the lock. The purse sprang open. Two flattened, crumbling chocolate cakes were clearly visible.

My cheeks burned with something that may have been shame, and I sank down on the unmade bed, staring at my loot.

It had felt so good, having those cakes to get me through the night. But right now, I felt nothing but bad. Embarrassed. Shameful. Fat.

Right at this moment, I felt fat in a way I'd never felt before. And this was saying something for a woman who had been fat all her life.

I TOOK my time getting ready, but eventually, there was nothing more I could pretend that I had to do. The cakes in my purse kept calling me, but after steeling myself, I transferred them into a bag and hid them under the bed, along with the soda bottles and three of the four pastries. I allowed myself one pastry, along with a large glass of water from the jug in the fridge, and ate it slowly and reverently, licking the wrapper to savor the smallest crumbs. That would have to do, for now. It was going to be another long night here at the cottage, and I couldn't be sure that Astrid would get me a ticket tomorrow. She'd come up with some excuse to make me stay another night. And another.

It would be fine, I told myself. I would get out of here sooner or later. She would have to give me the money for my half of the cottage. Once I had that, I'd go where I liked. Eat what I liked. When I liked.

Staring at the empty wrapper, I felt a sting at the back of my eyes. Had I liked it? I didn't know. How could I even tell anymore? The taste of raspberry filling lingered on my tongue, sticky and sickly sweet. I glanced over at the apple on the bedside table. If I was truly hungry, wouldn't I have eaten the apple? If I'd been starving, wouldn't an apple have been a better choice? There were vitamins and stuff in apples.

I turned the wrapper over and squinted at the content. The text was tiny and almost impossible to read, but I was pretty sure that it didn't say anything about raspberries anywhere. It was all chemicals and additives. What was wrong with me, what was wrong with my brain or my stomach or whatever part of my being that was in charge, that I would crave this garbage and not the apple?

Eventually, I made my way down the path toward the lake. I could hear Jonas and Elinor long before I saw them. Their pealing laughter and splashing. Had we sounded like that, Astrid and me? And Ellen?

Another pang and my chest started to constrict.

No. It was all right. Slowing my steps even further, I took deep, slow breathes. Pushing the images of the rag doll from my mind, I focused on memories from before that day. Ellen, living and breathing. Laughing and playing.

Sneaking off with Astrid to avoid having to play with me.

There. Crisis averted.

I covered the last part of the path with tired steps and stepped out into the sun.

Astrid was sitting on a vast picnic blanket in a garish but surprisingly beautiful pattern, looking out at her family. Fredrik and the children were out in the water, just past the pier, Fredrik standing in water to his waist and Jonas and Elinor swimming and splashing around him. Their laughter came bouncing off the glittering lake toward me, and I felt my eyes sting.

Had I ever laughed like that? So completely carefree and exhilarated?

If I had, I couldn't remember.

I had been a moody, difficult child; I knew that much. But there had been days when I'd played with other kids and enjoyed myself like that. I wished I could remember what that felt like.

Astrid noticed me standing there and glanced over her shoulder.

"Lisa!"

She almost sounded pleased to see me. I made my way over to the blanket. Astrid's and her family's belongings were scattered all over it, and there was no place for me to sit. That was fine by me. I had brought my towel and spread it out in a patch of shade, not too far from where Astrid was sitting. Lowering myself onto it, I forced a smile onto my face and turned toward my sister.

"How are you feeling?" she asked.

"Fine," I answered automatically. "Hot," I added and tugged at my dress to let some air inside the clinging fabric.

She smiled back and nodded. "Yes, it's a lovely day. Did you bring a swimsuit?"

I shook my head. Even if they made those in my size, I wouldn't want to wear one. "I don't really like swimming," I said.

Astrid's eyebrows rose half an inch. "Since when? You used to love swimming."

I frowned. Oh yeah. That's right. I used to. But I wasn't about to answer her question about when that had changed. It would only dredge up a lot of things I didn't want to talk about.

Fredrik came out of the water, walking toward the picnic blanket while tilting his head to get water out of one ear. He nodded toward me before turning toward my sister. "I thought I'd get started on dinner," he said.

I listened to them chatting about what he should make and whether or not they had any leeks left after yesterday's dinner, but my attention was directed toward the children. They were still out there, splashing away, frolicking like dolphins, back and forth right outside the pier. In the corner of my eye, I saw Fredrik bend over, grabbing a towel and his shirt from the blanket before setting off back toward the cottage. Astrid leaned back on her elbows, looking out at her children.

Her swimsuit looked sporty and new, and she had an even tan all over. I guessed they had spent a lot of time here this summer. Or perhaps they had been on holiday. Normal people did that, didn't they? They traveled. Saw the world. Collected experiences.

Looking out at the children, I sighed. I'd never been anywhere.

Pushing the annoying thoughts from my mind, I tried to think of something to say. This silence was too awkward, even for me.

"So … do you like being a lawyer?" I asked.

If Astrid was surprised by my question, it didn't show. The smile that spread across her face told me that she'd picked the exact right profession. She loved her work. I didn't understand half the things she told me about what her job entailed, but it was clear that she felt passionate about her career and accomplishments.

"How about you?" she said. "What do you do for a living? I mean, when you're working."

I shrugged. "I used to wait tables or work in shops,

when I first came to the States. A couple of months here, a few months there."

"Did you like it? Working with customers?" She looked closely at me.

I shook my head. "No. Not really." Still looking at the children, I was surprised to hear myself keep talking. "The plan was to see the world. Work long enough to make money to keep traveling, but the pay was lousy, and living was so expensive … In the end, I just never managed to save up enough to move on."

"Still …" she said. "You've lived in the States for almost twenty years. That's an adventure. I only spent that one year in Paris. Other than that, I've been living in the same part of the country where I was born and grew up." She shook her head, and for a moment, I thought she looked almost disappointed.

I wanted to tell her that my life had never been any kind of adventure. But I didn't know how to explain that I would have seen as much of the States if I'd just stayed on Mom and Dad's couch. Everything I had seen of the US, I'd seen on TV. I'd never gone to the Grand Canyon, or to Los Angeles or to New Orleans, or any of the places I had gone there to see.

I'd never done anything.

For a moment, I allowed myself to consider the possibility that there was still time. I could still do all of those things. I would have some money soon. I would have some options.

But then I thought about all of my maxed-out credit cards, and the faint glimmer of hope that had shimmered in the corner of my eye died out. Who was I kidding? I was never going to get ahead.

So far behind that I'd never even get close to catching up.

I hadn't thought about all those things that I'd wanted to do in so long; it felt weird when they all came crawling out of the shadows of my brain. Why was all of this happening now?

But I thought that I knew.

I had left my sagging couch and gone out into the world. Met people. Stepped away from the television.

And now, my brain was coming back to life. My whole body was. Thinking. Feeling. Wanting. Even dreaming.

It was the worst feeling ever.

WE SAT THERE FOR A WHILE, both silent, looking at the children. Then something hummed in the large tote on the blanket next to Astrid. She pulled out a cell phone and read a text message, squinting against the sun. "Dinner's almost ready," she said, dropping the phone back in the tote before pulling on a sundress over her bathing suit. "Kids!" she called out. "It's time to go."

Elinor made her way to the pier and climbed up the metal ladder with swift movements, hurrying along the wooden boards, leaving wet footprints on the weathered planks. Astrid held out a large towel toward her daughter, and she wrapped herself in it, shivering.

"Jonas!" Astrid said, her voice all Mom-like and stern. "Dinner's ready. Time to go."

"But Mo-om," he whined, but he was already swimming toward the shallows, paddling like a dog until he could crawl out of the water on all four. Collapsing in the sand, he rolled over, covering his face with one arm.

"It's still early," he said. "The sun hasn't gone behind the trees yet. We don't go home for dinner until the sun has gone behind the trees. You said so the other day."

Astrid sighed. "But this day is a bit different," she said, and her voice sounded a bit strained. "Get up now."

Jonas rolled over on his stomach and looked at her. "Because of Gammel-Mormor's funeral?"

Astrid picked up another towel and held it out toward him. "Yes. We had an early lunch, so now we're having dinner a little earlier than usual."

He got up and came over to her, allowing her to drape the towel around his shoulders. "I'm sad that Gammel-Mormor is dead," he said, his voice as solemn and serious as only a five-year-old boy could be.

"Me too," Astrid said.

Jonas wrapped himself in the towel and glanced over at me. "Are you sad that Mormor is dead?" he asked me.

For a moment, I didn't know what to say. "Yes," I said. "I am." But I wasn't sure that I was being entirely truthful. I was sad about a lot of things, but I had lost my grandmother a long time ago, and her being dead didn't feel as acute as it perhaps should have done.

Jonas kept looking at me. "And you're sad about your friend who died," he continued. "When you were little."

I stared at him. "You know about that?" I said, my voice sounding stilted and awkward.

He nodded. "Her name was Ellen. That's why we're not allowed to come here without an adult. Mom told us all about it."

I glanced at Astrid. She leaned forward and rubbed her son's arms through the towel. "Dry off now, or you'll catch your death."

Death. It felt so weird talking about death. About

Ellen. Just mentioning it so casually. I'd never spoken about what happened that day, and I couldn't imagine Astrid telling her children about it. Why would you want to let that into their carefree, happy world? It almost made me angry with her, and I had to remind myself that they were *her* children. She was the mom. Astrid knew best.

As always.

She had packed up all their belongings, folded up the giant blanket, and the kids had started walking back to the cottage, laden with their share of stuff. Astrid turned toward me. "Are you coming?"

I found myself reluctant to get up from the towel, even though it had gotten a bit chilly here in the shade. "In a minute," I said. "You go ahead."

She hefted the large tote onto her shoulder. "Dinner's almost ready."

"Don't wait for me," I said. "I might be a while."

Her eyes darted over toward the thick reeds before she looked at me again. "All right," she said slowly and nodded. "You take all the time you need."

A quick smile, and then she walked away.

22

CAROLINE

THE DISTRICT NURSE was getting Mother ready for bed, and I was standing in the kitchen, holding the refrigerator door open. Staring at the bag-in-box on the wire metal shelf. I didn't want to shake it, in case it was empty. But I also didn't want to pour a glass.

I was gagging for it, don't get me wrong, but that was the problem. I longed for the dull numbness it would bring, the fake calm that would spread through my body as my muscles relaxed.

But I needed a clear head right now. My mind was racing, and I had to think.

Mother's words still echoed in my mind. *It's your fault that the wench is dead*, she'd said. And yes, a lot of what she said these days made no sense, but right at that moment she had sounded so much like herself, so much like the mother that I had grown up with, that I couldn't shake the feeling that it was an echo from the past.

I'd tried different methods to get her to tell me, but none of them had worked. Her rant had taken off on a tangent and then faded out into a low grumble as we made our way back to the farm.

As I helped her into the house and up to her room, I had tried to think of a way to trigger her semi-lost memories, but at the same time, I hadn't wanted her to say something when the nurse was here, so I had let it go.

Still, I couldn't stop thinking about it.

The only dead girl I knew about was that girl who drowned in the lake when I was little. A friend of one of Britta's granddaughters that came to visit one summer. But it couldn't be her that Mother had been so angry about, because that had all been an accident.

It hadn't been anyone's *fault*.

And that's what Mother had said. *It's your fault that the wench is dead.*

Mother had always spoken like someone much older than her, perhaps taking after her own grandmother that she had been very fond of.

It was hard to picture Mother being fond of anyone. All my life, she had been so … disapproving. Of me, of Father. Of the neighbors. Of everyone.

But on the rare occasions when she had spoken of her grandmother, her grim features had softened. She had been almost unrecognizable.

I closed the fridge and walked over to the window. The house felt even more stifling than usual, and my whole body ached from fatigue, so I was surprised to see that the sun was still up. How was I ever going to make it until bedtime?

There would be another half hour or so before the nurse left, and I decided to grab some fresh air in the hopes that it would clear some of the confusion from my mind. Making my way through the gloomy house to the front door, I let myself out and walked around the corner, into the yard. It was still hot outside, as long as you stayed in the sun, but the tall trees cast long shadows over most of the open space. I took in the overgrown flowerbeds and the yellowing grass that no one had mowed in years. This place was a mess.

I stood there, looking around me, trying not to think about all the decisions that I would have to make. Soon. Whenever Mother passed away, all of this would be mine, but I couldn't imagine how I would be able to manage here on my own. The house was falling down around us, and it would be stupid to just sit here and wait for that to happen. I would have to do something. Get a job. Find a place to live.

Get a life.

Despite the sun, I shivered. Then I turned slowly and glanced over in the direction that my eyes always avoided. The concrete rectangle where the barn had been.

Where Father had died.

Just thinking about it made me groan out loud. That fire had changed everything, and I couldn't imagine what my life would have been like if that hadn't happened. If he had lived.

Maybe I would have gone to school like a normal kid. Maybe I would have made friends. Learned a trade. Got a job. Moved away.

Far, far away.

I slowly made my way over to the gray, cracked slab.

I could still do all those things, some small part of my brain suggested, but I knew it was too late. I was almost forty. Way too late for a lot of things.

Suddenly, I heard an unfamiliar sound. The pealing sound of children laughing. That was something you didn't hear every day around here. I turned my head back and forth until I could pinpoint where it was coming from. Down by the lake. It must be Britta's family.

Tugging my cardigan closer around me, I stared at the path that led down to the lake, picturing my neighbor's granddaughters. They couldn't have been more different from one another if they'd tried. One of them so perfectly put together, with her perfect, happy little family. And the other …

I cringed just thinking about her bulk. How did she even get around? I'd never had much of an appetite and couldn't imagine ever wanting to eat enough to put on all that weight.

There it was again. The laughter. For some reason, it made me move toward the path and then into the darkness between the trees.

I couldn't remember the last time I walked through these woods. It must have been as a small child, with Father, but Mother didn't like it when we went off alone, so it only happened once or twice. And one of those times had been to get a Christmas tree. I remembered following our tracks back to the house, Father dragging the tree behind him on the snow. I remembered feeling reassured by that, having those dark hollows to lead me back home, and then looking back, seeing that the branches had wiped out our trail, and my footsteps were gone.

I couldn't hear the children anymore but kept walking. There was a pier down here, I knew that, but I never came here. Mother was adamant that I'd never go near the lake. It wasn't safe, she said. You never knew what might happen.

Well, that wasn't true, was it. I knew exactly what might happen since it had actually happened, right on this spot. That poor girl drowning. I had heard them talking about it, late that night, when they thought I was asleep. Father had been part of the search party that had found her among the reeds. He had been upset, but in that understated way of his, his voice all tense and muttering. I'd never once heard him raise his voice. Mother had been so angry with him, and I hadn't been able to understand why. "Pull yourself together," she'd said, and her voice had been brimming with disgust. "Accidents happen. Britta shouldn't have let those children run around unsupervised."

Father had started to say something, but Mother had silenced him. "We will speak no more about it."

And we never had.

Of course, that girl dying, even though it had been a tragedy, had more or less been forgotten only a few hours later.

I came to the edge of the forest and stopped, still hidden in the shadows.

The children had gone. But there was someone there. Britta's granddaughter. The fat one. The one who had been gone for so long. In America, someone at the church had said. I had never been anywhere.

She was sitting on a blanket, staring out over the lake. The water was calm, but the sound of small waves hitting the poles under the pier carried over to me where I stood, feeling awkward. The woman slowly started to get up, and I took one step back to keep out of sight, but she didn't look in my direction. Her attention was directed at the water, and she slowly walked out onto the pier.

I should leave, I knew that. The nurse would be done soon. Mother was waiting. But my feet seemed glued to the spot, and I couldn't tear my eyes away from the giant woman as she moved out to the end of the pier. There, she paused for a while before grabbing the garish fabric of her dress and slowly lifting it over her head. I stared at the rolls of fat that were revealed as she pulled off the dress and had to swallow to keep from retching. Her thighs, belly, back, arms … Every part of her was covered in thick rolls of fat tissue. I had never seen anything like it. Mother had put on some weight as she got older, but her soft padding was nothing like what I was looking at now. I stared as the woman grabbed the handrails to the ladder and slowly lowered herself into the water. Out of sight.

Everything went quiet. Not a sound. I held my breath but eventually had to let it out slowly. I couldn't see where the fat woman had gone, couldn't hear her.

Had she drowned herself? Surely, that would be a lot more dramatic than what had just happened.

I should go. I wanted to go.

But I couldn't leave.

Getting a grip, I made my way over to the pier and walked slowly out to the end of it. I didn't know what I was more afraid of: that the woman would be floating dead in the water in front of me, or that she'd be swimming happily, perhaps annoyed at my intrusion.

She wasn't dead. But she was floating in the dark water, completely still, her hair spread out like a halo around her head, her arms stretched out and her legs spread wide. Like a starfish, if starfish could have been morbidly obese. They weren't, of course. Animals didn't get obese. Only humans seemed to lack the ability to regulate their caloric intake to the extent that would produce something like this.

I should leave. This was an invasion of her privacy; I knew that. I completely lacked interpersonal skills, and even I could see that this was wrong. Me standing here, staring at her grotesque body while she wasn't even aware of my presence.

But my feet wouldn't move. Mother's words kept echoing through my mind. *The wench is dead.* I might never be able to extract the meaning of those words from her addled mind, but perhaps there was another way. This woman had been here that summer, all those years ago. She must know what had happened to her friend.

Suddenly, she noticed me. Water splashed everywhere as she flailed and spun around in the water. I must have frightened her. She was treading water now, staring up at me, water dripping from the tip of her nose. She lifted one hand and wiped her face without closing her eyes.

For an extended moment, we just stared at each other, and I couldn't tell which of us was the more frightened. I knew my heart was pounding in my chest, and hers probably was too. Her massive breasts floated to the surface in front of her, and she pushed them down with one arm, shielding herself from my stare. My cheeks exploded with heat from the embarrassment. I finally looked away, raising one hand in apology.

"I'm sorry," I said, staring at the trees closest to the water. "I didn't mean to intrude. It's just ... I heard voices. And then …" Glancing down at my feet, I spotted her tent-like dress. "I saw this and I just wanted to make sure that you were okay." I pushed a fake smile onto my lips and glanced over at her. "Sorry."

The woman was staring at me. Then she ran her hand over her face again. "Fine," she said.

"I'll go," I said. "Give you some privacy."

I turned and walked slowly back the way I'd come. Behind me, I heard her climbing the ladder back onto the pier. I could picture the water trickling down the fatty rolls and had to force myself not to look back. She followed me back to her towel, and just as I was about to enter the woods again, I heard her voice behind me.

"You were at the funeral," she said.

I stopped, not turning around, even though I really wanted to. "Yes."

"Did you know my grandmother?"

I shook my head. "No. But my mother did."

It was quiet for a while. "Your mother," she said eventually.

I waited, but she didn't say anything more. I glanced over my shoulder. She had put her dress back on and was drying her hair with the towel. The synthetic fabric of the dress clung to her wet body.

"Yes," I said. "Vera." Gesturing toward the farm, I continued, "I'm Caroline. We live on the farm back there. My mother and I."

She nodded slowly but didn't introduce herself. Her scrutinizing gaze made me feel better about staring at her. I couldn't imagine what there was about me that was as fascinating as her un-human form but wasn't going to say anything about it. I was the intruder here. I was at fault.

As always.

Stupid, useless girl, Mother's voice echoed at the back of my mind.

"It was a lovely service," I said. "I'm so sorry for your loss."

She nodded again. "Thank you."

We stood there for a while, just looking at each other. We couldn't have been more different. She was so short and fat, me so tall and skinny. Her so dark, me so light-haired. But still … There was something in her eyes that looked … familiar.

Even just the fact that I managed to look her in the eyes was weird. I never did that. Had always avoided eye contact. But there was something about this woman that made it hard to look away. And it wasn't just about the fat. There was something in her eyes that seemed to mirror my own feelings of loss and grief.

Well, duh. She had just lost her grandmother. Of course, she was grieving.

But no. There was something more than that.

My eyes darted over to the thick reeds to the left of the pier. When I looked back, she had followed my gaze and was staring in the same direction. Slowly, she turned back toward me.

"This place must bring back many memories," I said, my voice sounding hollow and fake, at least to my own ears.

She looked me straight in the eyes before responding. "Oh, yes," she said. "You have no idea."

23

LISA

I DON'T KNOW what possessed me to get in the water. The sun was beginning to set, and the warmth had started to leave the air surrounding me, but I couldn't bring myself to go back to the cottage. Instead, I walked out onto the pier, stripped off, and lowered myself into the dark water.

I hadn't swum in a lake since that day with Ellen. Not in any lake, but definitely not in this one.

I more or less expected myself to panic, but instead, the chill of the water made me feel calm in a way I couldn't remember having felt before. The dark, murky water carried me, made me feel weightless and buoyant, and I lay back and looked up at the sky that was shifting from light blue to deep orange in an elegant ombre effect.

Swimming used to be my favorite thing to do, always nagging Mom and Dad to take me to the pool. I had been a good swimmer. A natural, one of my swimming instructors had told my mom. Now, I could barely remember what it had felt like to be good at something, but perhaps that swimming instructor had been right because slipping into the lake had felt like coming home.

As if I knew what that felt like.

A movement made me look over toward the pier, and my heart jumped into my throat. There was someone there, watching me, and suddenly, all the water's natural buoyancy disappeared. I splashed and struggled and finally managed to right myself in the water, shielding my naked breasts with one arm.

She looked so much like her father, standing there, I wanted to scream. The same steel-gray hair, even though she couldn't be more than a couple of years older than me. The same narrow face and sharp nose. The same weird stare.

But I was no little girl anymore. And she was not her father.

Slowly, I got my racing heart to settle down, enough to hear her apologize. As she turned to leave, I contemplated staying in the water, but the moment was lost, and I felt the chill in the water that I hadn't felt before. I made my way back onto dry land as the strange woman walked toward the path over on the right. I quickly dried off enough to be able to pull my dress back on, and then, just as she was about to disappear out of sight, I heard myself speak.

"You were at the funeral."

For some reason, I didn't want her to leave. There was something about her. Maybe she had some of the missing pieces of the puzzle I was trying to piece together.

She turned back and we spoke. For the first time in forever, I found myself feeling drawn to another person rather than repelled. There was something about her that felt strangely familiar, even though we'd never met before.

Strange really, considering all the time Astrid and I had spent here as kids. This girl had been living right next door all that time, and we'd never once played with her.

As we spoke, her eyes wandered over toward the reeds, and I looked over there as well, trying not to picture Ellen there. Her thin rag doll arms outstretched in the murky water.

When I looked back, she looked me straight in the eyes. For once, I didn't look away. It was like looking in a mirror, even though we couldn't have been more different.

"This place must bring back many memories," she said, and my mind was filled with images of her father. The Hunter. The way he had looked at Ellen. His gritty voice up in the hayloft. The way he moved along the path with Ellen slung over his shoulder, as if she had been a bag of potatoes or something.

Not a person. Not a little girl, like his own daughter.

"Oh, yes. You have no idea," I said, but then I wondered. Perhaps she did. What her father had done, it told me as an adult something about what kind of man he'd been. His death might have been the best thing that ever happened to her. The idea of growing up in the same house as a man who would do something like that made my skin crawl.

"She was your friend," she said, once again glancing over toward the reeds.

I nodded slowly. "My sister's friend, really."

She looked surprised. "Oh, so it was your sister who

was with her, when …" She stopped abruptly. "I'm sorry. That was …" She looked down at her hands, then back over her shoulder. "I should go."

"No," I said, more calmly than I'd ever thought I'd be able to talk about it. "It was me."

Her eyes darted back to my face. "It was you," she said, her voice breathy and vague. A small frown appeared between her stern eyebrows. So like her father. "That must have been … so awful."

I nodded slowly. "It was."

So many memories, all of them bad. The squirming kittens. The rag doll. The policeman. The taste of vomit.

And then the fire. The roaring, deafening fire.

It was all tangled up in the suppressed memories of Ellen, I could tell, but whether or not it was real, I couldn't figure out.

"Losing someone like that …" she said. "You can't have been more than … what?"

"Five," I answered automatically. Would there ever be a time when I didn't know exactly how old I was when everything in my life turned bad? Would there ever be a time when I could think about any of that without feeling like I was going to die?

"Five," she repeated. "That's rough."

I bit my lip, but in the end, I couldn't not say anything. "I only heard about your father today," I said. "I don't think anyone told me, at the time."

She looked slightly surprised but then nodded. "No, I can understand that. After what you had just been through."

There was something in her eyes that I suddenly recognized as curiosity. She was curious. She wanted to know what had happened to Ellen. The morbid cow!

Well, I wanted to know what had happened to her father. But that was different. Or so I wanted to believe.

She glanced over her shoulder again. "I have to go. The district nurse is with my mother, but she'll be done by now."

I nodded. "Well … It was nice talking to you," I mumbled and realized with a jolt that I had actually meant it. Almost. Perhaps nice wasn't the right word. But I had been able to do it.

She looked surprised again, openly this time. "You too," she said, and it almost sounded sincere. Was that possible? "Are you back for good, or …?"

I shook my head. "Just for a few days."

She took a couple of steps down the path to the farm. "Well … maybe I'll see you again, then," she said, "before you leave." She was glancing over her shoulder, suddenly looking awkward and embarrassed.

I felt the same way, but there was also something else. A curious excitement somewhere deep in my chest over having found someone that I could stand being near. The idea of speaking to her again should have repulsed me, but it didn't.

"I would like that," I said, and if my voice broke slightly, she didn't seem to notice or mind. "I'm Lisa, by the way."

Still looking more awkward than anything, she smiled a little. "Well, Lisa, I can't leave Mother for long. But you're welcome to stop by the farm for a cup of coffee or … whatever."

An invitation into a stranger's home. When was the last time I'd had that? Never, probably. Caroline couldn't have any idea how momentous that statement was. She probably had guests over all the time. This must be normal for her. This was what normal people did.

But me? Could I fake being normal for long enough to find out what had happened to the Hunter?

"Tomorrow?" I heard myself say. It was preposterous, me coming over for coffee, but I needed to find out what she knew. I needed Caroline's pieces to complete the puzzle.

"Come by anytime," she said. "I'm there all day." She pointed at the path behind her. "It's just up here."

I nodded. "I'll find my way," I said. But I already knew the way, of course.

After all, I had been there before.

24

ASTRID

I WAS STARTING to worry about Lisa when she suddenly stood in the doorway. Her hair was wet and tangled, and her cheeks were flushed.

"Did you go for a swim?" I asked.

She didn't reply. Just nodded.

"Great. Are you hungry? We've eaten already, but there's plenty of leftovers."

She glanced at the kids who sat at the table, Elinor reading a book and Jonas drawing with chunky colored pencils. "I need a shower," she said. "Maybe later."

She made her way past me and into Mormor's room. A while later, she came back out and went into the bathroom. I heard the shower being turned on.

Fredrik came down the stairs, dressed for a run. He ruffled Jonas' hair and gave me a quick peck on the way to the kitchen door. "I'll be back in half an hour," he said. "In time to read to you," he added, looking over at the kids.

Elinor grunted, but Jonas looked up with an eager

grin. "See ya!" he said and waved a little before returning to his drawing.

Fredrik jogged down the steps and disappeared out into the twilight. I walked over to the door, just in time to see him running up toward the road. I didn't like him running out here; there were no sidewalks, but his clothes had reflective bits here and there, and he was wearing a headlamp.

Turning back, I felt a restless itch. Normally, I would have run with him, but I didn't want to leave the kids. Or, I didn't want to leave Lisa. Or, I didn't want to leave the kids with Lisa.

I wasn't sure what it was, but I felt that I needed to be here. Lisa was going through a bunch of stuff; I realized that. It was obvious that this place brought back a lot of memories, and she was having trouble processing them.

The fact that she had gone in the lake had to be a good sign, though. If she could swim in the lake where Ellen had drowned … Talk about confronting your fears. I was proud of her. I was. It was just … I don't know.

I made myself some coffee and sat at the table, looking at my children. They weren't exactly close but compared to Lisa and me, they were practically Siamese twins. Looking at Jonas, I felt a stab in my chest. He was still so little, my baby, and I wanted to keep him this safe, this innocent forever.

But he was the same age now as Lisa had been that day when Ellen drowned. I couldn't imagine what a trauma like that would do to my baby boy.

All this time, I had been resenting Lisa for what happened. Blamed her, even. I didn't know what had happened, but surely, there must have been something she could have done. If nothing else, she could have run for help. She could have told us, as soon as she came back, what had happened. Perhaps it had already been too late. I don't know and would never know for sure.

But the idea of Ellen lying there among the reeds, all day and into the night … I shivered and got up to close the door. It was almost entirely dark outside by now, and I looked toward the road. No sign of Fredrik.

I pulled the door shut just as the bathroom door opened.

"Time for bed, you two," I said, hoping that the kids didn't pick up on the tension in my voice. I really had to struggle to sound normal, but I didn't want them to know how difficult this was for me. Did they see through my act? "Go and brush your teeth and get ready. Dad will be back soon. He'll read to you."

Jonas slipped off his chair and disappeared out into the hallway. Elinor looked up from her book. "It's not our bedtime yet," she observed, looking at the microwave display where red digits told her the time.

I walked over to the table, gathering up Jonas' colored pencils and putting them back in the box. "Could you take these with you upstairs when you go?" I asked, pretending that I hadn't picked up on her subtle objection.

She sighed but got up and took everything with her up the narrow stairs. I sat back down at the table. Took another sip of the coffee that had gone lukewarm by now. And waited.

Lisa appeared in the doorway. Her hair was wet, still, but combed out now, and she was wearing a T-shirt and sweatpants. I forced a smile onto my lips, but it was a struggle not to stare at the bulges and rolls of fat that pushed at the fabric. How could she have let herself go like that?

"Should I warm up your dinner?" I asked.

"I'll do it," she mumbled and walked over to the fridge. She removed the clingfilm from the plate and put it in the microwave.

I sat there, clutching the coffee mug.

"So, was it a nice swim?" I regretted the words as soon as I had uttered them. Oh, why did I have to keep poking her?

But Lisa just nodded, still staring at her plate, spinning inside the microwave. "Yeah …" she said. Then she was silent until the plate stopped spinning with a loud ping.

She got a glass of water and sat down across from me. Grabbing a fork, she took a bite. Then another. "This is good," she said. "What is that spice?"

I shook my head. "I'm not sure. Fredrik made it."

She nodded and took another bite. "Well, whatever it is, it's good." She glanced up at me. "I met your neighbor."

I frowned. "My neighbor?" I glanced at the window. "Do you mean Vera?" Remembering the old woman's outburst at the community hall, I gripped my mug harder. But Lisa shook her head.

"No, her daughter. Caroline."

I looked at my sister. She seemed focused on her dinner, but there was something else. Her cheeks were still flushed, even though she'd been out of the hot shower for at least ten minutes. "She was down by the lake?" I asked.

Lisa nodded. "She invited me over to the farm," she said. "Tomorrow."

"She did?" Releasing the ceramic mug, I pushed it away. "And ... you're going?"

Caroline or her mother had never invited me over, and we'd been neighbors for decades. I don't think Mormor ever went over there either. There was something weird about that family; I'd always thought so. Why would Lisa bond with them all of a sudden? They'd kept to themselves for decades. And my sister seemed to want nothing to do with anyone.

Or perhaps it was just me she didn't want in her life.

That thought stung; I won't deny it.

To my utter surprise, Lisa nodded. "I thought that I might."

My brain was struggling to connect the dots. It was an unfamiliar feeling, and I did not like it, not one bit. I'd had to drag Lisa back here, almost literally, bribed her even, to come to her own grandmother's funeral. She'd been ready to bolt as soon as we left the church. And now she was going for swims in the lake where her childhood trauma took place, and going next door for coffee as if nothing had ever happened to make her into the obviously dysfunctional monster that was sitting across from me?

No. This wasn't making any sense at all.

She had cleared her plate and was throwing glances toward the fridge.

"Do you want something more to eat?" I asked, and I couldn't entirely conceal the incredulity in my voice. She'd already had a large portion.

She shook her head and looked down at her empty plate.

"I thought we would spend the day together tomorrow," I said. "Just hanging out."

She pushed the plate away from her and leaned back against the chair. "How long do you think it will take? The paperwork?"

I shrugged. "A while," I said slowly. It hurt me that she couldn't wait to get away. We hadn't seen each other in decades. She was my sister. Why didn't she want to spend time with me? Why didn't she want to talk to me? Get to know my family. My children.

Except I didn't feel comfortable leaving her alone with them.

Another stab of uncomfortable truth hit me straight in the chest.

She stood up, gathering her plate and cutlery. "I need to get back," she said.

"Why?" I asked. "Why do you need to go back there? You don't have a job, no place to live? Is there someone special waiting for you there? Do you have a boyfriend? A girlfriend? Any friend at all." As soon as the words slipped out, I wished I could take them back. That had been cruel of me.

She put the dishes in the sink and then just stood there, with her back toward me. "No," she mumbled. "No, I don't."

"I'm sorry," I said. "Forgive me, Lisa. That was mean of me."

Still, she didn't turn around.

"I just don't understand …" I said. "Why you would rather be over there, all alone, instead of being here. With me." Those last two words sounded pitiful.

She turned around, finally, but didn't look at me. She crossed her arms across her chest, but it didn't look determined or even reserved. It just looked as if she was struggling to keep herself calm and together.

"I thought you were doing better," I continued when she didn't speak. "I thought you had begun sorting things out." Still, no reaction. "You went in the lake."

Her eyes flew to my face. "Yes," she said. "I went in the lake."

I leaned forward. "But surely that's a good thing," I said. "You're doing the work. You're processing."

Her face twisted in a grimace. "I'm what?"

I sat up. "You're remembering. And I'm hoping that you, as an adult, can see that what happened was just an accident. You were just a small child. There was nothing you could have done." I bit my lip. "I hope."

Her eyes were glued to my face. "What's that supposed to mean?" she asked. Her voice sounded frail. I was hurting her; I knew that on some level. But on some other level, I just couldn't stop myself. She had been hurting me all these years. Just leaving me, as if I was nothing. As if I meant nothing.

Perhaps I did.

I waved my hand in a gesture that I hoped would mitigate the sting in my comment. "I don't know what happened," I said. "No one does. You probably don't remember yourself, now, after all these years. If you had said something at the time ..."

She was silent for a long time. "It wouldn't have made any difference," she said quietly through gritted teeth.

"You don't know that for sure," I said. "Perhaps there was something we could have done. Perhaps she could have been saved. You should at least have tried. Not just run away."

A single tear ran down her round cheek. She wasn't flushed any longer. Instead, she had gone ghostly pale. "I tried," she said, and the words were so frail that they barely carried across to me. "I went back for her. It was too late." Another tear. She pushed away from the kitchen sink and walked toward the door.

"Don't walk away," I said. "We're talking."

She shook her head and kept moving.

"I need you to stay here and talk to me," I said. "It's the only way you'll be able to sort this out. It's the only way you'll be able to move on."

She paused on the threshold but still didn't turn around. "You don't understand," she said. "This … what you're doing … it's not helping. This is why I need to leave."

"What if I need you to stay?" I called out after her as she slipped into the darkness in the hallway. "What if I need you to tell me what happened? Could you do that? For me?"

But she kept walking.

"No, when did you ever do anything for anyone other than yourself," I muttered.

It was cruel, I know. Unfair, even. She'd been through so much. I couldn't imagine what it must have been like. And I could see what it had done to her.

But she probably hadn't even heard me. The door to Mormor's room closed with a soft click.

LISA

I ALMOST TURNED BACK TWICE on the short path to the farm. It felt so weird, doing something this normal. The fact that Astrid was angry with me had made the morning uncomfortable in the cottage, and I had mostly kept to my room. It had taken me forever to get ready, as well. I didn't have anything to wear that I felt comfortable in, not when I had to go outside and meet people. But moving through the quiet woods, I felt a strange twinge of excitement. There might be some answers to be found at the end of this path. I might be able to finally put an end to some of these questions, all this confusion.

I might finally know, once and for all, what actually happened back then.

Besides, I was as curious about Caroline as she seemed to be about me, and as much as the idea of telling anyone about Ellen repulsed me, I hungered for more information about the Hunter. About what had happened to him.

Coming out of the woods, I avoided looking at the

cracked concrete slab as I made my way over to the house. Just like the last time I'd been here, it didn't look inhabited. Most of the windows were dark and empty or had the curtains drawn, even though it was the middle of the day. When I came closer, I could see that some of the curtains had dark stains on them. Was that mold?

I had to walk around the corner to find the entrance. There was a smallish porch on the side of the house that faced the road. It had intricate wood decorations all around the roof, but pieces of them had fallen off, and the wooden steps leading up to the porch had collapsed and been replaced by some unvarnished boards some time ago. They were brown from dirt in the middle and would probably give way soon as well.

I placed my feet close to the edge, unsure if the weathered boards would hold my weight, but they did and I managed to make my way to the front door. There was no bell, no door knock, so I made use of my knuckles.

I waited, but nothing happened. I knocked again. The large house was silent. A car was parked next to the porch, so they should be here. Perhaps Caroline had changed her mind.

I had already turned to walk away when I heard steps from inside, rushing steps coming down a staircase. A key turned in the lock and the door opened. Caroline. She looked flushed, but she smiled at me.

"Lisa," she said, almost out of breath. "You came."

I knew she couldn't be that pleased to see me, but it still gave me a thrill. The idea of being so anticipated was alien, but at the same time very appealing on a primal level.

I didn't know what to say. "Hi." I waved a little. "Is this a bad time?"

She shook her head. "No, no. Not at all." She stepped back and to the side, gesturing at me to come in. "This is perfect. I just put Mother to bed for her nap."

Stepping inside the hallway, I was greeted by darkness and the musty smell of decay. There was an elaborate ceiling lamp, but it wasn't on, even though the small windows didn't let in much daylight.

Caroline pointed toward my left. "Through here. Please. Can I get you anything? Coffee? Tea?"

I shook my head but then thought that it might be impolite of me. "Anything is fine. Whatever you're having."

Moving in the direction Caroline had indicated, I found myself in a sort of sitting room, but it looked more like a cramped attic space, with boxes and extra pieces of furniture on almost every surface. Everything looked dull and muted, covered by a thick layer of dust.

"Through there," Caroline said behind me, and I spotted a door to my right, almost hidden behind a deep bookshelf packed with books.

My nose itched from the dust but seeing all the boxes and things made something click inside of me. Perhaps this was what I had recognized when I looked in Caroline's eyes yesterday. A fellow packrat. Glancing around the room once more, I thought that this must be what my house would have looked like, if I'd had one. Stuff everywhere. Signs of neglect. Of overwhelm.

Through the second door was a kitchen, a large farm kitchen with old-fashioned cupboards and a scarred table in the middle of the linoleum floor. It had probably been a quite nice kitchen once, but now it was worn and scuffed and grimy. It wasn't as cluttered as the sitting room, but there was a lot of random stuff in here as well, and quite a lot of dust in the air, even though the kitchen counter had been wiped down.

Caroline didn't seem bothered by the mess. I could understand that. Living like this, it became normal after a while. You didn't see the detritus. Even if it literally blocked your path, you'd just step over it, rather than deal with it. The story of my life. I had never met anyone else who was like this. It was fascinating but also disturbing. Like unexpectedly catching your reflection on a shiny surface.

Caroline switched on an old coffee maker. The plastic top looked more yellow than the original white, and we sat at the kitchen table. The chairs were sturdy and oversized, much more suited to someone like me than skinny Caroline.

"It was so nice of you to come," she said, fingering a potholder that sat at the middle of the table along with a saltshaker and a roll of paper towels. "We don't get many visitors."

I didn't know what to say. Here I was, pretending to be a normal person doing something normal like visiting a new acquaintance, only to discover that the person I was visiting also was a bit of a freak. Not as bad as me, but there were definite similarities.

Something brushed up against my leg and I jumped. Looking down, I saw a large black-and-white cat with matted fur. Its belly was grotesquely distended on both sides. "Oh," I said. "You have a cat."

Caroline leaned back and looked under the table. "Yes. A couple of them." She sat up again, shrugging.

"You must have cats, living out here. They keep the mice out of the house."

I nodded, but my heart was pounding. This cat was the spitting image of the cat I'd seen out in the barn all those years ago. And judging by that belly, there would soon be a new litter. Mama Cat would have to find some other place to build her nest, though. Through the window behind Caroline, I could see the tall trees behind the space that had once been occupied by the large barn. I shivered as images of the squirming kittens in the hay flashed before my eyes. And then, the hollow between the bales had been empty. There were kittens in the barn. There were no kittens in the barn. Was I making all of this up? Had I dreamed it? Had I dreamed all of it?

Well, no. Because Ellen had died, for real.

And the Hunter had too.

Focus, Lisa! You came here for a reason!

I folded my hands on the table and forced myself to look at Caroline. "So … You live here with your mother?" I said, trying to sound casual. Just making conversation. "Did you move out and then come back, or have you always lived here?"

She didn't reply. Instead, she stood up, rather abruptly, and walked over to the coffee maker. She opened the cupboard above and retrieved a couple of largish mugs, filling them both. "Do you take milk or sugar?" she asked, her back toward me.

"Black is fine," I said.

She turned around, one mug in each hand. Placing them on the table, she sat down and then immediately wrapped her hands around the mug, as if to keep warm, even though the kitchen was rather stifling. "I've always lived here," she said with a slight grimace.

"That's nice," I said. "It's a great house."

There was an awkward silence. Then Caroline sighed. "I suppose," she said. She looked around the kitchen and her shoulders sank, as if in resignation. "Great as in big, for sure. It's a lot of work." She leaned back, staring at her coffee mug. "I haven't managed to keep up with the maintenance."

"Well, you have your mother to care for," I said.

She nodded. "That's true."

For a moment, she seemed to get lost in her thoughts. I tried to think of a way to ask about the Hunter, without asking about him.

"It must have been tough for your mother as well," I said, "alone in this big house with a child."

Caroline's eyes flew to my face. "You know ..." she said. "Sometimes that's exactly what *I* feel like, now that Mother is ..." She bit her lip. "I helped out a lot when I was little. And Mother can't really do much of anything. I'm sure she struggled, but at least she had me. I ..." She didn't finish the sentence, but then, she didn't have to.

Was it possible that she, too, was all alone? I had always thought of other people being connected in a myriad of ways. That I was the only one left out of that web. Perhaps I wasn't.

I nodded and forced myself to focus on the conversation, steering it in the direction I wanted it to go. "It must have been different ... before."

Caroline let out a heavy breath. "Oh, goodness, yes. Father was really good at fixing things, and he always kept the house looking nice." She blinked a few times quickly. "He'd be appalled if he saw the state of the house now. I've really let him down."

I leaned forward, eager to keep her talking about him. "Of course, you haven't," I said. "I'm sure you've done the very best you could."

She shook her head slowly. "It's never enough, though, is it?" she said, her voice thin. "I can't seem to get a handle on things."

I didn't know what to say. I knew exactly how that felt. But I had never met anyone like me before; I didn't know how to deal with that as an outsider. Heck, I didn't know how to deal with that within myself.

"You're doing just fine," I said, hoping that it sounded somewhat authentic. "Of course, you're overwhelmed, caring for your mother and looking after this big house all by yourself." I sipped the coffee, but it was still too hot. "When was the last time you had a break? Went on a holiday?"

She looked confused, as if the concept was new to her. "I've never been anywhere," she said. "And as for breaks … This is it. When Mother takes her midday nap. Or when I've put her to bed in the evenings."

"What do you do then?" I asked, searching her face.

Her face went tense, and she looked away, but not before I'd seen the shame in her eyes. There was something she didn't want me to know. Then she shrugged. "I don't know. Nothing."

I nodded. "Tell me about your father," I heard myself say. Keep her talking. "What was he like?"

A tiny smile lit up her stern face. "He was great," she said. "Sure, he could be strict, and he wasn't around a lot of the time because he was always working, always busy. But he was a kind man, and he was very good with the animals. I miss him so much."

She seemed sincere, but I found it difficult to believe that she was talking about the same man who had haunted my nightmares for decades. A kind man? I shivered, remembering the stern features and that intense look in his eyes. Kind? No! He'd been a monster.

A monster who had deserved to die.

26

CAROLINE

I COULDN'T BELIEVE she'd come. That she'd wanted to come. It felt so weird sitting here in our kitchen, drinking coffee with a visitor. A proper visitor. Apart from the district nurse, no one had come to the house for years, and she only hurried through her tasks before rushing off to the next name on her list. We hadn't spoken more than a few phrases to each other over the years, usually the same ones. *How's she doing today? See you tomorrow, then.* Sitting here, engaged in a conversation, I became painfully aware of the fact that I wasn't any good at this. I had to search for the right words, think through every statement to make sure that I didn't overshare or say something inappropriate.

But Lisa didn't seem to mind my awkwardness. She looked calm and collected and she did a great job at hiding her disgust over the chaos that was my home. I liked her even more for that.

Perhaps, if I didn't mess this up, this was someone who might become ... a friend?

Careful, careful, Caroline, I admonished myself.

Don't get your hopes up. You don't want to seem too eager. No one likes a clingy, desperate woman.

Especially not a stupid, useless one like me.

"So," I said, leaning forward slightly. "Are you back for good, then?"

She shook her head, and I felt my heart sinking like a lead balloon.

"No, just for a few days," she said. "There's some paperwork that needs to get sorted, that's all. My grand-mother's will and all that."

I could feel tears stinging at the back of my eyes and swallowed hard to get the lump in my throat out of the way so that my voice wouldn't sound too emotional. "I see," I mumbled and hurried to take a sip of coffee to break eye contact. The disappointment was even more acute than I would have expected. Of course, she wouldn't want to stay here. She had a life somewhere else. Probably friends too. Real, proper friends who lived in houses that didn't look like a hoarder's paradise.

"Caroline!" My mother's keening voice came through the ceiling. "Caaaaroline!"

I put my mug down and stood up abruptly. "I'm sorry. I'll just pop up and see what she wants. I'll be right back."

Running up the stairs, I felt panic rising. I'd tried so hard not to get my hopes up, but here I was, daydreaming like a stupid schoolgirl about making a friend and having someone to talk to. Someone who could perhaps teach me how to be a real person, so that I wouldn't have to stay here all alone once Mother had—

I stopped myself in my thoughts outside the door to Mother's room.

Once Mother had passed away.

No. No, that wasn't it.

Once Mother had *died*.

"Caroliiiiiine!" she keened, more annoyance than desperation in her frail but grating voice.

I placed my hand on the door handle but waited another beat before opening the door. Mother was dying. It was only a matter of time. And once that happened, everything was going to change.

Except that I didn't need to wait for her to die before I started making changes.

I could start today.

In fact, I had already started, yesterday, when I invited Lisa over for coffee. Just like a normal person would do.

I could feel the pull from the kitchen downstairs. There was a person down there that I … liked. That interested me. That I felt almost comfortable with. I wanted to be there, with her. Not up here, not with Mother.

I opened the door before she could shout again, determined to get her what she needed as quickly as possible, and return to the kitchen before Lisa got bored and left.

I did *not* want her to leave.

LISA

CAROLINE WAS GONE for so long that I had time to finish my coffee. I waited, but still no sound of her footsteps coming back down the stairs. I felt stupid just sitting there but didn't know what else to do.

In the end, I got up, put my coffee mug in the sink and walked back out into the sitting room. Not that anyone would want to sit there. There *was* a sofa in there, a brown two-seater covered in a coarse fabric with a definite 70's vibe. A couple of boxes and a rolled-up carpet that smelled slightly of mildew stood on the sagging seat cushions, and it was obvious that no one had sat on that sofa for many, many years. There was a matching armchair, also mostly concealed underneath stacks and stacks of magazines and some folded-up tablecloths of various sizes and hues, mostly retro ones. There was no TV, only a black transistor radio on a table next to the window, the cord strung along the wall to an awkwardly placed outlet at waist height. The pull-out antenna pointed almost straight toward me. On a table in front of the window, someone had started laying a puzzle but then abandoned it after finishing the frame and one corner. The motif seemed to be some kind of nature scene, but it was hard to tell. A plant on the windowsill had died and felled all its leaves over the table, and they had withered into frail fragments that had more or less merged with the cardboard puzzle pieces. A red wooden candelabra next to the plant held five candles that had melted in the sun and drooped awkwardly in all directions, like something in a Dalí painting.

Turning toward the bookshelves, I could see why they hadn't bothered with a TV. The shelves that ran all along the wall, floor to ceiling, were packed with books of all sizes, jammed in wherever they could fit. Most of them older, properly bound books, but some paper-backs as well and also some library books with stickers on the spine. I pulled one of them out of the shelf right in front of me and turned it over. The cover, wrapped in protective plastic, hadn't faded like the other books, but it was an old-fashioned design, and the title didn't ring any bells. I leafed through it and noticed the pocket at the back, with a slot for a card with stamped return dates. I vaguely remembered those from when I was little, before the libraries computerized everything.

Pulling the card out of the pocket, I studied the numbers. There were half a dozen dates, the last of them the fifteenth of August, thirty years ago.

Staring at the dates, all a bit crooked and faded, with slightly different shades of ink, I couldn't help but be transported back to that summer. Looking around the room, I realized what I was looking at. It was a time capsule. Time had stopped in this room, in this house, on that day when the Hunter had died. I didn't remember the date, but it had to have been early August, because it was only a week or so before school started.

My chest tightened and I struggled to catch my breath, not just because of the dust and debris that surrounded me, but also from some other feeling.

He was a kind man, Caroline had said.

And when he died, everything in this house, *in her life*, had stopped, broken down. Died with him in that barn.

Slipping the card back inside the book and the book back on the shelf, I moved toward the front door. The thunderous roar of a blazing fire pounded my eardrums and my face felt hot from the flames. Poor Caroline. Her life had also ended that same weekend, all those years ago.

That was what I had recognized when I looked her in the eyes.

She was also a rag doll, not a real person.

Like me.

Hearing her talk about her father had felt uncomfortable, even painful. I hadn't wanted to hear those things about him. The Hunter hadn't been kind, he had been a *cruel* man, a ruthless killer, but I was the only one who knew that. If Caroline hadn't been aware of his inhumanity, if she hadn't known that side of her father, that was good for her, I guess. I certainly wasn't going to be the one who told her what he had done to Ellen. She didn't need to know about that. Let her believe that her father had been a good man. What did it matter now, all these years later?

Moving out into the hallway, I stopped at the foot of the stairs, listening. Voices came from upstairs, but they were too muffled for me to make out what they were talking about. Glancing at the front door, I hesitated. Should I just leave? Perhaps that would be best. For me, at least.

And since when did I care about anyone other than myself?

Astrid's words stung; there was no denying it. But she was right, in a sense. Me leaving home hadn't been about getting away from them, it had been about getting away from here, from me, from the person I had been back then, but I'm sure my family couldn't have seen it that way. And the reality of it was that I *had* abandoned them and never looked back.

I'd been so determined never to return to Mormor's cottage and look at me now. Not only was I back here, but I was actually standing *in the Hunter's house*, waiting for his daughter.

Shaking my head, I turned and moved toward the front door. I should just leave, before Caroline came back downstairs. It was for the best. There was no way I was going to be able to have a normal conversation with this woman. I wasn't normal, and I hadn't been for so long; I couldn't even fake it anymore. Sure, there had been some kind of recognition, some kind of connection between us down by the lake; there was no denying that. I guess we were just broken in the same kind of way, but matching scars was not something to build a friendship on.

A friendship? I shook my head and placed my hand on the door handle. You're getting way ahead of yourself there, Lisa, I admonished myself. Who'd want to be friends with you?

I was just about to leave when I heard a door open

and close upstairs. Footsteps over creaking floorboards. My heart skipped a beat. Should I just go? Make a run for it? Glancing down at my belly that was pressed up against the door, I almost laughed. Yeah, like I was going to be able to outrun skinny Caroline. She would catch up with me before I'd made it down off the porch, and then what would I say?

No. I had to pretend to be a normal person and say goodbye.

I let go of the door handle and turned toward the stairs. Caroline's face dropped when she saw me by the door. It was almost as if she was sad to see me go, but I knew that couldn't be true.

"Are you leaving?" she asked, her voice breathy, as if she'd run down the stairs.

"You're busy," I said, gesturing vaguely in the direction of the room upstairs where her mother must be. "I should go."

She shook her head and wrapped her arms around herself in a hug, as if she was cold, even though the hallway was stifling and almost void of air. "I'm not busy," she said, glancing down. "You only just got here." She looked up at me again. "Unless you've got somewhere to be?"

I should lie, I thought. I should make up an appointment or just some excuse. Family obligations. Anything. "No," I heard myself saying. "I don't have any plans this afternoon."

Her face lit up. I couldn't believe it, and I told myself that it couldn't mean what I thought it meant, but a soft warmth spread throughout my chest. I couldn't remember the last time anyone had been glad to get to spend time with me.

How was I supposed to walk away from that?

"Stay a while," she said, and there was something in her eyes that resembled hopefulness. It couldn't be real, but it was irresistible, nonetheless.

We walked back through the cramped sitting room. "Are you hungry?" she asked over her shoulder toward me, but before I had time to answer, a weird noise came from somewhere in the corner behind the armchair. We both stopped and stared. It sounded primal, like someone was dying. Caroline turned and stared at me, and I stared back.

"What is that?" I whispered. There was nothing I could think of that would make such a creepy noise. Caroline took a couple of steps toward the armchair and peeked over the backrest.

"It's just the cat," she said, laughing a little.

"The cat?" I had never heard a cat sound like that. "What's wrong with it?"

Caroline turned and continued toward the kitchen. "She's having her kittens," she said as if that was the most normal thing in the world.

I just stood there, staring after her. "But w—" I took a step toward the armchair, wanting to take a look for myself, but then I stopped, afraid for what I might see if I looked down into the darkness. "Should we do something?" I called out after Caroline, who stood at the refrigerator, staring into it. "Call a vet?"

She shook her head, slamming the fridge shut without having taken anything out. "She'll be fine," she said. "It's her third or fourth litter. She knows what to do." She gestured at the kitchen table. "Are you hungry? I could make us something."

I shook my head. "No. Thank you." My eyes kept

being pulled toward the armchair, but my feet moved in the other direction, into the kitchen.

Caroline pulled out her chair and sat down again. "I'm glad you stayed," she said, and I was taken aback by her forthrightness. I waddled toward the table, the hairs at the back of my neck standing up straight at the pitiful sounds coming from the sitting room.

"Three or four litters," I said, feeling faint and relieved to sit down again. "You must have a ton of cats around here then."

Caroline chuckled. "Oh no," she said. "We only keep one or two from each litter."

"Oh." I hadn't a clue how many kittens a cat usually had. The only time I'd seen a litter had been up in the hayloft across the yard outside, and I had done my best to forget that experience, but I seemed to recall that there had been many of the small whimpering creatures.

"I wanted to talk to you," she said, and I pushed the unpleasant memories from my mind. Stay in the present, Lisa. Forget about the past. Move on. "About what happened to your friend. Or, your sister's friend, rather."

My attempts to stay in the present were futile; I could see that. Whatever I did, however far I ran away, it would always be with me. Ellen would always be there, right by my side. Ellen, the mermaid. Ellen, the rag doll.

"To Ellen?" I asked, swallowing.

Caroline nodded. "It was a long time ago," she said. "And you were very little. But I'm sure you remember everything that happened, the same way that I remember what happened to Father. I was a little older than you, but not a lot."

I didn't know what to say, so I just nodded.

She glanced up toward the ceiling. "I hope you don't think me heartless," she began, fingering the potholder again. "But for me, what happened to your friend was overshadowed by what happened to my father. As far as I recall, the two events happened almost at the same time, and when Father died, everything just ..." She looked up, blinking rapidly. "Everything just stopped," she continued. "And it never really started back up again after that."

I wanted to look over my shoulder at the sitting room, frozen in time, preserved for eternity in that thick layer of dust. There were no words, so I nodded again.

Caroline glanced at my face but then quickly looked down at her hands again. The cat gave out a pitiful wail somewhere behind me, and my arms were covered in goose pimples, even though the house was warm.

"Mother ..." she began but then paused and swallowed. "She has been slowly but surely losing her grip on reality. Dementia is a cruel disease, and just as hard on the family as on the afflicted." She sighed. "Anyway, she is more or less completely lost in the fog by now, but once in a while, she'll say things that sound so ... clear. And most of the time, those phrases are things that I've heard her say before. Echoes of her voice from when I was little. Things that she said, that got stuck somewhere in her brain, only to come unstuck now, as her memory is disintegrating." She glanced up at me again, as if to see if I was following her reasoning. I nodded.

"And yesterday, after the funeral, she said something that made me a bit confused. It may not have anything to do with your friend, but …" She shook her head. "I just wanted to talk to you and see if I could make some sense out of what is going on inside of her demented brain."

My mouth was so dry, I wasn't sure if I could speak. "What did she say?"

"She said …" She paused for so long that I thought she'd decided not to tell me. Then she raised one hand in a helpless gesture. "She said, 'It's all your fault that the wench is dead.'"

CAROLINE

LISA LOOKED BLANK AT FIRST, and I felt stupid. I shouldn't have said anything. It was just the dementia talking. But Mother had sounded so much like her old self …

Then I noticed how Lisa's face slowly paled, and her breath could barely be heard, even though she normally breathed with heavy, chesty rasps. "She said that?" she whispered. Her brow was pulled together, and she looked confused, then worried, then angry, before she pulled herself together with a slow intake of breath. "What do you think she meant?"

I leaned back, feeling the edge of the backrest press against my shoulder blades. "It might just be something she dreamed or heard somewhere. Something from a book, perhaps. She used to read all the time before her eyesight deteriorated. It's just …" I smiled to conceal my embarrassment, "there's this tone of voice that she only ever used with Father, when she was angry with him. I haven't heard it since he passed, and it was so weird hearing her scolding him for something like that."

Lisa didn't look me in the eye. Instead, her eyes had wandered to the window behind me, looking outside. "You think it was something she once said to your father?"

I didn't want to admit that I had heard my parents fighting about Ellen. Didn't want to think about what that might mean. But I was anxious to know what had happened to that little girl. If it was possible that Father somehow could have been to blame for the accident. I didn't see how that could be, but still. For Father's sake, I needed to make sure.

"I think it might have been," I said, trying my very best not to let my desperation seep out into my voice. "And the only dead wench that I know of was your friend."

Lisa's eyes darted to my face and then back outside again. "Your father was among the men who found her," she said, her voice thin.

I nodded slowly. "Yes. Yes, he was."

"There was a search party," I said. "I was watching them from the loft."

I wanted to scream at her. Wanted to shake her. Yes, that was all well and good, but all that happened *after* the girl had gone missing. By the time the search party went out, she had already been dead for hours.

What I needed to know was ...

What had happened before. Earlier in the day.

Before that little girl had drowned, helpless as a kitten in that big, dark lake.

LISA

MY CHEST FELT SO TIGHT; I could barely breathe. So many old memories, so many old feelings, fears, nightmares. I didn't want to think about any of this. Didn't want to remember.

I could see that her mother's statement had caught Caroline's attention, though. What a weird thing to say. I don't know when I'd last heard the word 'wench'. But I remembered the Hunter's wife, the little round white-haired woman at the mall. Scolding her little girl. Caroline.

"Do you think," she said, "that you could tell me a little about what happened. I'd just like to know." She sat upright, leaning forward, her elbows on the table. "Please don't think that I'm morbid or nosy. It's just that ..." She glanced down at her hands, seemingly surprised to see them folded tight. "I can't imagine Father having done anything to endanger a child, or anyone, for that matter. He wasn't at all that kind of man. But I would like to understand what is going on in Mother's head. If there is some unfinished business, something unresolved from back then, I don't have much time to set it straight." She looked up, straight at me. "She is dying," she said, almost apologetically.

Several slow, deep breaths and I was amazed at how calm I was. "It was a long time ago," I said. "Does it really matter now? Your father is gone." Her leaning forward made me pull back, but the solid backrest kept me in place.

Caroline shook her head, chuckling joylessly. "Oh, I'm very much aware of that fact." She gestured toward the sitting room behind me. "There is no way of living in this house and not constantly being reminded of the fact that Father is gone."

"It's been thirty years," I said slowly. "Perhaps it's time to move on."

As if I knew anything about moving on. Running away, yes. Maturely moving on with one's life, not so much.

Caroline slumped back against her chair, her head moving slowly from side to side in a soft protest. "I know that I have to," she said, looking up at me with eyes that seemed to shine with tears. "And I'll have to, soon. When Mother ..." She swallowed hard. "I honestly have no idea what I'll do. When she's gone, I mean."

Looking at her, it was obvious that the truth about Ellen's death was the last thing Caroline needed. She was already trapped in this messy house because of her mother's inability to deal with her husband's death. And perhaps also his guilt, if the statement that had gotten Caroline so riled up was an actual echo of a fight long ago. Had the Hunter's wife known about what he'd done? Had she known what kind of man he was?

It didn't seem possible. She'd had a young daughter,

for crying out loud. How could she have lived in the same house as a monster like that, letting him close to her innocent child? What kind of woman could do such a thing?

I sighed. "You'll figure it out," I said, hoping that it didn't sound as hollow as the words felt to me. I'd never been able to figure anything out, so why should she?

Caroline shook her head, blinking the tears away. "I don't know," she whispered. Pulling herself together, she sat up, clearing her throat. "But I'll have to, I know that. You're right."

Thin, squeaky mewling noises came from the sitting room. Then an almost as thin, almost as squeaky voice from upstairs. "Carooooline!"

Caroline looked ready to crack from the strain. "Oh god," she muttered under her breath. "What is it *now*?"

I pushed my chair back. "I should leave," I said. "You're busy."

"No!" she protested. Then she pulled back, giving me a crooked smile. "Why don't you come upstairs with me, say hi? Mother doesn't get many visitors." Glancing at the large clock on the wall, she straightened her back. "The nurse will be here in half an hour or so. Then we can talk some more without being disturbed." She must have seen the reluctance on my face. "Oh, please stay," she said.

I nodded, but as we made our way out into the hallway and up the creaking stairs, I wished I'd had the guts to say no. I did not want to meet the Hunter's wife.

On the landing upstairs were lots of doors, all of them closed. Caroline walked over to one of the doors on the left and pulled it open.

"Mother?" she said. "I've brought a visitor." She

glanced over her shoulder at me. "Come," she said eagerly, gesturing at me to follow. "Come and meet my mother."

We stepped inside the room. As soon as I crossed the threshold, the stench of urine assaulted my nostrils. The room was dim, only a narrow sliver of daylight sneaking in between the heavy curtains. An upholstered armchair with a small, round table stood in front of the window, but it was empty. I looked around the room.

It was sparsely furnished, with hardly any decorations. No trinkets, potted plants or paintings. A large woven tapestry covered a big chunk of one wall, but its muted yellow and brown tones didn't exactly add any color to the room. In the darkest corner stood an old bed with a bed frame of dark-stained wood. A low muttering could be heard from the shadows.

"I can't sleep," a woman's voice said impatiently. "It's too hot. Get me out of this bed, girl."

Caroline hurried over to the bed and proceeded to maneuver the old woman from underneath the covers and across the floor over to the armchair.

"Mother," she said as soon as the woman was seated. "This is Lisa. Vera's granddaughter, you know. We met her at the funeral. You remember her, don't you? She's come for a visit. Isn't that nice?"

I took a step closer, opening my mouth for a greeting, but the Hunter's wife beat me to it.

"I thought I told you to stay out of my yard!" she almost shouted, raising the same gnarled finger that she had threatened me with, in the church hall yesterday.

"Mother!" Caroline said, shocked and embarrassed. "Lisa is my guest. I invited her to come."

"Worthless girls running around where they don't

have any business to be," the old woman continued, but she was staring out into space now, and her words didn't seem to be directed at me, or Caroline for that matter. "Poking their noses in other people's business, that's just asking for trouble. Stupid, useless girls always getting in the way..." Her voice tapered off into an unintelligible mutter.

"Mother!" Caroline admonished, but then she leaned in closer, glancing over her shoulder at me. "What on earth are you talking about?"

But her mother had run out of steam. The muttering continued, but it was impossible to discern any words. Caroline backed away.

"Are you all right there then, Mother?" she asked. "The nurse will be here soon. Do you want your tea now, or after she has left?"

The old woman sat with her head slightly turned away from us, muttering so quietly that I wouldn't have been able to tell that she wasn't silent if I hadn't seen her wrinkly lips move. Something was clearly upsetting her, but I wasn't sure if it was my presence or if it was something from the past.

Caroline shook her head, clearly exasperated at the lack of communication. "The cat had her kittens," she said. "Not that you care," she said under her voice and gestured me toward the door.

"Wretched vermin," the old woman growled, her voice suddenly a lot clearer. "Just drown the lot of them, I say. We've got too many cats running around here. They'll eat us out of house and home before long, I shouldn't wonder. Get rid of them!"

Caroline sighed. "Yes, Mother," she said, shooing me toward the door, but I had stopped in my tracks and turned back toward the old woman. She was staring out through the gap in the curtains again.

I turned toward Caroline. "Do you actually *drown* them?" Her words from before, 'We only keep one or two from each litter,' echoed through my brain. I had assumed that she'd meant that they gave the rest away or even sold them, but this? Distant memories of squirming, blind little creatures flooded my mind. So small. So helpless.

And don't get me started on drowning.

I had issues with drowning!

Caroline didn't seem to notice my revulsion. "Yes, it's the fastest way. So easy. They don't have time to feel anything."

So easy?

Had it been *so easy* for her father to kill Ellen? Was this whole family completely deranged? Were they all psychopathic killers, or was it just me who was imagining things again?

I took a step back toward the door, but I struggled to pull my eyes away from the old woman. What did she know? And was she too far gone to be able to tell me, if I could manage to get some time alone with her?

Did it matter, really, what had happened to Ellen? I mean, she had died. I knew that much. And I knew that she had died here, on the farm. I had left her here, and I had seen the Hunter carry her down to the lake, where she'd been found later that night.

I knew enough. I knew who the bad guy was.

And I knew that he had been punished for it. The fire. Burning so hot. So loud. He'd gotten what he deserved.

It was over. So why couldn't I just walk away? Why was I still here?

I was crossing the threshold when the Hunter's wife had another outburst. "Stupid, useless girls," she ranted. "Sticking their noses in other people's business. I'll teach her some manners, I will. Nosy brat!"

I stopped. Caroline had already started to turn toward her mother, opening her mouth to say something, but I beat her to it. "What brat?" I asked.

"That wretched wench! No manners, I tell you. Screaming at me like a little banshee, she was. Well, I shut her up. Useless girls. What's the point of them, I swear I don't know."

Caroline looked stricken. "Mother," she said, but there was no strength behind the admonishing this time. Her words barely carried across the floor over to the armchair where her mother sat, fuming at the enraging memories of her distant past.

I moved slowly toward the old woman, even though I wanted nothing more than to leave. I didn't want to know any more. I already knew far too much. There was no way of being certain if this old woman's demented brain would divulge any actual information or if it would just be random, garbled imagery.

Like my own memories. Like how I could remember the kittens in the barn and remember them not being there, at the same time. Like how I could remember Ellen, the rag doll, slung over the Hunter's gaunt shoulder, and Ellen the mermaid, swimming around in her underwater palace, searching for pearls. Like how I could remember the fire that killed the Hunter, even though I couldn't have seen it.

I didn't want to know.

But I had to ask.

"The useless wench," I said, staring at the wrinkled lips. The white hair. *Has she seen a ghost, Mormor?* I had asked at the mall. Had she? Or had she just married a killer? A monster? A predator who preyed on little girls, like her own daughter? "What useless wench?" I asked. "Are you talking about Ellen?"

The Hunter's wife turned toward me, staring in my direction with eyes that looked blind, but must have seen me somehow. "Get off my property, you grotesque fatso," she said, and her narrow lips curled in disgust. Yep. Not entirely blind then.

"What did she do that upset you so?" I said, not letting my feet move toward the door, even though they really, really wanted to.

"Those darn vermin," she spat, "those mewling kittens. We didn't want any more mouths to feed."

"What did you do to the kittens?" I asked, feeling as if I witnessed the interaction from above. So aware of my placement in the room, between the old woman and Caroline. Somehow wanting to shield Caroline from the truth about her father. She had suffered enough, hadn't she?

Hadn't I?

Just leave, the rational sliver of my brain urged me. Please just walk out that door. Nothing good will come of knowing.

"What did y—" I repeated, but before I could finish the sentence, she interrupted me with another garbled tirade.

"Lisa," Caroline said behind me, "please, let's just go. She doesn't know what she's saying."

But looking into those cataract-dimmed eyes, I

thought that wasn't entirely true. Caroline's mother knew *something*, all right.

"We drown the kittens," she said, her voice suddenly completely crystal clear, right in the middle of all that garbled muttering. "We've always done it that way. My father taught me. And I taught my daughter. That's how we do things around here. I told her. Go back to the city if you can't deal with the reality on a farm, I told her."

"Who?" Caroline said behind me. "Who did you tell?"

3 0

CAROLINE

MY MOTHER WASN'T MAKING any sense. I didn't hear most of what she was mumbling about, and the parts that came out clear were warped, somehow. It didn't make any sense. I had no idea what she was talking about. When she started up about the kittens, I sighed. I'd deal with them, like I always did. What did she care, anyway? I was the one buying the cat food. I was the one feeding them. She didn't do anything around the farm anymore, hadn't for years.

But when she started talking about that wench again, I pricked my ears.

"Who?" I asked. "Who did you tell?"

Lisa was standing between Mother and me, and she raised one hand toward me, as if to make me be quiet. I didn't understand why she would do such a thing. *She* was the guest here. This was *my* mother.

"That wretched girl that your father brought here," she said, and the world collapsed around me.

"WHAT?" I said. Or perhaps I screamed. I moved

252

forward, pushing Lisa out of the way. "What are you talking about?"

But Mother didn't seem to register my anger. Her head lolled over toward the window and her low mutterings started up again.

"That pitiful man," I heard her say, and I bristled. I hated when she spoke about Father in that way. Father was kind, not weak. He was gentle, and she was always bossing him around. Father was loving. And Mother was hateful and spiteful and …

"Oh, why don't you die already?" I muttered and turned toward the door. "Let's just go," I said to Lisa, but she didn't move.

"You knew," she said to Mother, and there was something strange about her voice. So … angry? Why would Lisa be angry with Mother? That didn't make any sense. "You knew all this time, and you never told anyone." She took a couple of steps toward Mother, who didn't seem to register anything of what was going on.

"What did she know?" I asked. Could someone please explain to me what was going on? It felt as if everyone else was in on a secret, and I was the only one walking around like a naive fool, blissfully ignorant. "What? Tell me!"

Lisa stood bent over the table, her face almost too close to Mother's for it to look entirely suitable. I walked up to her and placed one hand on her shoulder, pulling her back. "Lisa?" I said. "What are you talking about?"

Lisa slowly stood up, but she didn't take her eyes of Mother.

"Lisa!" I said again. "What was she saying about Father? About him bringing a girl here?" I tugged at her shoulder again, forcing her to look at me. "What is it that you're not telling me?"

She stared at my face, her expression a mix of anger and desolation. She started to shake her head, but I gripped her shoulder even harder. It probably hurt her, but she didn't even flinch. "You don't want to know," she said between narrow lips. "Trust me, Caroline. Don't listen to her."

I stared at her round face, the features blurred by fat. "This is my father we're talking about," I said between gritted teeth.

She nodded slowly. "Exactly. And you loved your father. You don't want to sully those memories of him. They're all you've got now."

I felt my throat constrict. It was true. It was just Mother and me now, and soon it would be just me. Just me and my memories in this monster of a house, falling apart around me. She was right. I didn't want to know. Not if it was anything bad. I didn't want to hear anything unkind about Father.

But still ... I needed to know.

"Tell me," I said, and my voice sounded surprisingly determined and forceful, considering that I could barely stand. My legs felt like jelly, and I could feel the entire structure holding my sanity up crumbling under the weight of this. "Please, Lisa. You have to tell me what happened."

She looked at me for a long time and I could tell that she was wavering back and forth. In the end, she glanced over her shoulder at Mother, biting her lip.

"I don't know exactly what happened," she said. Her voice brittle, as if she was a little girl, not the massive, fully grown woman standing in front of me. "I wasn't here when it happened. But we came here that day, Ellen and I." She swallowed. "Your father was down by the lake, and he told us that his cat had kittens. Ellen wanted to see them."

I pulled back, shaking my head. "You were *here*?" I looked around me. "In this house?"

She nodded toward the window. "We were in the barn. Up in the hayloft."

I couldn't believe it. Why would Father do something like that? I had never been allowed to play with other children, never had any friends. Why would he bring Lisa and Ellen here? It didn't make any sense. "You're lying," I said. "Or you're not remembering it right. Why would he do that?"

Her shoulders slumped, and I was worried that she wouldn't say anything more, but then she continued. "I was afraid of your father," she said, and when I opened my mouth to protest, she raised her hand to stop me. "There was something about him that freaked me out, and I kept begging Ellen that we should go back. But she didn't want to. She wanted to stay with the kittens. She wanted to watch them sleep." A deep breath and a slow exhale.

I tried to picture them out there, up in the hayloft. How could there have been children here at the farm without me knowing about it? If I had seen any other children around here, I would never have forgotten about it. "I ... I don't believe you," I said. "No one ever came here. You must have dreamed it."

Lisa shook her head. "I thought so, for the longest time. Or I wanted to believe it. Because I felt so guilty about leaving her here. I left Ellen with the kittens and went back to Mormor's." Another ragged sigh. "I made it almost all the way back, but then I felt too bad, so I turned around to come and fetch her. On the path to the lake, I saw … your father. And he was carrying Ellen over his shoulder. Her arms were dangling down his back."

She closed her eyes, and I could see that remembering was hurting her. Still, I couldn't let her stop now. What she was saying didn't make any sense.

"He was carrying her?" I echoed to try and get her to keep talking. "Was she hurt or something, so she couldn't walk?"

She blinked quickly and stared me straight in the eyes. "I don't know for sure," she said. "But I think that she was already dead."

LISA

I COULD TELL that it was painful for Caroline and how she fought to make sense of what I was saying in a way that didn't reflect badly on her beloved father. I didn't want to tell her. But I had kept it all in for so long.

"What are you saying?" she asked, her voice a frail croak. "I don't ..."

She pushed past me, over to her mother, falling on one knee in front of the old woman. "Mother?" she pleaded. "Tell her that it isn't true. They were never here, tell her, Mother."

Caroline's mother kept staring out through the gap in the curtains. "He should never have brought her here," she said, and her voice was dripping with contempt. "Wretched brat."

"Mother?" Caroline said, still on one knee. "Why did he bring her here? And what did he do to her? You said ..." She paused, glancing over one shoulder at me. "I heard you arguing, Mother," she continued, her voice lowered. "I heard you screaming at him, after that girl had been found dead." She leaned against the table and covered her face with one hand. "Tell me it isn't true, Mother," she pleaded, but her voice was muffled, and her mother didn't seem to register the plea.

"That pitiful man," the old woman said, a sudden outburst. "Always going on about how it was important for a child to have friends. As if I'd want those awful brats running around here all hours of the day. Get rid of her, I told him. Get rid of her before Carro sees her. Or we'll never hear the end of it."

Caroline fell back, landing heavily on her narrow behind on the hardwood floor. "You told him to—" She was staring up at her mother, shaking her head. "Mother, what did he do?"

The old woman chuckled, a cracked, evil sound. "That useless man. He could never do anything right. Wouldn't hurt a fly, that witless wimp."

Caroline's shoulders slumped. "No, that's what I thought," she muttered, more or less to herself. "But Mother?" she asked, looking up at the old woman. "What happened to the girl?"

"Always such a mess out in that barn!" the Hunter's wife exclaimed, "always leaving things laying around, such a messy, hopeless man."

"Mother! What did Father do to the *girl*?" Caroline repeated, but her mother just kept muttering about things not being put back in their place and filthy, filthy barns.

I grabbed Caroline under the armpits and helped her to her feet. "I'm sorry," I said. "I don't think she wants to tell us. Or perhaps she can't."

Glancing over at the demented old woman, I felt a pinch of frustration. The truth might be locked inside of that white-haired head, with no way of getting to it.

"What did your husband do?" I asked her. "And how come you never told anyone?"

If she heard me, she didn't show it. She was mumbling about the kittens again now. About how they bred like rabbits, and you had to get rid of them, or they would be everywhere.

"I'll deal with the kittens," Caroline murmured and turned toward the door. "I'll take care of it, Mother." Her voice was heavy with grief and confusion. My heart ached for her.

"I told that wench, I did," her mother said, all of a sudden. "I explained it to her, but she wouldn't listen. Kept shrieking at me, and I couldn't stand the noise she made. It was going to give me a migraine; it was. And your father just standing there, useless as always." She shook her head. "No help at all."

Caroline stood as frozen, her back against her mother, her head hanging against her chest. "What did you do, Mother?" she asked, but it was almost as if the words weren't directed at her mother. As if she didn't expect a coherent answer. No wonder, after so many years of living with a demented old woman.

"I didn't *do* anything," her mother protested abruptly. "I just pushed her out of the way, so that I could get on with it. It wasn't *my* fault."

Caroline's head snapped up. "What wasn't your fault, Mother?" she asked, staring straight ahead of her. I held my breath.

"That useless man always leaving his things lying around, I've told him a million times to put things away in their rightful place. I've told him! I have!"

"Yes, Mother," Caroline said. "You have. I know you have."

"But would he listen? No."

"No," Caroline said, her head sinking toward her chest again. "No, I don't think he did, after a while."

"It wasn't my fault," the old woman said again. "The rope was just lying there, and she tripped over it and fell. And then the bucket was standing right in the middle of the floor for no reason at all."

I shivered, remembering the sound the tin bucket had made against the concrete floor inside of the barn. "The bucket?" I said.

The old woman raised one hand to the back of her head. "Whack!" she said, her cracked voice surprisingly strong. Or perhaps it was just the impact of what she had said that hit me so hard.

"She hit her head on the bucket?" I whispered.

The old woman rolled her eyes. "One minute, she was screaming blue murder at me to leave the kittens alone. And then ..." She paused, looking up into nothing at all. "Everything went quiet. The kittens stopped squirming, and everything went quiet."

Caroline turned and stared at her mother, her face ashen. "*You* killed that girl?" she said, her voice cracked with disbelief.

"That useless, useless man," her mother said as if she hadn't heard her daughter's words. "Leaving his things lying around like that. It was all his fault. And I told him. He'd better clean up his mess before our Carro saw what he'd done."

Caroline's eyes widened. She turned toward me and stared at me. "I'm sorry I didn't believe you," she said. "Oh my god," she groaned. "He carried her down to the lake and left her there, in the water." Her hand flew up and covered her mouth. Then it slowly sank back down to her side. "She killed that girl, and Father helped her get away with it." She turned and stared at her mother, who sat there muttering as if nothing had happened. But the air in the room was electric with tension.

"Your father didn't kill Ellen," I said, and my voice sounded as if it came from a place far away. My ears felt as if I'd been on a plane. "He didn't do it," I whispered. A roaring sound built and my ears popped. My cheeks were burning, hot, hot. The Hunter, the monster from my childhood and adult nightmares, was not a killer, after all.

I'd gotten it all wrong.

My stomach twisted and turned, and I felt bile rise in my throat. Spinning around, I hurried toward the door, out onto the landing and down the stairs.

I only made it halfway. On a creaking step in the middle of the narrow stairs, my legs gave way and I collapsed. One hand managed to grip the handrail at the last minute and kept me from tumbling headfirst down the rest of the stairs. My stomach convulsed and a thin white trickle of vomit flew out of my mouth. I stared at it as it slowly seeped down the brown paneled wall.

He didn't do it. He didn't kill Ellen.

She hit her head on the bucket.

The bucket.

The bucket that I had left in the middle of the floor.

3 2

CAROLINE

I COULDN'T BELIEVE what I was hearing. I'd always known that Mother was a cold woman, a heartless woman even, and that she had a temper, but I'd never have imagined that she could hurt someone. Actually kill someone.

This was too unreal. Like something from a book. Except, books usually had happy endings, and I couldn't imagine how this could end in any other way than disaster.

My mother had killed a little girl.

The thought felt alien in my mind, painful like a sharp piece of grit in my shoe.

Lisa bolted for the door, and I was torn between wanting to follow her and trying to get some more information out of Mother's unreliable memories.

But what more did I really need to know, apart from what I'd just discovered? That poor girl had died in our barn all those years ago, and it had been Mother's fault.

Poor Father had covered for her.

Swallowing a sob, I turned toward the door. The last

262

day of his life must have been awful. He must have felt so bad about what had happened. He'd done something nice for his daughter, for me, because he had wanted me to have friends.

And Mother …

It was dark out on the landing, but I could make out the shape of Lisa halfway down the stairs. She was sitting down, clinging to the banister, sobbing.

I couldn't imagine what that experience had been like for her. Seeing her friend dead like that, alone out in the woods. Unbelievable that she'd never told anyone.

But oh, how glad I was that she never did.

Because if she had told someone, the police would have come for my father.

And knowing him, he probably wouldn't have told them the truth. Rather than giving up his wife, he would have taken the blame.

What would that have been like, growing up with a father in prison for the murder of a child?

I shivered as I made my way down the stairs, sinking down on the step next to Lisa. Her warm bulk was trembling, and a sharp stench of vomit made me grimace. I put my hand on her shoulder and she flinched.

Well, I could hardly blame her. I couldn't even imagine what she'd gone through that day. And then she had lived with those nightmares for thirty years. I just found out about it now, as a grown woman, and I was struggling to deal with it.

"It must have been awful for you," I said quietly. "I can't imagine what that must have done to a child. Seeing something like that."

She groaned and shook her head slowly.

"What are we going to do?" I asked her. "Should we tell someone? Call the police?" I looked back up the stairs over my shoulder. "They won't be able to do anything now."

Lisa ran one hand over her face and struggled to her feet. "I'm so sorry," she croaked, "so very sorry…"

A small pool of sick glinted at the edge of a tread.

I shook my head. "Don't worry about it," I said. "I'll clean it up later."

The sound of a car pulling up outside made me snap out of the confusion. "Damn. It's the district nurse." I got up and hurried past Lisa down the stairs, opening the door to the cupboard underneath. "Go and wait in the kitchen," I said. "I'll just let her in, and then I'll come and make you some tea or something."

"I-I c-can't—" she stuttered and turned toward the door.

"No!" I said, grabbing a rag from the bucket on the floor of the cupboard and hurrying to clean up the sick. "You can't leave now! We need to talk about what just happened."

She took another step toward the door, but I hurried back past her, threw the stinking rag in the cupboard, slammed the door shut, and then grabbed her by the arms.

"Please, Lisa. You can't leave now," I said, pushing her toward the kitchen.

She just stared at me, her eyes wide with fear. Shock, even.

On some level, I could understand that, sure, but at the same time, she had known all these years, and I was

264

just finding out about this now. If anyone had the right to look shell-shocked, surely it was me?

"Wait in the kitchen!" I told her, frog-marching her over the threshold into the sitting room. Footsteps came up the porch, and there was a knock on the door. The sound seemed to wake Lisa up, and she tore out of my grip, hurrying toward the kitchen.

I turned back and let the nurse in.

She was brusque, as usual, and for once, I was grateful that she didn't have the time or inclination for small talk. I could not have managed that today. As soon as she had disappeared upstairs, I hurried out into the kitchen. Lisa was standing at the sink, staring out the window at the spot where the barn used to be. She didn't seem to register my presence.

I walked over and stood behind her. "I'm so sorry," I said. "I'm so sorry that you had to experience that. I can't imagine what that must have been like."

I'd had nightmares every night for years after Father died. And even during daytime, I'd sometimes get panic attacks, thinking about the thundering fire closing in on me from all directions. What a horrible way to die!

Glancing up at the ceiling, I was surprised at how calm I felt, considering what I'd just been told. But really, what difference did it make? I'd lost my mother many years ago, and soon she'd be gone for good.

If anything, it was a relief to know that Father hadn't been responsible for that little girl's death. I'd never seriously believed that he could do something like that, but the relief I felt now must mean that a small part of me had had doubts.

I placed my hand on Lisa's shoulder again, and again

265

she tried to pull away, but I didn't let her. Instead, I pulled her into an awkward embrace. Not that I thought that I could make up for thirty years of nightmares, but still …

"I'm so sorry you had to see that," I said and felt her stiffen.

"It's all my fault," she said hoarsely, pulling away from me, raising one arm as if to shield herself from me. "I thought that he …" She shook her head. "I—"

"You were just a little girl," I said. "Please don't blame yourself for any of this."

She stared straight at me. "But it is all my fault," she repeated. "Ellen. I killed her."

33

ASTRID

THE SUN HAD REACHED the treetops across the lake. That meant it was time to get out of the water and make our way back to the cottage for dinner.

"Come on, you two," I called out to Elinor and Jonas. "It's almost dinner time."

They came grudgingly and dried off with the towels that I held out to them. I slipped on a sundress over the bikini, stretched languidly, and realized that I felt more relaxed than I'd done in weeks. Ever since Mormor died, probably. The funeral was over. Lisa was … doing better, I hoped. And she had been gone most of the day, so I'd had time to just be. For a moment, as I lay here in the sun, I hadn't worried about her.

I still thought it would be best if she didn't go back to the States. If she stayed here, where I could keep an eye on her. But I couldn't deny that having her back had been a strain.

"Is aunt Lisa having dinner with us today?" Jonas said, tugging a T-shirt over his head. The yellow fabric turned dark where it got wet from his hair.

I glanced over at the path that led to the Johansson's farm. "I don't know. She isn't back from her visit with the neighbors yet. She would have had to come this way."

"How come we never visit the neighbors?" Jonas said.

That boy and his questions. Usually, I loved that about him, but today it frustrated me that I didn't have an answer. Yes, how come?

We never bothered the Johanssons, that's what Mormor had always said. Well, we didn't have to keep doing everything the way that Mormor had done. The cottage was mine now.

I gathered our things in the large totes that we used for our lake excursions. "Let's go over there now," I said. "We'll introduce ourselves properly, and then we can let Lisa know that dinner's ready."

Elinor raised her eyebrows in that annoying way that Fredrik said she got from me. "But we never bother the Johanssons," she said.

I put the bath towels on top of the tote bags. "We're not bothering anyone. We're their neighbors, at least over the summer. Mormor and Mrs. Johansson might not have been the best of friends, but I'm sure it would be nice to get to know the daughter. They came to Mormor's funeral, so there can't have been any bad blood."

Jonas grimaced. "Ugh, blood!"

"It's just an expression, silly," I said. "Come on. Have you got your crocs on? The path is bound to be covered with pointy needles and stuff."

We made our way over to the farm. I'm sure I'd been this way before, at least as a child when we used to play all over these woods, but it didn't seem familiar to me at all.

Running around in the woods had stopped abruptly, of course. After what happened to Ellen, I'd been alone here at the cottage. Lisa had refused to come. And playing alone in the woods wasn't as fun, as much as I'd complained about having my little sister tagging along everywhere that I went. Plus that I'd been getting older, more into books and stuff rather than playing make-believe games outside.

The farm was closer to the lake than I'd expected, and as we crossed the yard, I was shocked to see the state of the house. I seemed to recall that it had been an impressive home, but now it looked almost haunted.

"What a creepy house!" Jonas said, echoing my own thoughts. "Does someone actually live here?"

"Yes," I said, rounding the corner to the front of the house. "Mrs. Johansson and her daughter."

Jonas shuddered. Elinor didn't say anything, but her nose was wrinkled with disgust. I was starting to regret having brought the children. I should have told them to go back to the cottage, but it was too late now.

We made our way up onto the rickety porch and over to the front door. I knocked gently. After a while, when nothing had happened, I knocked a little harder.

The door flung open. Mrs. Johansson's daughter stood there, looking flustered. Her face was even paler and more drawn than at the funeral. Her wide eyes stared straight at me.

"Yes?" she said.

"Hello," I said. "I thought I'd come by and introduce myself. I'm Astrid. We met at Britta's funeral, but we didn't get a chance to speak, so ..."

I held out my hand. The woman stared at it as if it were a snake. Then she slowly reached out her own hand and took it. Her palm was damp with sweat and slightly sticky. I wanted to pull away but didn't dare. There was something not right with this woman, and I didn't want the children to be frightened. Especially not Jonas. He had enough phobias.

"Nice to finally meet you properly," I said. "Er …?"

"Caroline," she said.

"Nice to meet you, Caroline."

She finally let go of my hand but didn't move.

"I was hoping to speak to my sister," I said. "She told me she was coming to see you today."

Caroline pressed her lips together and glanced over one shoulder. "She's in the kitchen," she said, but she still didn't move.

I felt awkward just standing there and again wished that I hadn't brought the children. "Well, I don't want to intrude, but I'd like a word with her if you don't mind."

Caroline backed away slowly and we stepped inside the hallway.

The first thing I noticed was the smell. Or rather, stench. Rot and decay with undertones of something acid, almost like vomit. I hoped my face didn't show my reaction, but I couldn't help but place one hand on Jonas's shoulder to keep him close by me. "The kitchen, did you say?" I said.

Caroline gestured to my left. I walked that way.

This house was more than dilapidated. It was a hoarder's paradise. Everywhere I looked, there was stuff and more stuff, and it felt as if no one had even tried to clean this place in decades.

Such misery. I couldn't imagine living like this, but Caroline didn't seem to notice.

We came into what once must have been a sitting room but was now a dumping ground. There was a strange noise coming from over in the corner. Oh my god, was it mice? Or even ... Rats?

"What on earth?" I said before I could stop myself.

"It's just the cat," Caroline said behind me. "She had her kittens today."

"Kittens?" Jonas said. "Can I see them?"

Caroline stared at him as if she'd never seen a child before, but then she nodded. He made his way over to the armchair in the corner, and I was grateful that he'd had all his shots. This place was a health hazard. No wonder Mormor hadn't wanted anything to do with these people.

Elinor stayed by my side initially, but when Jonas had crawled up onto the dusty armchair and peeked over the back, his excited squeals made her look up at me questioningly.

"Go ahead," I said. The words 'but don't touch anything' came as far as the tip of my tongue. There was no way of moving in this room without touching anything. I'd have to scrub myself with chlorine to feel clean again after just standing here.

I looked over at Caroline. "My sister?" I said.

She gestured toward another door. "She's in there."

I walked toward the door and looked inside. Lisa was sitting at the table with her back toward me. She wasn't moving.

"Lisa?" I said. She didn't seem to hear me. I turned to Caroline. "What's wrong with her?"

Caroline just shook her head. "I don't know. She's

not making any sense. She keeps going on and on about a bucket or something."

I checked my kids. Jonas was hanging over the back of the armchair, and Elinor was leaning over it, careful not to touch the muggy fabric. The kittens would keep them occupied until I'd checked on my sister.

I hurried into the kitchen. Lisa didn't get up or even turn around. I'm not sure she even noticed me being there. She was just staring ahead, out the window. Had she seen us come? Then, what was she doing just sitting there?

"Lisa? Are you alright?"

No reaction.

I grabbed her shoulders and she flinched, but the chair was too close to the table for her to be able to get away from me. She stared up at me with haunted eyes. They were shiny with tears.

"My mother said something that upset her," Caroline said. "But I'm sure she'll be fine. I'll make her some tea and she'll be right as rain."

I looked over at her. "What did your mother say?" I found myself strangely protective of Lisa, as if she'd been one of my children instead of my grown-up sister.

Caroline waved one hand dismissively in my direction but didn't look at me. "It was nothing. Mother has lost her marbles completely, she didn't know what she was saying, but Lisa took it the wrong way. She completely overreacted."

Well, that sounded like my sister. "Lisa?" I tried again. "It's time to go now. Dinner is almost ready."

Caroline spun around. "Lisa is welcome to stay for dinner," she said, almost defiantly.

"Well, that's nice," I said. But when I looked at Lisa, I

could tell that something was seriously wrong. I leaned forward. "Lisa, what is it? Talk to me!"

Lisa stared up at my face, but it was almost as if she didn't see me. "He didn't kill her," she croaked. "He was innocent."

I glanced over at Caroline, but she hadn't reacted to Lisa's weird statement. Had they talked about this? Why would Lisa want to talk about Ellen with a complete stranger when she hadn't wanted to talk to her own sister? Never, in all these years?

I'm not going to deny it. That hurt.

"Of course, he didn't," I said. "We all know that. It was an accident. Don't worry about that now, Lisa. It was a long time ago."

She didn't look reassured by what I'd said, though. In fact, she looked completely distraught. "It was all my fault," she whispered. "Everything. All of it. The bucket …"

I had no idea what she was talking about. "I'm sure that's not—"

Jonas appeared in the doorway. "Mom! Can we have a kitten?"

"Not now, baby," I said to him, at the same time as Caroline replied, "Of course. Pick anyone you like. Your sister can pick one too."

I glared at Caroline but couldn't think of a polite way of telling her to fuck off and not give my children any pets. Instead, I turned back to Lisa. "I don't know what happened here, or what Mrs. Johansson said to you, but I think we'd better leav—"

"Lisa is welcome to stay," Caroline interrupted. "She can have dinner here with me."

I looked up at her. It was strange. She looked kind of

normal, if a bit dowdy and old-fashioned. But there was something in her eyes, something in the pitch of her voice, that made me think that she was a bit … disturbed. Judging by the state of this house, I wasn't surprised. This was not a good environment for my sister. Lisa was still so very fragile and confused about what happened to Ellen.

"That's nice," I said slowly. "But as I said, my husband has dinner ready. We should be going. Jonas?"

But my son was gone from the doorway. I heard his excited squeal from the other room. "She said we could get one each!" and my daughter's skeptical but cautiously excited reply. "Really? She said that?"

Fredrik was going to kill me.

I tried to get Lisa out of the chair, but she didn't want to move, and I didn't have the strength to shift her. "Come on, Lisa. We really need to go now." Nothing. Not an inch.

I let go of her and walked over to the doorway. "I did not say that you could each have a kitten," I explained. "We'll have to talk it over and discuss it with your dad as well. Maybe, someday."

"But Mo-om!" Jonas was not going to let go that easily.

"Those kittens were born today," I explained, "They can't leave their mommy."

His eyes widened. "They're cat babies?"

I nodded. "And babies have to stay with their mommy; you know that."

He pointed excitedly at the dark corner behind the armchair. "They're suckling on her teats! All lined up like the piglets in that book you used to read to me when I was little."

274

'When I was little'? We'd read that book just a couple of months ago. Was my baby in such a rush to grow up? "That's good," I said. "They are just like human babies. They can't eat cat food yet. They need their mommy. So, no, you can't have a kitten. Not today. Perhaps some other time."

His face fell like an anvil and his shoulders slumped. "Whenever you say that, it means 'never.'"

"That's not true!" I protested.

Elinor turned toward me and nodded solemnly. "It is, too," she said with a disappointed sigh. "You haven't even looked at them."

I took a deep breath but regretted it immediately when I got a nose full of dust. "Fine," I said and made my way through the wreckage over to the armchair. I hated to think what molds and fungi would be thriving in this environment.

It was dark in the corner behind the armchair. I could barely make anything out, apart from some soft shapes. I pulled my phone out and lit the flashlight, holding it up. The cat mom glared at me, her eyes glowing by the reflected light, but she didn't move. She couldn't. A neat row of little kittens was lined up, side by side along her soft belly. Just as Jonas had said, they were suckling and pressing their little paws repeatedly into their mother's fur to stimulate milk production. I wished I could say that they were cute, but they looked more like rodents than kittens at this stage.

"Very cute," I said unconvincingly. "But we really have to go now."

I turned around and started to make my way back to the kitchen. Caroline was standing by the table.

"Do you want the kittens or not?" she said, rather aggressively, I thought.

"I don't know," I replied. "I'll have to speak to my husband. I'll get back to you."

"I'll need to know by tomorrow," she said. "I'm not keeping them unless there's someone who wants them."

"Oh," I said. "That's a shame." I glanced over my shoulder toward the armchair where Jonas was still bent over the back. "If you don't want kittens, you should have neutered the cat."

Caroline shrugged. "Better to let nature take its course," she said. "We keep one or two from each litter."

"Still," I said. "It must get expensive to have so many animals put down. A co-worker of mine had to have his cat euthanized, and the vet charged him a pretty penny, as I recall."

"Oh, I don't take them to the vet," Caroline said.

"She kills them," Lisa said, completely out of the blue. "So easy. So easy to kill someone."

"Lisa?" I said. "I think we should go now." I turned around and called out to the kids. "Jonas? Elinor? We're leaving."

34

LISA

EVERYTHING WAS wrong and there was no way I could ever put it right again.

It had been wrong all this time.

All this time, I had been blaming the Hunter. And all this time, he'd just been this nice and meek guy who tried to do something sweet for his daughter.

It had never been about the kittens or about wanting to be alone with Ellen so that he could do something unspeakable to her. He had only wanted to bring a couple of kids to the farm so that his daughter could make some friends. He must have seen us running around in the woods. I'm sure we weren't as stealthy as we'd thought.

That such a random thing could have such devastating consequences.

I just moved the bucket out of the shadows, so that I'd have somewhere to put my towel.

I just. I just.

I couldn't wrap my mind around it.

It was all my fault and I couldn't live with that.

Ellen. Poor Ellen. Poor feisty Ellen, who wouldn't have balked at telling some strange lady to stop hurting those helpless kittens.

Ellen hadn't been a helpless kitten. Ellen had been a fierce, strong girl.

And still she'd ended up dead.

So wrong. So very wrong.

I couldn't deal with it. My head felt as if it was going to explode. Implode. Spontaneously combust.

Burst into flames. Oh god.

The fire.

The Hunter, or rather, Mr. Johansson, hadn't hurt Ellen. He had only wanted to be kind to his daughter. I had to stop thinking of him as the evil Hunter. He had been Caroline's father and she had loved him.

Everything had been something completely different from how I had perceived it.

I slowly became aware of voices. Here in the kitchen.

I was sitting in Caroline's kitchen, but that annoyed voice sounded like Astrid.

Using all my strengths, I pulled myself away from the maelstrom of thoughts that coursed through my broken mind and blinked against the sunlight that struggled to push through the dirty window.

Yes, my sister was here, and she was tugging at my arm. "Lisa," she said. "I think we should go now." She turned away. "Jonas. Elinor. We're leaving."

I couldn't move. There was no way I could go back to Mormor's cottage now. Not while those children were there. Not now that I knew what I'd done.

I had killed an innocent little girl.

Sure. Mrs. Johansson had done the actual pushing, but if I hadn't left that tin bucket in the middle of the floor, Ellen would have just fallen over. If it hadn't been for me, she would have gotten up again. Probably not even with a scrape or a bruise.

Instead, she had died.

No. I had to stay away from Jonas and Elinor. I had to stay away from my sister and her husband and their perfect life.

I couldn't do anything other than cause anyone pain.

I had already killed my sister's best friend.

As much as Astrid claimed to have gotten over it, I'm sure there must be scars somewhere deep inside of her as well. There had to be.

Astrid turned to me. She looked frazzled. "Come on now, Lisa. We have to go."

"She doesn't have to," Caroline said. "She's more than welcome to stay."

"Lisa, come on!" Astrid said angrily. Then she walked over to the doorway. "Jonas, get away from those kittens now!"

I could hear his little voice coming from somewhere in the other room. "I've decided. I want the black one. The one on the end."

"We're not getting any kittens, stupid," Elinor said, and she sounded so much like her mother at that age that it made me nauseated.

"But she said—"

"Jonas, I won't tell you again." Astrid was really angry now.

Caroline came to my nephew's rescue. "The black one, you said? I'll keep that for you then. You can come back for it in eight to twelve weeks."

"I told you that we'll have to discuss it—" Astrid tried to be firm, but Caroline wasn't listening.

"And if your mother doesn't want you to have a cat," she said, her voice raised to speak over my sister's objections, "you can keep it here. You're welcome to come visit it anytime you like."

Somehow, I managed to turn around and I saw Astrid through the doorway. Her face was red and I could tell that she was near the breaking point. No way in hell she'd want her children coming here.

This was *not* her kind of place.

Jonas didn't see it, though. Or if he did, he was blissfully ignorant of what Astrid's facial expression meant. "Can I really? Oh, thank you!"

My sister made a noise deep in her throat. It might have been funny under different circumstances. But no one was laughing now.

"Can I speak to you in the kitchen, Caroline?" Astrid said, and there was a tension in her voice that would have frightened anyone.

Caroline wasn't scared, though. I'm not sure she understood what she'd done. She didn't seem that entuned to nuance. Growing up with only her mother would do that, I supposed. If someone didn't constantly yell at you that you are useless, then that must mean that they like you, right?

They both came back into the kitchen and Astrid began to close the door, but then she seemed to change her mind.

"Lisa. Take the children and go ahead back to the cottage, please. I left my phone down by the lake and Fredrik must be wondering where we got to."

She gestured at me to leave, and somehow, I managed to get up off the chair and move out the door into the sitting room. I wasn't going back to the cottage, though. I was never going back there. I just needed to get out of this house. This maudlin memorial of all the things that had gone wrong all those years ago.

So many lives, wasted.

Elinor was standing by the door to the hallway, her arms crossed and her brow wrinkled in an exact replica of her mother's frown. Jonas was over by the armchair, constantly glancing over his shoulder at the corner where the kittens were.

"Come on, doofus," Elinor said to her brother. "We're leaving."

Jonas took a step back and leaned against the armchair. "I want to stay here with the kittens. I'll go with Mommy later."

Elinor didn't want to give in. "She told us to go ahead."

"Yes, we're all going," I said and was surprised at how calm my voice sounded. I felt nothing but calm. "Come along now, Jonas."

I ushered Elinor before me out into the hallway, but when I looked back, Jonas was still standing by the armchair.

"I'm just going to say goodbye to my kitten," he said.

"All right," I replied. The walls were closing in on me and I needed to get out of here, now. "We'll wait for you right outside."

He turned around and clambered up on the armchair, and I followed Elinor out the front door. Just as I stepped across the threshold, I heard Mrs. Johansson from upstairs. Her pitiful "Caroliiine" gave me chills. That dreadful woman.

Elinor walked over to Caroline's car and shoved her

hands in the back pockets of her cutoff shorts. "We're not getting any kittens," she said again.

"You might," I said, but she shook her head.

From inside, I could hear Mrs. Johansson's cries from upstairs. Caroline would be frantic. But that was good because then she'd be too busy to notice that I left.

Sneaking away without saying goodbye didn't feel quite right, but at the moment, that was the best I could do.

35

CAROLINE

LISA'S SISTER was angry with me. I couldn't understand why, though. I thought that she'd be pleased.

"I think we got off on the wrong foot," she said. "And I don't want that. We'll be keeping Britta's cottage as a summer home, and I want to have good relationships with all the neighbors. That is important to me."

I nodded slowly. "That is important to me too. Mother was never much for mixing with the neighbors, but I want things to be different."

Astrid frowned. "Good. That said, my children will not be getting any kittens. And I don't want them coming here."

From upstairs, my mother's keening voice penetrated the floorboards. "Carooooline!"

I buried my face in my hands and groaned. How was anything ever supposed to change if everything always stayed the same? I wanted things to be different. I wanted to have friends. I wanted there to be children here at the farm.

That little boy. So adorable. So open. So ... pure.

Of course, I wanted to give him a kitten. I wanted to give him anything he asked for.

"I just wanted to do something nice for your little boy," I said, pulling my hands away from my face. "There's no need to be angry."

"My son doesn't understand how much responsibility a kitten entails," Astrid said. "It was kind of you to offer, but I really would have preferred if you'd checked with me first. Now he's got his hopes up."

"But he can have a kitten," I gestured toward the closed door, but Mother's wails continued and I couldn't ignore them anymore. "I'm sorry," I said. "I'll just go and check on my mother real quick."

"That's fine," Astrid said. "We're leaving."

"No, no," I said and hurried past her. "Don't go. Please don't."

I flung the door open. Jonas startled on top of the armchair. He looked guilty. "I'm sorry," he said. "I just wanted to say goodbye to my kitten."

"That's fine, sweetheart," I said, my heart swelling. Such a dear boy. "You can stay as long as you like.

"We're not staying," Astrid said behind me as Mother called out for me again.

My head was throbbing and I couldn't think straight. "But he's welcome to," I said to Astrid. "Please don't make him leave. Don't tell him he can't come here. I'd love to have him. He is more than welcome."

Jonas pointed at the candlesticks on the windowsill. "What happened to your candles?" he asked.

Through the dirty window, I could make out the bulky silhouette of Lisa, standing over by my car with the little girl. Was she going to leave without saying goodbye? "Oh …" I said. "The sun melted them."

He jumped down from the armchair and made his way over to the window, gently prodding the nearest candle. "But they're not soft."

"No, they melted on a really warm day. Today hasn't been as warm, so they hardened again."

"I didn't know candles could do that," he said. "I'm the one who lights the candles."

Mother keened again and my head felt as if it would split in two. I wanted to run outside and talk to Lisa before she left, but I also wanted to stay here with this darling little boy. Angry Astrid was behind me, and even though I couldn't see her, I was sure that she was making angry faces at her little boy.

And Mother ...

Again I wished she would just die already. And then I was immediately assaulted by shame. What a terrible thing to think about one's own mother. I gritted my teeth and started toward the hallway stairs.

"I'm really good at lighting candles," Jonas said. "I can usually get the match lit on the first stroke."

"That's great," I told him, but my attention was elsewhere. If Mother didn't let me get back downstairs right away, Lisa would leave, and she probably wouldn't come back. Even if she'd want to—which she probably wouldn't—her sister might not let her. "I'll be right back," I told him, or her, or anyone who would listen.

Then I ran upstairs to see what Mother wanted.

36

ASTRID

THE WOMAN WAS DERANGED. That much was clear. I had to get my kids and my sister out of here.

This was seriously beginning to undermine my love for this place. As much as I'd looked forward to our summers here at the cottage, I was afraid that things would become different from now on.

It might be a good thing to just leave. Rude, of course, but this Caroline person was not someone I wanted in my life, or in my children's lives.

Mormor had known this all along, I guess. That's why we never bothered with the Johanssons.

I stood in the doorway into the kitchen, staring at the mess in front of me, vaguely aware of Jonas over by the window, poking the melted candles. Lisa and Elinor were outside waiting for us.

"Come along now, sweetie," I told Jonas.

"Just a minute," he said. "I just want to see ..."

I made my way over toward the door, my eyes wandering around the piles and piles of stuff. What a nightmare! I couldn't imagine ever living like this.

"Oh!" Jonas said, and there was something in his voice that made my head spin around in his direction.

My son was standing by the window, a box of matches in one hand and a lit match in the other. He had tried to light one of the melted almost-up-side-down candles. The problem was the dusty spiderwebs that covered the entire window, all the way from the radiator beneath to the thin, withered synthetic curtains. The small flame of the match had ignited just a few threads at first, but by the time I'd turned my head, the whole window was engulfed in bright yellow flames.

"Jonas, no!" I yelled at him.

Jonas didn't move. Instead, he just started screaming, his high-pitched hysterical scream that always drove me up the wall.

"It's fine, Jonas," I said loudly. "Just back away from the flames."

I looked around to try and find something to put the fire out with, but there was nothing in this room that wasn't at least as flammable as the curtains. The net curtains melted and dripped down onto the table where an ancient jigsaw puzzle lay, covered in dry leaves from a long-diseased potted plant, and all of it just ignited with a surprisingly loud poof. Tall flames shot up between me and my son.

There was something about seeing him there, behind the flames, that just broke me.

"Jonas!" I screamed at the top of my lungs.

I tried to reach him, I did. But as I got closer, the flames leaped and spread over to the sofa, to a stack of boxes, down to the woven carpet on the floor. They weren't just in front of me anymore; they were behind me and on both sides.

"Jonas!" I screamed again.

My son hadn't stopped screaming. I don't know where he found the breath to keep going because I already found it difficult to breathe. I tried to push some things out of the way so that I could reach him, but it was just too hot. Flames shot up everywhere and singed the hairs off my arms.

This wasn't the way it was supposed to be. This wasn't what was supposed to happen. I'd had a plan, but this wasn't it. This was wrong, and I didn't know how to make it right.

I made my way back toward the kitchen door, thinking that I'd be able to make my way to Jonas from that direction, but by the time I got there, I realized my mistake. The bookshelves had caught fire, and there was no longer any way to get to the front door.

Even if I could get to Jonas, there was no way for us to get out of here.

37

LISA

ELINOR GROANED BESIDE ME. "JONAS!" she said crossly in a voice that echoed her mother's voice from thirty years ago. "What did you do?"

I turned my head and saw flames inside the window. Before I'd even taken it in, Jonas started to scream. It was the most awful sound I'd ever heard.

"Jonas!" Elinor screamed, but the annoyance from just now was gone. "Moooom!"

I patted my pockets, but my phone was back at the cottage, next to Mormor's bed. "Have you got a phone, Elinor?" I asked.

"No," she whined. "No screens at the cottage, Mom says."

The flames had completely engulfed the window, and I could barely hear Jonas's screams. I grabbed Elinor's arm and turned her toward me.

"I need you to run back to the cottage," I said, staring into her wide, frightened eyes. "Back to your dad. Tell him to call the fire department. Tell him to hurry."

She just stood there, her eyes wide with fear. "B-but, Mom is in there …"

"Go now, Elinor," I said, pushing her toward the corner of the house. "I'll go and get them out of there, but you need to get the fire department. Run home to your dad, now!"

Another push and she set off. I staggered toward the porch and back inside the house. The heat came toward me on the threshold, like a fist right in the face. Jonas was still screaming somewhere in there. And Astrid.

I never even hesitated. Not this time. Of course, I was scared. Panicked, even. But Astrid and Jonas were in danger, and this time I was not going to chicken out.

Even if it killed me, I was going back for my sister and her son.

Shaking off the fear, I took a couple of steps toward the fire and then stopped. I could barely breathe, and I wasn't even in the room yet. Unbelievable.

The whole sitting room was already filled with flames and smoke. A thick, black smoke that stank of toxins and carcinogens. We're never going to get out of here alive, I thought. And then I felt it.

The resigned acceptance.

Yes, this was bad, but I could see the danger now. I could hear it, smell it, taste it.

Fear of something tangible was a completely different beast compared to the general anxiety I'd been living with most of my life. If anything, seeing the horrific sight in front of me made me almost calm.

This was it. My chance to, if not make things right, then at least do something to make up for that terrible thing that I'd done when I had left Ellen behind. I might not be able to save them, but I would die trying.

I looked around and spotted the door underneath the stairs. Where Caroline had fetched the rag when I was sick. I hurried over and pulled it open. Yes. It was a utility closet, with a large stainless-steel sink. A bucket on the floor had rags draped over the edge. I turned the tap on and soaked both rags, as well as a thick knitted cardigan that hung from a hook out in the hallway. Then I splashed water all over my face and hair and the front of my dress.

With the sopping wet cardigan over my shoulders, I returned to the hallway. Jonas had stopped screaming. As eerie as that sound had been, the silence was worse.

"Jonas!" I called out. "Astrid!"

No reply.

I covered my mouth with the sleeve of the wet cardigan and breathed through the fabric. It didn't help, not much. But I didn't care. I had to get to my sister. And to Jonas.

If it was the last thing I did.

The bookshelves were on fire and burning books tumbled to the floor on my right as I made my way around the armchairs and the sofa. One of them hit my arm and I cried out, but then bit down on the fabric. There was no air in this room. No air at all. But somehow, I kept going.

This is it, I thought. This is where I die. This is the end of me, the end of it all.

Well, not quite yet. I have something I need to do first.

The fire was hot. And so loud. Just like in my dreams.

Not dreams. Memories.

Oh, please no, I thought. No more. Not now.

Somehow, I made it over to the kitchen door. A cough came toward me through the darkness.

"Astrid?" I called.

"Lisa," she croaked. "No, Lisa, no! Get out of here!"

Her face was black and her arms were streaked with soot. She had grabbed some dishtowels and soaked them and was trying to make her way to Jonas, but the towels were thin and flimsy and didn't hold as much water as my thick rags. The flames and the smoke from the couch forced her back. "Jonas!" she screamed. "I'm coming. Mommy's coming."

No reply. She made another attempt to push through, but some sparks ignited her dress and flames licked her arm. I wrapped my arms around her and put the fire out with the sopping rags. She tried to pull out of my grip, but I turned around and pushed her toward the door.

"I'll get Jonas," I said. "You have to get out of here before you catch fire. Go! Now!"

She shook her head. "Jonas!" she screamed. No reply. She turned toward me. "Where's Elinor?"

"She went back to the cottage," I said. "She's getting Fredrik to call the fire brigade." I pushed her toward the door again. "You have to go now, Astrid. You have to get out of here." A final push. "I'll get Jonas and meet you outside."

She looked at me, her eyes squinting from the smoke. "Do you promise?" she said, and her voice sounded so weak. So completely unlike her.

"I promise," I said, not meaning a word I said. I just had to get Astrid out of here. We were all going to die. Jonas and me. And Caroline and her evil mother. The only tragedy there would be my beautiful nephew. But I could still save my perfect sister. She could go on. She still had Elinor. And Fredrik. She could still have a good life. "Go, Astrid. Hurry."

I gave her one of the wet rags to breathe through and draped the other over my hair. The whole room was burning now, and sparks were coming at me from all sides.

"He was over by the window!" Astrid said, pointing. I nodded and started moving in that direction. When I glanced back, I saw her backing reluctantly toward the door. I waved at her, and then she finally left.

This was it. Jonas hadn't made a sound for several minutes. He'd been in the thick of it from the start, and I was pretty sure that the smoke inhalation had already killed him, but I wasn't about to leave him in here to burn. That poor child.

And if I failed in my attempt to get him out of here, at least he wouldn't have to die alone.

Pushing the burning rug off the couch created an opening in the wall of flames in front of me. I couldn't see anything at all. The smoke was in my eyes and in my nose, and my throat was closing up. I'm pretty sure that my hair was on fire, despite the wet rag, but I couldn't reach to put it out. Somehow, I managed to find enough air to call out one last time. "Jonas!"

"We're over here," a thin little voice said, all the way over in the corner. I made my way toward him, coughing.

I stumbled on something and fell to my knees, crying out from the pain. It turned out to be a blessing in disguise because I found some air underneath the thick smoke. Right. That's what they'd told us in the fire drills in school. Stay low.

Now, where was my nephew? I peered into the smoke. Was that him over there?

"Jonas, come here!" I pleaded.

Jonas didn't move. He was behind the armchair, where the kittens had been. In his arms, a squirming little hairless rat-like creature. He was staring at me. "I'm sorry," he said, his bottom lip trembling. "I didn't mean to do it."

"I know," I said. The lack of oxygen was making me light-headed. We had to get out of here. Him being alive changed everything. I couldn't let him burn.

I had to save him.

"Come here," I said again, crawling forward on hands and knees before reaching in behind the armchair. My fingers found fabric, and I pulled him toward me by his T-shirt. My back was so hot; the wet fabric of the cardigan was boiling against my skin. I wrapped my arms around him and started to back away from the corner when the window exploded behind me. Shards of glass flew in all directions. Some of them hit me, but that was the least of my problem. I was running out of time. Running out of air. Running out of … life.

Staggering to my feet with the small boy in my arms, I turned around and felt a gust of fresh air coming from the place where the window had been. The air was fanning the flames, but the oxygen was more than worth the burns as I made my way over to the empty window frame. The slats had more or less burned through, and with the glass gone, it was easy to knock out the remnants of the wooden window frames. The wall was on fire, though, and the ground outside was quite a long way down, even though we were on the ground floor. Even worse than that, a pile of rusted old scrap metal, car parts, and farm equipment created a deadly moat underneath the window. Astrid was nowhere to be seen. She must have run back to the cottage.

I would never be able to climb out of the broken window. There was just no way. There was nothing for me to stand on that wasn't already on fire, and even if I'd managed to get up on the burning windowsill, I'd be staked on the rusty iron junk outside. But maybe I could throw Jonas far enough that he could clear the pile? Children were resilient; I'd read that somewhere. They often survived falls from high windows because they were so relaxed.

Jonas was stiff as a board in my arms, though, and he was clutching the wet cardigan with a death grip. "You'll have to jump, Jonas," I said. "Go on! You have to."

"I can't," he whimpered and didn't let go.

My strength was waning fast. "Please, Jonas. We have to get out of here. The whole house is going to burn down," I pleaded, but he refused to let go of me.

"It's too high up," he said. "My kitten will never make it."

Oh, the kitten. Poor helpless kittens. Something moved underneath his T-shirt, and I realized that he had stuffed the poor animal under his shirt when I'd pulled him away from the corner. The poor animals. They didn't have much of a chance, did they, Caroline's wretched kittens. If they didn't burn, she'd drown them. So easy. So easy to kill. Just dunk them in a bucket.

Oh, god. Buckets.

I staggered and leaned against the burning wall but then yanked back when my skin started to fizzle. "Jonas, you have to be a big boy now," I said. "You have to jump."

"No!" he protested and clung even tighter to me.

I leaned over the windowsill, pulling as much of the outside air as I could get into my lungs. It wasn't enough, and I could feel myself starting to black out. Someone appeared around the corner of the house. Fredrik.

"Over here!" I called to him. "Fredrik! Over here!"

My brother-in-law was a runner. I never thought I'd appreciate that in a person, but in this moment, I was truly grateful for his ridiculous lycra outfits and healthy lifestyle. He had probably run all the way from the cottage, but he was barely winded when he came up to the window, right beneath us.

"Your dad is here," I said to Jonas, and that was the magic word because Jonas turned around in my arms and almost dove out the broken window, howling like an animal.

"Oh, god, Jonas!" Fredrik shouted and grabbed his son midair, backing away from the house, checking him. "Are you alright?"

Jonas clung to his dad. "I didn't mean to," he whimpered.

The roar of the flames. His tiny little voice. I didn't mean to. No. No. No. My brain was going up in flames. I couldn't take it. But at least, now they were all safe. Nothing mattered anymore. I could let go. Just breathe in all the deadly smoke that surrounded me and let it all be over.

Fredrik looked up at me. "Where's Astrid?" he shouted over the roar from the flames.

I pulled myself back to the present and stared at him.

"Isn't she with you?" He shook his head. "No, Elinor came to find me. I haven't seen Astrid." He stared up at the burning building, his hands still moving over Jonas' body, checking him for injuries. "Oh, god, Astrid …"

I leaned out the window and looked over toward the porch. My sister wasn't there. She wasn't anywhere. Oh, no. She must have gone upstairs to get Caroline.

"I'll get her," I said.

And then I turned and walked back into the flames.

38

CAROLINE

MOTHER HAD WET HERSELF, again. This was the final straw. I was tempted to just leave her sitting there, but the nurse would be able to tell, probably. We couldn't have that.

I fetched clean clothes and wet wipes but had only just managed to peel off her sopping underpants when I heard someone screaming. It sounded like a child. Like that darling little boy.

"You've left the pot on the stove again," Mother muttered. "You'll burn the house down, one of these days, you useless—"

"Oh, shut up," I said, and for once, she did as she was told. Well, well, wonders never seize. I wiped her down, wrinkling my nose at the acrid smell of urine. Not until I stood up and turned to pick up the clean underpants did I see it. Thin wisps of smoke curled in through the gap under the door. It almost looked beautiful in the semidarkness. Like something magical.

Then it hit me. The choking sensation that comes

from a lack of oxygen. Like something tight wrapped around my throat.

I should have run; I know that. But I didn't. Instead, I just stood there, staring at the smoke. The child kept screaming. It was surreal. All these years, with just me and Mother in this big, awful house. And now Lisa and her sister were downstairs, and her sister's lovely children.

And the awful house was going up in flames.

I wasn't especially brave in general, but fire frightened me more than anything else. This was how he must have felt, I thought. This was how he'd died.

I turned and stared at Mother. She was coughing and leaned over toward the window, fumbling for the latch. The window was stuck, of course. Just like everything in this house. I pushed her to the side and managed to get it open, gasping in the clean air in large gulps.

Once my head stopped spinning, I pulled myself together.

"We have to get out of here," I said. "Come on, Mother."

"What did you do?" she scolded. "You useless piece of—"

"STOP IT!" I screamed. "I didn't DO anything. I never DID anything. I was a GOOD GIRL!"

She stared at me, uncomprehending. Then she coughed again. And a thought struck me.

Slowly, I backed away from her, toward the door.

"What are you doing?" she croaked. "Where are you going?"

"I'm just going to pull the pot off the stove," I said,

and I was surprised at how calm I sounded. This was it. This was my chance. I could just walk out the door and leave her here. The house would burn. Mother would burn.

And I would be free.

The idea was exhilarating. Intoxicating. It made me dizzy. Or perhaps that was the smoke.

"It's only fair," I said, looking at the woman who had ruined my life. "You're the one that should have died that night. You're the one who deserved to die." I placed my hand on the door handle but yanked it back when it burned my palm. "You should have died, not Father. We could have been happy without you. But without him, I never had a chance."

I pulled my cardigan down over my hand and made another attempt at opening the door. Thick, black smoke welled into the room.

"Caroline!" Mother wailed. "You can't leave me here!"

I started to leave, but as soon as I'd stepped out onto the landing, a shadow came toward me through the smoke.

It was Lisa's sister. "The house is on fire!" she choked through a wet rag that she held in front of her mouth. "We have to get out of here."

I started to move toward the stairs, pushing her in front of me, but Mother called out for me again, and at the sound of her voice, Astrid stopped at the top of the stairs.

"Your mother," she said. "We'll have to carry her. I don't think the fire department will get here in time."

She turned around and hurried into Mother's room.

I didn't know what to do. There was a roar coming from downstairs, and the smoke had filled the entire landing.

"We have to get out of here," I shouted at Astrid. "Leave her!"

She'd been almost all the way over to Mother's chair when she heard me. She spun around and stared at me. "We can manage her, between us," she said, leaning over the table to fill her lungs over by the window. "Come on, Caroline!" She gestured at me to come back.

"She was going to leave me here!" Mother wailed. "My daughter was going to let me burn!"

"Don't be silly," Astrid said. "She was just going for help." She stared at me. "Weren't you, Caroline?"

Every part of me wanted to just run down the stairs and out of the burning house. The screaming from downstairs had stopped and I was sure that everyone else had made it out. It was just the three of us in here now.

And the best thing would be if only two of us made it out of here alive.

"You don't understand," I said, leaning against the doorpost. The smoke was making me light-headed. "You don't know what she's like."

Astrid frowned at me. A sound as if from an explosion came from downstairs. "We have to get her out of here," she said. "Come on, Caroline. Help me carry her."

I didn't move. "She killed your friend," I said. Four little words. A part of me couldn't believe that I'd said them out loud. Another part of me felt giddy with relief. I had done it. I had spoken the truth.

Would it set me free?

Another cough from Mother. I took one step inside the room, beckoning to Astrid, who was staring at me. "Come," I said. "Leave her. It's better this way."

But Astrid didn't move. She just stood there, looking from me to Mother and then back at me again. "You're insane," she said. "If you're not going to help me, I'll have to carry her myself."

"No!" I said. "Get away from her!"

It was so frustrating. Why had she come? She was going to ruin everything. This was my one chance. I had no idea what had happened downstairs, but this house burning to the ground could be the best thing that had ever happened to me. If Mother burned too.

There was a nice symmetry to it, I guess. One fire, one dead parent, had ruined my life.

Another fire, another dead parent could set me free.

Heavy steps came up the stairs behind me. I groaned and pushed my hair from my face. What was this? Rush hour? After all the years of just me and Mother, the house suddenly felt crowded. I couldn't wait to get out of here.

Get out and watch it burn, as I'd watched the barn burn to the ground all those years ago. I could still recall the hollow feeling in my stomach, the intense heat. The deafening roar.

I'd never known that fires could be so loud.

That same roar was coming from downstairs now. Time to get out before it was too late.

"Astrid!"

I spun around and saw Lisa come staggering across the landing toward me. She looked like she'd been through hell, all covered in soot and grime. The skin underneath her nose was completely black, and a cut above her eyebrow seeped dark red blood down the side of her face. Was that my cardigan she was wearing? It was many sizes too small for her. It looked ridiculous.

"Get out of here, Lisa!" I said. "You have to get out."

She didn't seem to hear me. She didn't even look at me. Pushing past, she repeated her call. "Astrid!"

Her sister just stared at her. Then she pointed to Mother. "Caroline says ..." she said, her voice faint. "Ellen?"

Lisa crossed the floor, grabbing her sister by the arm. "I know. But you have to get out of here, now."

Astrid's eyes darted to the door. "Where's Jonas? Couldn't you get to him?"

"He's fine. He's outside, with Fredrik," Lisa said, dragging her toward the door.

"Fredrik's here?" Astrid let herself be pulled halfway across the floor, but then she stopped and tore her arm from Lisa's grip. "But we can't leave her here," she said, pointing at Mother. "Help me carry her." She scowled at me. "Caroline was going to leave her."

Lisa grabbed her sister again and tugged her toward the door, putting all her considerable weight behind it. Her skinny sister didn't stand a chance. "Forget about them," Lisa said. "You have to get out of here."

Forget about *them*?

My heart broke, hearing her say that. That she'd let Mother burn, that I could understand. After all, Mother had made her life hell as well.

But I had thought that Lisa was my friend.

The smoke inhalation was really starting to get to me, but I managed to stagger out onto the landing and grab the door, slamming it shut behind me. Then I stood outside on the landing, staring at it. I didn't have a key. Looking around, I spotted an antique chair that mother had placed in the nook at the top of the stairs many years ago. No one had ever sat there. I grabbed it and jammed it under the door handle.

Then I turned and walked down the stairs.

39

ASTRID

I STARED at the closed door. The old woman behind me coughed and then coughed again. This day had taken a turn.

Lisa pushed past me over to the door and grabbed the door handle. It must have been hot because she pulled her hand back as if it had burned her. She used the other hand, where she had a thick rag, but the handle didn't turn. She put her elbow against the door and pushed, but it didn't budge. Again, with more force.

"Lisa," I heard myself say. "You're bleeding."

She looked over at me. Her eyes were empty with fatigue and lack of oxygen. Her skin gray underneath a thick layer of soot. "I'm sorry," she said. "I shouldn't have come back."

I pulled myself up and tightened my fists. "Not now, Lisa. We'll talk later. But not now."

She shook her head slowly. "Now might be all we've got," she said, and her voice sounded coarse. "Unless we can find another way out of here."

My mind was racing, trying to process all this new

information and come up with a solution. Come on, I told myself. This is what you do best, Astrid. Find a way.

That fire, though. It was making it impossible to think clearly. The smoke hurt my throat and I suddenly understood my son's terror at the sight of an open flame. Standing here, I regretted having been so dismissive of his fears. This was what he had been afraid of, and I couldn't blame him. This was a nightmare. Being inside of a house as it burned to the ground.

But no, I was not going to give up. There had a be a way out.

Pushing Lisa out of the way, I tried to open the door. It was jammed shut. Fine. Find another way.

Hurrying over to the window, I pushed the thick drapes to one side in a cloud of dust and leaned out. The ground was disturbingly far down. The fire was roaring, but I could hear voices. My children's voices, screaming for me.

"Fredrik!" I hollered. "Fredrik! I'm over here!"

Leaning out as far as I could through the window, I gasped for air, but the smoke was everywhere, and the heat coming up through the floorboard was stifling. We didn't have much time.

Fredrik came running around the side of the house. "Astrid!" he screamed. "You have to get out of there."

Oh, my darling husband. Stating the obvious was his biggest flaw. "The door is blocked," I yelled. "We can't get out."

Elinor and Jonas came around the corner as well. Seeing them brought tears to my eyes. Lisa had managed to get Jonas out of that hell. I glanced over my shoulder at her. She was still trying to open the door.

She had gotten my son out and come back inside for me.

She had put herself in harm's way for us. Biting my lip, I blinked the tears from my eyes. Only yesterday, I had accused her of being selfish. But she must care about us; otherwise, she wouldn't be up here. She could have left.

My sister had come back for us. I'd gotten my sister back after all these years.

Now, I had to get her out of here, or we would both perish.

The old woman coughed again and tried to push me away from the window. I turned toward her. "Is there another way out of here?"

"My daughter was going to let me burn," she whined. "That useless girl. That hopeless, useless girl."

I didn't understand how this frail creature could have had anything to do with what happened to Ellen all those years ago, but I pulled away from her withered hands all the same. There was something about her that gave me the creeps.

"Is there another way out of here?" I said again, louder this time.

"We're all going to die," the woman wailed. "That stupid girl just left us here to die."

"Astrid!" Fredrik shouted from outside. "The fire department is on their way, but you have to get out of there now!"

"Find a ladder," I shouted back.

He looked around the yard, but even I, who had a much better view than him, could see that there was nothing there. Nothing useful, at least. Piles of overgrown trash here and there, rusted iron and farm equipment from when the farm had been run properly, decades ago. Probably things that had been in the barn over there when it burned. I remembered the barn as being huge. There must have been a ladder in there, surely?

"Look over by the barn!" I shouted again and pointed.

Fredrik ran across the yard and started to scour the ground over by the cracked concrete slab. The grass was almost to his thighs.

"Mommy!" Elinor wailed. "You have to get out of there!"

"I'm trying, baby," I said. The wall underneath the window was too smooth, with no ledges or anything to put my feet on. And even if I could have climbed down, there was no way that Lisa would be able to.

Lisa came up behind me, leaning out as well. "It's not too far down," she said. "I'll lower you down. Fredrik will catch you. You'll be alright."

I shook my head. "But what about you?"

My sister stared at me as if I'd said something stupid. "Yeah," she said slowly. "What about me?"

Fredrik came running back toward the house. "I can't find a ladder," he hollered. Elinor shrieked hysterically, both hands against her face. Jonas just stared up at me mutely. Oh, God. My children would see me die if I didn't figure this out.

"You'll have to catch her," Lisa called to him. She turned toward me. "Go. You have to go to your kids, Astrid. They need you." She glanced at Elinor and Jonas. "Listen to them." I opened my mouth to protest but she shook her head. "Go. Be with your family. It's OK, Astrid. It's for the best."

I shook my head. "No," I mouthed. "No," I said, louder, but then I choked on the heavy smoke and started coughing.

By the time I had caught my breath again, Lisa had yanked the heavy drapes off the rods. She tugged on the fabric. It was gray with dust and smelled hazardous, but it didn't disintegrate immediately, as I would have expected.

"I'm not leaving you here," I said, my voice hoarse. "I can't do that, Lisa."

She lowered one of the curtains out the window, holding on tight to one end. Closing her eyes, she swayed slightly. Then she pulled herself together and opened her eyes again. The blood from the cut on her forehead had dried, a dark red crust in a Rorschach shape all down the side of her face. She looked awful. But I finally recognized her. My sister. My fearless, determined sister, as she'd been before … I turned and stared at the frail old woman in the armchair. She was still muttering to herself, but her head was slumped to one side. She didn't look strong enough to swat a fly. Oh, God. Ellen.

I didn't know what to think. And for me, this was literally a first.

"Go," Lisa said, bracing herself against the wall by the window. "Now, while I can still help you."

"I'm not leaving you here!" I screamed. This was insane. How could she expect me to—

"If you stay here, we both die." Lisa looked me straight in the eye without even blinking. How could she not be afraid? And, yes, she might be right, but you never knew.

"The fire department is on its way," I said.

Lisa nodded. "I know. And they may or may not get here. But you need to get out of here now. Go, be with your kids. They need you, Astrid."

She shook the curtain and leaned out the window to see how far down it reached. I followed her gaze. Fredrik was standing underneath the window, his arms reaching up toward me.

"I'm right here, Astrid," he called up to me. "Just jump. I'll catch you!"

My eyes stung, and it wasn't just because of the smoke. He was always there for me. Even now, when I was in more danger than I'd ever been, I felt safer, knowing that he was here. Blinking rapidly, I climbed out the window, holding on to the thick curtain fabric. It creaked and tore a little but didn't give way.

Lisa held on to the other end of the curtain. Our eyes met just before I started to lower myself to the ground. She smiled faintly. As if this was ok. Like there was any way this could ever be ok.

"The fire department is coming," I said.

She nodded quickly. "Hurry," she said, her voice strained from the effort. "I don't know how much longer I can hold you."

My eyes blurred and I swallowed hard but did as she'd said and climbed as quickly as I could down the thick curtain. Just when I started to run out of fabric, I felt Fredrik's fingers against my bare leg.

"I got you!" he said, and I let the last few inches of moldy curtain fabric slip through my fingers.

Fredrik grabbed me, but the impact knocked him to the ground, and we fell, one on top of the other in the tall grass. I rolled off him, gasping for air. I barely had time to fill my lungs before Elinor and Jonas threw themselves on top of me. They were both crying hysterically, and I wrapped my arms around them, hugging them tightly.

Safe. I was safe. We were all safe.

I wiped the tears from Jonas' sooty cheek. A part of me had thought that I'd lost him in that inferno, and I could hardly believe that he was here, seemingly unharmed.

"It's alright," Fredrik said, to the kids or to me, I wasn't sure. "We're all alright."

I sat up, still clutching my children, and looked up toward the window I had climbed out of. Gray smoke welled out through the open window that gaped like an empty eye socket now that the curtains were gone.

No. We weren't all alright. Not all of us.

Not my sister.

40

LISA

W<small>HEN</small> A<small>STRID</small> <small>LET</small> <small>GO</small> of the curtain, I fell backward, collapsing onto the floor behind the armchair where Mrs. Johansson was sitting, muttering and coughing. The room was hot and filled with smoke, and as I lay there, I thought that this was it. I had done what I'd come here to do. I had found out the truth about Ellen. And I had made sure that Elinor and Jonas were safe.

Staring up at the dark ceiling, seeing the swirls of thick smoke above me, I felt life draining from my body. It hadn't been a good life, but I had at least done something right in the end. It wasn't much, but it would have to do.

Saving Astrid and Jonas hadn't been an act of heroism. It turns out, none of them would have been in danger if it hadn't been for me. But at least they were safe now.

I rolled over on one side and coughed. The floor underneath me was sizzling hot, and the flames had started to break up through the boards here and there. Not where I was laying, thankfully. This was going to

312

get worse before it was over; I understood that. It was a horrible way to die.

Jonas' words echoed through my mind. *I didn't mean to.* And the last of the barrier to my blocked childhood memories crumbled.

I hadn't meant to, either.

A sob racked my body, and I blinked the tears from my eyes. It was too much to bear, but fortunately, it looked as if I wouldn't have to bear it much longer.

Staring across the room, I saw that the ugly wall hanging had caught fire. Spreading from the lower right-hand corner, it burned fast, like a thin sheet of paper instead of the thick wool that it was. One minute it was there. The next minute the wall behind it came into view.

It was the same kind of rough-hewn planks as all the other walls in the house, but in the middle of them was something I hadn't expected.

A door.

I lay there, looking at the door, breathing slow jagged breaths that probably pulled more smoke than oxygen into my poor lungs. My head was spinning and I was starting to fade. Why was there a door there, behind the wall hanging? And where did it lead?

It didn't matter; I knew that. Nothing mattered anymore.

But slowly, a couple of the messed-up pieces of my mind fell into place.

I was trapped in here. There was no way out.

Except …

Now, there was a door.

Getting up off the floor wasn't easy. I had inhaled a lot of smoke and my head hurt so bad. Everything hurt so bad. If I just stayed here, surely it would all soon be over. All the pain would go away.

But no.

Something made me get up off the floor. I made it onto my knees and then fell over. OK. Try again. Up on one knee. Then the other.

One foot. And the other.

The whole room keeled over, and I fell, hard, hitting the floorboards with a dull thud.

Okay. Walking was apparently not an option. Besides, down here by the floor was where the last oxygen was.

I crawled on my hands and knees across the floor. Perhaps the door wasn't real? Perhaps it was just a figment of my imagination? Yes, that must be it.

But the figment had a handle that felt solid and not as red-hot as the handle on the door to the hallway. The figment of a door opened to reveal the ugliest bathroom I'd ever seen. Poop brown vanity and toilet, and an orange-colored vinyl mat on the floor that not even the most rabid retro lover would want to bring back.

I looked back at Mrs. Johansson. She was still sitting in her armchair, staring out the window. A couch racked her wizened body, but she almost didn't seem to notice. Her gnarled fingers rested on her lap, and her face was distorted by a hateful grimace.

Astrid had wanted to save her, but I saw nothing that deserved saving. If she hadn't been such a bitch to her daughter, Ellen wouldn't have died. Yes, I placed the bucket in the wrong place, but there was no way I could have known what would happen.

As much as I felt to blame for Ellen's death, I hadn't killed her.

Mrs. Johansson probably hadn't meant to kill her either. She just hadn't cared if Ellen lived or died. Just another worthless girl. As useless as a litter of kittens and just as easy to kill. Mrs. Johansson had been a bitter, nasty woman, and so many lives had been ruined because of her actions. If she had taken responsibility for those actions and called the authorities, instead of having her husband hide what had happened, my life would have turned out differently. Ellen would still be dead, but I might have had a chance.

Maybe there had been a way to make me a real girl again, back then? Before I turned into a rag doll for good?

There were probably reasons why Caroline's mother had turned out the way she had. But try as I might, I couldn't find any pity for her.

And I couldn't bring myself to want to save her.

Crawling across the threshold into the dreadful bathroom, I pulled the door closed behind me.

41

CAROLINE

THE HOUSE WAS BURNING. I stood by the road, staring up at the façade. So much smoke. Flames came out of the windows that exploded in glittering fragments of glass as the fire moved from room to room.

Tears ran down my cheeks in silent grief. So many emotions, all tangled up, and I didn't know what made me more upset. Losing my home. Or gaining my freedom.

Glancing up the road, I felt a lump in my throat. Still no sirens coming. I should be able to hear them for miles, but the only sound was the roar of the fire.

Just like that night.

I remembered standing with Mother by the side of the house, watching the barn crumble. I'd been confused and muddled by sleepiness, and even when the tall building collapsed, I hadn't understood the importance of Father not standing there with us.

The fire department had shown up, but they had directed their hoses at our house to protect it from the sparks. The barn had been left to burn.

And not until morning had anyone told me that Father had been inside those collapsed walls.

Now I stared up at the house where I'd lived all my life and sobbed. Not for Mother, no.

But for Lisa and her sister.

It had been wrong of me; I knew that. And if I had been a braver person, I would have gone back in again to try and save them. But I wasn't.

I heard a noise from inside. An ominous creaking noise, and then a burst of sparks from the windows. Something had collapsed in there.

I wiped the tears from my face and tried to pull myself together.

This was it. It was over.

I was finally all alone in the world.

The idea made me feel dizzy. Untethered, as if gravity was releasing me and I was starting to float away.

Or perhaps it was just the smoke.

The front door flew open. Black smoke welled out from the hallway and from that smoke emerged a frightful sight.

It was all black and grimy and looked like something out of a nightmare. It staggered across the porch and down the broken steps, coming toward me.

It had made it halfway across the driveway before I realized what it was and started to run toward it.

"Lisa!"

Her legs gave way and she collapsed on the gravel just as I reached her. I fell to my knees and stared at her. She looked dead. There was blood and burned bits of flesh, and the stench was one of death; I was sure of that.

"Lisa?" I whispered.

She groaned.

I sobbed.

"I'm sorry," I whispered. "I didn't mean to. I just …"

She didn't move.

Slowly, it dawned on me. She was dead. And I had killed her. Her and her sister, along with Mother.

My newfound freedom wouldn't get me anywhere other than jail.

I sighed. Perhaps that was for the best.

There was no way I was going to manage alone out there, anyway. In prison, there would be rules, and someone else would be in charge. And perhaps they wouldn't even be mean about it, like Mother.

I would do fine in prison.

Glancing up at the burning building, I thought that it would be better than this.

Something touched my knee, and I opened my eyes. Lisa was staring up at me, her hand on the gravel in front of me.

"Lisa! You're alive!"

She took a deep breath, raspy and wet but still, a breath.

"Hang in there! Help is coming." Her hand was burned and bloody, but I took it gently and held it in mine. "And I'm so sorry. So, so sorry."

She tried to speak but a cough overtook her.

"It will be okay," I said. "Just hold on. Someone will come, soon." I glanced up the road, but still no sirens. "Just hang on for a little while longer."

The cough subsided and her lips moved again. I leaned forward to try and hear her over the roaring fire. "What was that?"

"Not your fault …" she whispered.

I bit my lip. "It was all my fault," I said. "I shouldn't have—"

"No," she croaked. "Never stood a chance …"

"Your sister," I said. "I never meant for either of you to—"

"Astrid …" she said, struggling to catch her breath. "… is fine. She's fine."

I stared at her, then up at the building. Part of the roof caved in with a loud crash and sparks rained down around us, stinging my bare arms like searing bug bites. How could she be fine? How was that possible?

As the crash rang out, I could finally hear sirens echoing through the woods.

"Help is coming," I said, squeezing Lisa's hand gently. "They're coming now."

Just as the firetruck pulled into the driveway, I saw movement by the side of the house. Lisa's sister and her husband came into sight. Her husband was carrying the little boy and steadying his sobbing wife. The girl was clutching her mother's arm. Her face was distorted, as if she was wailing, but I couldn't hear a thing over the sirens and the fire. The man said something to his wife, and she looked up. She spotted Lisa and me and froze. Three long seconds of pause, while the doors of the firetruck opened behind me, and men came running.

Then Astrid broke free from her husband's embrace and bolted toward us. She reached us at the same time as a paramedic appeared, placing a large bag on the gravel next to Lisa's head.

People, people everywhere.

There hadn't been this many people at the farm since Father died.

319

They were running, shouting, rolling out fire hoses across the yard, but it was too late. There was nothing they could do but spray water on the trees closest to the house to prevent a forest fire.

One of them came up to us.

"Is there anyone left inside?" he said, looking from me to Lisa, to Astrid, and then back again.

"Mother," I mumbled.

"Your mother is inside?" he asked, glancing behind him at the inferno. "Do you know where?"

"Upstairs. The second door to the right," I said.

"Right," he said. "Anyone else?"

I shook my head, looking at the people in front of me. "Everyone else made it out."

Astrid lifted her head and glared at me. "No thanks to you!" she spat. "She locked us in a room upstairs," she said to the fireman. "My sister and I. We could all be dead if it hadn't been for my sister."

The fireman turned around and gestured to someone behind me.

The paramedic placed a mask over Lisa's face.

"Is she going to be okay?" I asked, but no one heard me. "Is she?"

Someone wrapped a blanket around my shoulders and grabbed me by the arm to pull me up off the gravel. "You'll have to come with us," they said right next to my ear. I looked up and saw a policeman. Tall, imposing, but with kind eyes.

A female police officer came over to us and grabbed my other arm. "Are you in need of medical assistance?" she asked.

I shook my head.

"Alright then," she said.

They walked me over to the police car that was parked up on the road, behind the fire trucks and the ambulance. I kept glancing over my shoulder to see what happened to Lisa.

The female police officer helped me into the back-seat of the car, holding my head so that I didn't bump it. There was something so sweet about that gesture that brought tears to my eyes.

The door slammed shut and I leaned my forehead against the window, trying to see past the ambulance, but I couldn't see Lisa. The fire was still roaring, though. The house would be gone before the end of the day. The house and Mother, all gone.

Everything had worked out just fine. Lisa and her sister and those cute kids were safe, and Mother was gone.

I leaned back and closed my eyes.

And the best of all was that I didn't have to decide what to do next. The police officers up front would do that for me.

42

ASTRID

I COULDN'T BELIEVE it when I saw Lisa lying there in the driveway. We'd heard the sirens and came around the house to meet them. My legs barely carried me, but Fredrik held me tight and kept me upright.

You'd think that losing my sister wouldn't be such a trauma. After all, I had lost her many, many years ago. But the idea of my little sister inside that burning building while I escaped unharmed ... It crushed me. I'd had to climb out that window, for the children if nothing else, but still.

The guilt.

Seeing Lisa made hope spark to life inside me, but when I reached her, that flame was almost smothered. There was so much blood and burned skin, and her breathing sounded like something out of a horror movie. At least there was a couple of seemingly capable paramedics among the first responders, and I pulled back to let them help her.

I'd meant to tell the fire chief that Caroline had locked us—along with her creepy mother—in a room inside that burning building, but Lisa said something, and I leaned forward to hear her.

"Please don't," she rasped.

I stared at her. "We have to tell them," I said.

Lisa moved her head slowly from side to side. "Please don't," she said again. "Promise me …"

I swallowed the tears that welled up at the sight of her and nodded. Of course. I owed her my life. My son's life. Whatever she asked of me, from now on. Anything at all.

And what did I care what happened to Caroline? Not one iota, to be honest.

The paramedics and a couple of the firemen lifted Lisa onto a gurney and started to roll it back toward the ambulance. I stood up and watched her lying there under a metallic rescue blanket, an oxygen mask strapped to her face. Fredrik appeared by my side and wrapped an arm around me again. Jonas was still in his arms, his head slumped against his dad's shoulder.

"My wife has inhaled a lot of smoke," he said, and one of the paramedics stopped and turned around.

"There's another ambulance coming," he said.

"That's her sister," Fredrik said, nodding toward Lisa.

The paramedic hesitated, then nodded back. "Fine. She can ride with me in the back."

I had barely any strength left in my body, but Fredrik led me over to the ambulance and helped me climb in. There was a seat next to the gurney where Lisa was, and I sat on it, strapping on the seatbelt. The paramedic gave me a small canister with a mask and showed me how to use it. Then he turned his attention to Lisa, hooking her up to a drip and various sensors and monitors. Screens all along the wall came to life and started displaying graphs and numbers. I spotted one line with a red heart beside it.

My sister was still alive.

I turned and looked out the backdoors, just as one of the firemen went to close them.

"Wait," I said. "My son, he was inside that building as well. There was a lot of smoke."

I placed the oxygen canister on the blanket covering my sister's legs and held out my arms for Jonas. Fredrik handed him over. Jonas felt rigid and heavier than ever before. Perhaps it was just because I was weak from the exertion.

I leaned back and placed the mask over my son's face. He stared up at me, his eyes large and dark with despair.

The fireman closed the backdoors and the ambulance started moving. Jonas didn't react.

"I don't have any more oxygen canisters," the paramedic said. "You'll have to share that one."

But I kept the mask pressed to my son's face all the way to the hospital. My chest hurt, but it was only partially because of the smoke inhalation.

43

LISA

I DIDN'T REMEMBER much from the ambulance ride or the emergency room. They pumped me full of pain relief, and I was pretty out of it for days. Then started the long and arduous process of healing the burns and cuts that covered most of my body. It would have been hell for anyone, but with a body like mine, it was even more of a challenge. The hospital staff were great, though, and they took really good care of me.

Because I had to have so many operations, I was on a liquid diet for weeks, and even though it's not a method I'd recommend, it was certainly an efficient way to lose weight.

By the time I was well enough to get out of bed, Astrid brought Elinor and Jonas to see me. Jonas was a shadow of his former self, and I could tell that Astrid was worried about him. The previously bubbly and talkative boy was now almost mute, staring at me with large, worried eyes where I sat in the armchair in the visitors' lounge, covered in bandages from head to toe like an obese mummy.

325

When Astrid took Elinor to get some snacks from the vending machine, Jonas stayed behind, entranced by the fish tank that some genius had installed in the visitors' lounge. I studied the back of his head. His hair had been cut short instead of the floppy hairstyle he'd had when I first met him.

He seemed lost in the underwater world, but once his mother and sister had gone, I heard his voice.

"I didn't mean to," he said, and his voice sounded hollow and frail.

"No, of course not," I replied.

He turned his head slightly, glancing at me out of the corner of his eye. "That woman died," he said, his voice barely a whisper. "And you nearly died."

"Mrs. Johansson didn't die because of you," I said softly. "I think your mom told you about that. We could have gotten her out of the house if it hadn't been for Caroline."

He looked in the fish tank again, tracing the movement of one of the fish with the tip of his finger against the glass. "She was sick," he said matter-of-factly. "Mom said she'll be in a hospital for a long, long time."

"Yes," I said. Caroline's destiny was still undecided by the legal system, but Astrid had told me that she'd probably never get out of the psychiatric hospital where she'd been admitted. I intended to go and visit her once I got out of here.

"Still," Jonas said, and there was a tremble in his voice. "I started the fire. It was all my fault."

I stared at him. His narrow shoulders. The sneakers with led lights and curly laces that I secretly envied him. He was so little. Even though I'd only just met him, I could still see the baby in him. There was no way I, or anyone else, could blame him for what happened.

"You lit a candle," I said. "That's all you did."

He glanced toward me. "But …"

"No," I said. "You just lit a match. Everything that happened after that … There was no way you could have known what would happen after that. No one could have known."

His bottom lip trembled. "You got hurt because of me."

I smiled at him. "I was outside when the fire started," I said. "I went back inside to make sure that you and your mom got out of there."

He shook his head. "That was so brave. I could never have done something like that."

"You did do something like that," I reminded him. "You could have run outside when the fire first started. But instead, you went back to save your kitten."

A light flickered in his eyes. "I saved him," he said, thoughtfully. A quick glance toward the door. "Mom says I can keep him. We got cat baby food from the vet, and I feed him with a tiny bottle, like the ones that Elinor had for her dolls when she was little."

I smiled at him. "That's great."

"I've named him Little Frog."

I laughed but stopped myself when I felt a stab of pain. "That's a great name for a kitten."

He looked sad again. "I wanted to bring him, but Mom said that kittens aren't allowed at the hospital." He bit his lip. "Will you come and see us when you get out of here? Or are you going back to the States?"

I shook my head. My head was spinning, and I

hoped that Astrid and Elinor were on their way back. "I don't know, sweetie," I said. "We'll see."

AFTER MY TREK to the grocery store, I was so exhausted that I barely made it up the stairs to my apartment. No wonder. Even though it had been more than two months since the fire, the recovery process had been slow and arduous. Today had been the first day since leaving the hospital that I'd gone out on my own. I had been impatient to do this, but perhaps it had been too soon.

I stopped in the middle of the stairs and shifted my shopping tote from my right hand to my left so that I could grab hold of the railing. Breathing deep, I closed my eyes and did an assessment the way the physical therapist had taught me. Yes, I was tired. Yes, there was some pain, mostly from the excessive scarring after the many skin grafts. Quite a lot of pain, actually.

But I was doing OK.

Another deep breath, and then I continued to climb the last few steps up to my apartment. Seeing the front door made me smile. A newspaper holder mounted on the wall next to it had my name on the printed label. My apartment. My home.

I found my keys in the pocket of my new jacket, two sizes smaller than the old one, and unlocked the door.

The door swung open into a bright hallway. I placed my tote on the floor as I removed my jacket and shoes and then carried it into my kitchen.

It wasn't big, but it was bright and clean, and there was a small dining table by the window. When I sat in my favorite spot, on the right, I had a partial view of a park.

I unpacked the groceries—mostly fresh fruit and veg, milk and eggs—and had just closed the refrigerator when my phone beeped.

It was a text from Astrid.

I'M WORRIED ABOUT YOU.

I sighed. My older sister still didn't think that I could do anything. DON'T BE. I'M FINE.

A second later came the reply. I'M HEADING INTO A MEETING. TALK MORE LATER!

Something brushed against my leg and I glanced down.

"Hello there," I said.

The kitten made a noise that was halfway between a meow and an accusation. Glancing over at the food bowl in the corner, I saw that it was empty. I made my way over to it, refilling it from a large box standing on the counter. Then I collapsed on a chair by the table and watched my little cat eat.

Once he was finished, he came over and brushed against my leg. I pushed out of the chair and walked into the living room. A large gray sectional in the corner was dotted with brightly colored sofa cushions and a couple of fuzzy throws. I grabbed one of the throws and curled up in the corner. The kitten jumped up and nestled in the crook of my arm, after having walked in circles for a while. I scratched the spot behind his ear and he immediately started purring. The sound vibrated into my chest, and I smiled.

"Yeah, let's take a nap," I said and stroked his striped fur. He lifted his chin to let me scratch underneath it.

We dozed off for a while, but by the time the doorbell rang, I was back in the kitchen. I had been awake for twenty minutes or so.

I went out into the hallway and opened the door, checking to see that the kitten wasn't around.

Jonas burst in through the door. His sister and Astrid were standing outside.

"Jonas!" my sister said reproachfully.

"It's fine," I said. "Come on in."

We all went into the kitchen, where Jonas was sitting on the floor, petting the cat.

He had refused to give up the kitten that he'd saved from the fire, and had bottle-fed him several times a day for weeks. Unfortunately, Fredrik had turned out to be quite violently allergic. I'd offered the kitten a place to stay as soon as I'd gotten out of the hospital, and after two months of itchy eyes and a runny nose, Fredrik had insisted that Jonas let Little Frog move in with his aunt Lisa. I'd mostly offered to take care of the kitten for Jonas's sake, but Little Frog had turned out to be good company, and on the days when my scars were giving me trouble, he gave me a reason to get out of bed.

I invited Astrid to sit. They had brought yet another cat toy, and Jonas and Elinor went into the living room to play with Little Frog. My sister looked me up and down.

"Are you alright? You shouldn't have gone to so much trouble just because we were coming over. I'd be happy to order groceries for you online for a while. Until you feel stronger."

I shook my head. "I'm fine. It was nice to get outside." Flicking the switch on the coffee maker, I pulled cups from the cupboard and set the table. "Little

330

Frog and I took a nap when I got back, and now, I'm as good as new."

Astrid watched me move back and forth between the table and the cupboards and refrigerator. "You look good," she acknowledged. "You're barely limping and I can tell that you've lost a lot of weight."

"I told you," I said. "I'm doing much better."

And I was. As soon as the burns had healed, the hospital's physical therapist had offered me a session in their pool. I'd jumped at the chance to get back in the water and had been swimming every day since. With the support of the buoyant warm water of the rehab pool, my body had finally gotten the exercise that everyone had told me that I needed all my life, and I felt stronger than I'd done in decades. Being limited to the hospital's meal schedule and offerings had also made a huge difference. Funnily enough, I hadn't had any cravings while I was in the hospital. My body and my brain had been too busy with other things, I guess.

I placed the cookies and braided cinnamon buns on the table and called out to the kids. "Time for fika." I could hear their excited laughter from the living room, but they appeared almost immediately, plonking down on the chairs opposite their mother.

I poured them each a glass of juice, and coffee for my sister and me. "Did you want milk?" I asked Astrid. "I've got some."

She shook her head. "Black is fine."

We all sat down, sampling the baked goods. Jonas kept glancing under the table for Little Frog, and as soon as his cookie was gone, he slid off the chair and went searching for the kitten again. I almost expected Astrid to tell him to get back in his chair until he'd been excused, but she just smiled and sipped her coffee. Elinor finished her juice and looked expectantly at her mother. Astrid nodded, and Elinor left the table as well.

Astrid and I sat there in silence for a while, drinking our coffee.

"He's doing so much better," she said softly.

I nodded. "I can see that."

She placed her hand on mine and squeezed it gently. I didn't pull back. Didn't even want to. Instead, I turned my hand and gripped hers, squeezing it back. She leaned toward me, pressing her shoulder against mine in a sideways hug. It felt good.

Hearing Jonas's laughter from the living room, I felt assured that he'd be able to put what had happened behind him. That was comforting. Enough pain had come out of that house, but it was gone now.

I looked at the cinnamon buns that were left on the table and noticed that I didn't feel the need to take another one. The one I'd eaten had been yummy, and I'd savored it, every bite. And now, I was fine. Astrid let go of my hand to take another sip of coffee, and I leaned back.

There was still a long way to go, but for the first time, I thought that I'd be OK. Seeing Jonas bounce back had given me hope for my own recovery. I wouldn't be going to therapy, like him. And I wouldn't need to be drugged, like Caroline in her awful hospital room. I'd been to see her twice, and she'd barely known me, her eyes glazed over from the drugs. I intended to keep visiting her and do what I could for her. Us rag dolls had to stick together, after all.

I didn't want any drugs and was glad that I'd been

able to stop taking the pain medication. I was done hiding from my emotions. Hiding from my life.

I looked past Astrid, out the window. The trees in the park down the street were just starting to change into their autumn colors. Summer had ended and I was still here.

This apartment might not be much, but it was the first place in as long as I could remember that felt like home, and I wasn't going anywhere. I didn't know what I'd do with whatever was left of my life, but I would have plenty of time to figure that out. Recovery would take months, perhaps even years. I was in no rush. My body might be visibly broken, but my mind had a lot of catching up as well. In many ways, I was still five years old.

I'd swore that I'd never come back here, but now I was glad that I'd come. Perhaps that traumatized and guilt-ridden five-year-old would finally get a chance to grow up?

Honestly, I had forgotten most of what happened back then. It had been too much for my little brain to cope with, and there hadn't been anyone else around that had known the truth and could have helped me process all of it.

I was intent on helping Jonas get over what he did, and in the process, I seemed to be helping little Lisa as well.

The last of the memories that had flooded my brain when I was locked in Mrs. Johansson's room, upstairs in that burning building, had been locked away in the dark recesses of my mind for thirty years.

I hadn't thought I'd be able to deal with it, to live with it.

But here I was. Living with it.

Hearing Jonas's thin voice saying: "I didn't mean to" had brought it all back.

I hadn't meant to either.

And perhaps, with time, I'd be able to help little Lisa get over what she'd done.

44

LITTLE LISA

ALL I WANTED WAS to go back home to Mommy and Daddy and never ever come to this place again.

It was really late. Even Astrid was asleep, had been for a long time. I didn't know if Mormor was sleeping in her room downstairs. Perhaps not. Was she awake, tossing and turning, thinking about what she could have done differently? Did she believe that it was all her fault?

My stomach turned at the idea of Mormor being upset over this. None of it was her fault. Perhaps it was mine. I wasn't sure. It was definitely the Hunter's. That was the only thing I knew for certain.

I could picture him, still, shaking the policeman's hand, without a worry in the world. He probably slept by now. I couldn't imagine him lying awake, feeling bad about what he did. I didn't think you could turn little girls into rag dolls if you were the kind of person that felt bad about hurting other people.

I lay in that bed for hours and hours. It was as dark outside as it would ever get, and still, I couldn't sleep.

Even if it hadn't been my fault, I still felt bad about what had happened. I should have done something. I should have said something.

But all the words that swirled around inside my head were words that would never want to come out. Somehow, I knew that I would never be able to tell anyone about what had happened.

And if I didn't tell … What was to say that the Hunter didn't do it again? To some other little girl? What if he did this sort of thing all the time, and lots and lots of little girls that went out for a swim or to play just never came back. It was a nightmare.

He was a nightmare.

And I was afraid that I would never be able to wake up from this one.

All day, I had been lying there in my narrow bed, as if paralyzed by what had happened, but now I could feel my legs itching to get moving. Slowly, soundlessly, I crept out from under the duvet, found some warm clothes in the suitcase under the bed, and pulled them on. Then I sneaked down the stairs, making sure to not step in the middle of the steps, where they creaked the most. Once I'd made it downstairs, I stood for a long while in the hallway, listening at Mormor's door. I didn't hear anything. Then I moved on into the kitchen. I opened the kitchen door.

It was so dark outside. Unbelievably dark. In the city where I lived, it was never dark like this. There were always streetlights and neon signs and cars and houses with lights on in the windows.

There were no streetlights here at Mormor's cottage and there was no moon tonight either. I turned and started to go back upstairs, but then I spotted it. On the windowsill next to the kitchen table stood the stable lantern that Mormor used when the power went out. I had borrowed it last December for our Lucia pageant, and Mormor had taught me how to light it. It was what they used before flashlights were invented.

I took the lantern and carried it over to Mormor's wood stove. On the small shelf next to the stove, she kept her matches. A large matchbox with a boy on the front. I lifted the hook on the side of the lantern and opened it. Cranking the small wheel on the side made the wick come up a bit. I lit a match and held it to the wick, holding my breath until it caught fire. Then I quickly shook the match and put out the flame before it burned my fingers.

The lantern filled the dark kitchen with a soft, warm glow. I closed the glass and carried the lantern toward the door. Seeing the compact darkness outside, I hesitated. Then I turned back and grabbed the box of matches from the shelf. Just in case the lantern went out. I slipped the small box into the pocket of my jeans and went outside.

I half expected Mormor to come running out after me, in her dressing gown and her hair in curlers, but the small cottage was completely silent when I moved away from it.

I hurried along the path, keeping my ears pricked for footsteps, but none came. Everyone was at home, sleeping, I guess. It felt as if I was all alone in the world, and in a way, I probably was.

I was never going to be the girl that I had once been again; I knew that. The Hunter had turned Ellen into a rag doll, and me into … I didn't know what. Perhaps I was a rag doll too. Perhaps not quite as dangly, but certainly as weak.

I walked and walked for a long time. Now and then, I thought I heard something, and I stopped and stood completely still, holding my breath, waiting for someone to come toward me in the darkness. But no one did.

After a while, I kept walking.

The path was longer at night, or at least it felt like it. My body felt numb, though, and I could have walked forever. I just had to go back. Of course, I knew that it was too late now. I should have gone back right away. Perhaps then it would have made a difference. Now, there was nothing I could do. Ellen was gone, and no one would ever believe me if I told them what the Hunter had done to her.

Eventually, I saw the barn ahead of me. The doors were still wide open, and I stepped inside with my heart in my throat. The smell of hay brought back all the horrid images, and I felt sick again. Breathing was difficult in a way it hadn't ever been before, but all around me were ordinary things. Ropes and buckets and shovels and a ladder, hanging on two big hooks along the wall. Glancing up toward the house, I almost expected the Hunter to come toward me, but all the windows were dark. The Hunter slept.

On numb legs, I walked over to the ladder. I couldn't climb with the lantern in one hand, so I placed it on the bucket where I'd put my towel earlier. It felt like a million years ago. Then I started to climb. Don't ask me how I managed to get all the way to the top of the ladder with my fingers all numb, but I got up there and made my way over to the place where the kittens had been.

The light from the lantern that I'd left downstairs didn't reach the corner where the cat mama had made her nest, so I couldn't see a thing, but as soon as I got closer, I knew something was wrong.

It was too quiet. Even if it was the middle of the night, I didn't think that kittens were all that silent, just because it was dark. After all, they couldn't tell night from day, right?

But the mewling noises that I'd heard the last time I was up here were gone, and when I felt around in the spot where the kittens had been, they weren't there.

I called out, Here, kitty. Here kitty, kitty. But the cat didn't come, and her babies were nowhere to be found. I couldn't see anything, but surely, I would have heard them if they were here. Where could they have gone to?

Suddenly, I had an idea. I pulled the box of matches from my pocket, opened it, and took out one match.

I lit it and held it up in front of me. It lit up a surprisingly large area, in such a dark barn. I wouldn't have thought that such a small match could make such a difference, but it really did. I leaned over and held it over where the kittens had been, but it was as I had suspected. The cat was gone, and her squirming babies too.

I held the match high, checking all the nooks and crannies in between the hay bales, but there were no kittens anywhere. The match burned down, and when it reached my fingers, I swore and dropped it.

I thought for sure that the flame had gone out when I dropped the match because it went all dark up in that hayloft again. But then I saw a glow under the hay. A warm, pulsating heart that grew and grew.

When a tall flame burst out from under the dry stalks, I stood up and took a step back. It happened so quickly, just as I'd been sure that it wouldn't catch on.

But it did.

And it spread quickly through the dry hay bales. I felt the heat pressing me back, over toward the ladder, and then I scrambled down, not trembling anymore now.

As I stood on the concrete floor of the barn, looking up, I could see the glow and smoke coming down through the gaps between the floor planks in the loft. It wasn't dark anymore. The fire raged and spread, but for some reason, I wasn't afraid. When the heat from the flames made my cheeks glow, I sighed with relief, and when a plank collapsed and fell down among the rubble and farm equipment that was stored underneath, I actually smiled.

No little girl was ever going to be turned into a rag doll up there, ever again.

In the end, the heat forced me to back out through the large open doors and move over toward the forest. I stood there watching the flames break through the outer walls and light up the entire farmyard.

Suddenly came a shout, a loud curse, and I pulled back behind a tree.

The Hunter came running from the white house, pulling on his overalls as he ran. He stopped for a moment and just stood there and stared at the flames, tugging at his hair in a gesture of despair. I didn't feel sorry for him.

Then he ran over to the large doors on the opposite

side of the barn and pulled them open. I could see straight through the cavernous building as he held an arm up to shield his face and moved cautiously into the fire. He grabbed as much as he could of the tools and things that were hanging there and then ran out, throwing the stuff on the ground out in the yard before he ran back in for more things. He threw a bunch of stuff into a wagon and pushed the wagon toward the doors, but the wagon was already on fire, and in the end, he had to grab some of the items on it and save those, letting the wagon stand there and burn in the middle of the floor.

The third time he went in, he looked up at the hayloft for a while, but then he rushed in underneath it, desperate to save whatever he could. But before he came back out again, I heard a loud creaking sound, and a large part of the roof came in, shooting sparks up into the night sky like fireworks.

I stood there, clutching the tree until my hands went numb, but once I was certain that the Hunter wouldn't come staggering out through those doors ever again, I started moving away from the barn.

It wasn't completely dark any longer, and I easily found the path down to the lake, even though I'd left the lantern on the bucket in the barn. Just as I stepped out on the grass next to the dock, I could hear the sound of sirens far away. A firetruck. An ambulance, maybe.

It didn't matter.

I walked over to the dock, sat down with my legs dangling on the side toward the reeds and watched them slowly appearing through the darkness as the sky went from black to dark gray, to lighter gray, and then indigo.

The sun came up, and I watched the yellow glow on the reeds. It was so quiet. All the noises and all the nightmare images in my head were gone.

The only thing I could think about was those fire-work sparks against the night sky.

No little girl was ever going to be made into a rag doll in that barn again.

Or anywhere else, for that matter.

The Hunter was dead.

It should have felt good. Or perhaps it should have felt terrible. I wasn't sure anymore.

I didn't feel a thing.

But as I got up from the dock and started walking back toward Mormor's cottage, at least I knew why that was.

I wasn't a little girl anymore.

I was a rag doll.

THE END

ABOUT THE AUTHOR

If you enjoyed this story, a review or rating would be greatly appreciated. Or tell a friend about it.

If you want information on new releases or special offers, **please sign up for my newsletter,** only used for new releases or special offers. No photos of my pets or meals, I promise.

Keep reading for info on other titles by Sydney James.

I've been running for so long, moving from town to town, changing my appearance, starting over. Trying to get away from my painful memories, and from him.

The man with the dragon tattoo on his chest.

Arriving in Boulder, Colorado, things seem to fall into place in a way that they've never done before. Is it a sign? Is it finally time to stop running? Perhaps, I can finally start to rebuild the life that the Dragon destroyed, all those years ago.

But my past catches up with me, and I am forced to make a choice – keep running or find a way to make sure that the Dragon never hurts me or anyone else ever again.

Slaying the Dragon is a psychological thriller novella with a twist you'll never see coming.

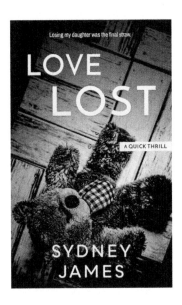

I was in hospital being patched up after a nasty fall when my daughter disappeared from the playground, and my already horrible day suddenly turned unbearable.

My husband John only turned his back to our 2-year old daughter for a moment. But sometimes a moment is all it takes.

I loved John so much, once upon a time, but all that love is now gone. The question is, can I find my baby girl before she too is lost forever?

Love Lost - available now!

If you want to read more stories like this,

sign up here!

Printed in Great Britain
by Amazon